REVIEWS FOR *GREY'S AWAKENING*

Joyfully Recommended

"…*Grey's Awakening* is like a thunderstorm – powerful, glorious, and seemingly alive with raw emotion…an enthralling story that no words can do justice to (though I will try) with two heroes that will wrap themselves around your heart and not let go…Their love story was as touching as is it was spellbindingly erotic…"

—Shayna from *Joyfully Reviewed*

"…This novel is well-written and intensely sexual…a passionate and emotional ride…characters with enough aggression and physical dominance to strike sparks off each other at each encounter…is intense and affecting and very high in entertainment value. And did I mention hot? Keep a fan close by, and maybe an ice bucket or two."

—Bobby, from *BookWenches Reviews*

5 Lips

"…Cameron Dane has an amazingly well done story with *Grey's Awakening*. I loved the emotional pull and intensity of this story. I felt really invested in Grey and Sirus…When you want a story that will grip you and not let you go pick up *Grey's Awakening* you will not be disappointed…"

—Tina, a 5 lips review from *Two Lips Reviews*

GREY'S AWAKENING

CAMERON DANE

ISBN-13: 978-1467973274
ISBN-10: 1467973270

GREY'S AWAKENING

Grey's Awakening originally released as an e-book by Liquid Silver Books in June 2009

Cover Art, Print Design, and Formatting by April Martinez
Grey's Awakening edited by Chrissie Henderson
Manufactured in the USA

PROLOGUE

His twin was a dead woman.

Grey stiffened at the sight before him and did his damnedest not to salivate.

Not. My. Type.

Grey repeated that mantra silently, even if the man before him was half-naked, full of gorgeous muscles, and standing in the archway that led to the bedrooms in *Grey's* cabin. The tattoo of a rearing mustang on the man's left pec gave away who had sent him here. Only Grey's sister Kelsie would think this kind of rough-looking guy was for Grey. Well, his sister, and maybe his best friend John too. In moments like this one, Grey cursed the week a couple of summers ago that his sister and best friend had finally hooked up and admitted to each other they were in love. To think Grey had provided the cabin that had allowed it to happen. *This* cabin.

Kelsie was so, so dead.

Grey never should have told her he'd planned to drive up to the cabin.

From across the living room the stranger clutched the towel at his waist and started stalking in Grey's direction. "Who the hell are you?" the guy growled. Dark, wet hair lay plastered to his forehead, and his flesh glistened with moisture. Heat from his body mingled with the frigid air breezing in through the open door at Grey's back and created a shimmer of steam around the man's skin. "Get the hell out of this cabin right now."

That got Grey out of his paralysis and standing upright, going toe-to-toe with a hulk of a man who had to be at least six-feet-four. "*Excuse* me," Grey would have bumped the guy's chest to get him out of his personal space, but he guessed the giant of a man wouldn't even budge under the shove, "but this is my goddamned cabin, and *you're* the one trespassing on *my* property. So go pick your clothes up off the floor, or wherever the hell they are, and get the fuck out of here before I call the authorities."

"Oh." His head tilting, the guy took a step back, and much of the rigidity left his stance. "You're Grey? Kelsie's brother?"

Grey took a breath, and resisted the urge to grit his teeth. Of course the guy knew his sister. "Yes." Everything on the *outside* settled and calmed. "I am."

"No offense," the man scratched the stubble on his hard -- *fucking sexy* -- jaw, "but can I see some ID?"

One, two, three, four, five, calm, calm, calm ... stay calm. "Yes." Grey slid his wallet out of his back pocket. "Fine." Producing his North Carolina driver's license, he handed it to the big man. "There you go. One Greyson Cole. See the picture? That's me. Would you like me to produce a phone number so we can call my sister to confirm it? Or can you deign to tell me what the hell you're doing in my cabin, now that you know it's mine?"

"Sirus Wilder." The man stuck his hand out, the appendage yet more big and rough stuff. "I own the cabin across the lake. I had a pipe leak in my bathroom three days ago." Sirus grimaced. "The shower tile and wall is going to have to be broken through in order to fix it, and the floor in the bathroom is going to have to be replaced. There's only one guy I trust to do it, and he can't clear enough time for a few more days. Anyway, with the valves to the house shut off, I don't have any water. I called Kelsie, and she sent me her key for your cabin. She told me I could stay here so that I have a toilet and shower, until mine is repaired."

Okay, so not exactly a setup after all. Grey ignored the sense of deflation that sighed through him as he accepted this man didn't bat for his team. Didn't matter. Stunning, defined muscles and a thick head of dark hair notwithstanding, everything about Sirus Wilder screamed that he wasn't Grey's type. Even if -- *Jesus Christ* -- he did have the most insanely wide chest, with a line of hair that trailed down his tight-as-hell stomach, where it disappeared under the towel. Grey's towel. *Shit.*

Grey shifted his stance to cover the twitch from his cock. Geez, he'd been celibate for too long.

Not. My. Type.

Sirus cleared his throat, startling Grey into tearing his gaze off the man's thick chest and quarter-sized, copper-colored nipples.

"Sorry," Grey covered quickly, "I was just wondering if you were ever going to give me back my license." He held out his hand.

"Right." Red slashes cut through the guy's pronounced cheekbones. "Sorry." Sirus handed over the ID and then backed up. "Let me go throw my clothes on and I'll be out of your hair."

Grey paced the length of the cabin while he waited for Sirus to return. *Fully clothed this time. Please, God.* After the disaster of his last relationship, Grey reminded himself that he had sworn off men for good. Since women didn't crank his carburetor, he had gotten very acquainted with his left hand over the last three years. Damn, though, he missed sliding into a man's tight ass and fucking until he could barely move.

"Okay, sorry again about the mix-up." Sirus emerged, fully clothed, with a black bag slung over his shoulder -- a very wide shoulder, covered in midnight blue flannel now. *Shit.* Grey wasn't into guys who wore faded jeans, work boots, and flannel. "Your sister must not have known you were going to be using the cabin," Sirus added.

"I wouldn't bet on that," Grey muttered under his breath.

Sirus glanced up, the slate in his eyes deepening to smoke. "What?"

Swallowing past the sudden thickness in his throat, Grey rubbed his chest, smoothing the black leather jacket covering his suit and tie. "Nothing. Just mumbling to myself."

"If you say so." Sirus tossed his duffel on the couch, and moved to grab a coat off a hook by the front door. When Sirus shrugged into the camel-colored, suede, Shearling lined jacket, Grey almost came in his dress pants. The guy was just so damn big. Grey didn't go for big. At least, not bigger than himself. He had no interest in someone overpowering him, in bed or out.

Turning his gaze down, the only way to stop staring, Grey moved out of the line to the front door, watching discreetly as Sirus made his way across the floor.

"So," Sirus paused at the threshold, "thanks for the use of your cabin for a few days, even if you didn't know about it. Your sister raves about you, so it was good to finally meet you. If you need anything while you're here, I'm right across the water. Have a good one."

No, no, don't do it. He's a big boy and can take care of himself. "Do you need to stay here a few more nights?" Grey's fists clenched at his sides, even as he made the offer. Damn the man for mentioning Kelsie. "You would know by now there are two bedrooms. I don't need both. There's plenty enough room to share for a short while."

"I don't want to put you out."

"You said you don't have water." Grey made the words sound like a curse. A flash of taking a bath in an aboveground pool rocked a small shudder through him; early memories from childhood he would rather not remember. "It's really not a problem." Years of negotiating with people who could buy and sell him ten times over brought Grey's focus up from the floor and onto a man he wanted out of his cabin more than just about anything in the world. Dark slate eyes connected with his, and Grey stuffed down the immediate desire to retract his offer. "Any friend of Kelsie's is welcome here. You can use the second room until your cabin is repaired."

"Thank you." Sirus stepped back inside, and Grey's heart sank. "I appreciate the kindness."

"No problem." *Big problem.* Why couldn't this man be one of those people who protested a kindness until the other person gave up? He wasn't supposed to say yes. "Go ahead and get yourself settled back in," Grey offered anyway, "and we'll just work around each other for a few days until you can go back home."

"Okay." Sirus moved across the floor, his body something of incredible fluid grace for such a big man. He paused, right back where he'd started, and Grey slipped back those few minutes to the guy in a towel and nothing else. Damn it, Grey had gone too long without seeing a naked man in person. That had to be it. He didn't like thickly muscled men. He preferred sleekly sculpted and streamlined, maybe a few inches shorter than his own six feet of height.

What in the hell had he been thinking, inviting a person he didn't even know, into his home? It was more than stupid, it was downright risky. Grey took a step back, and then another, until he bumped up against the door. He wanted to tell Sirus to get out, but he couldn't. Not now. Jesus, Grey didn't know what the fuck to do.

Live with it.

This had disaster written all over it.

Shit.

CHAPTER ONE

S irus Wilder stood inside the cabin, silently cursing and calling himself ten kinds of foolish for agreeing to stay after getting a look at Greyson Cole. Kelsie had never said her brother was so damned gorgeous. Six feet of stunning, perfect, sinewy body, thick brown hair, sun-kissed skin, and the most piercing hazel eyes with flecks of amber Sirus had ever seen.

Of course, why would Kelsie mention her brother's near physical perfection? It wasn't as if Grey enjoyed bending over for a stiff dick, had wet dreams about a mouth full of thick cock, or had fantasies of coming like a geyser all over another man's body.

Sirus imagined himself standing naked, and Grey moving

to him, sinking to his knees… *No.* Not again. Sirus was not in the market for a relationship, and he did not do casual sex. Not that it mattered. Buttoned-up, neat, and trimmed-out on all corners, Kelsie's brother was clearly the exact opposite of hot, raunchy animal sex -- gay or straight. This guy probably put a double-thick towel under his woman in bed so the sheets didn't get messy. Hell, in Sirus's mind, one of the best things about losing control was seeing all the damage done in the aftermath. Falling over into that wet spot, knowing he'd drawn that reaction out of his partner, was pure bliss to Sirus.

At least, it used to be. Not anymore.

No more lusting after straight guys.

No more convincing himself lust was love.

A heavy ache twisted Sirus's chest, but he quickly berated himself for letting his mind drift to Paul, his previous partner. He snapped himself back into the present in a shot. The first thing that registered in his brain was Greyson Cole edging his way outside.

"Oh, hey," Sirus dropped his bag on the floor, "do you need help bringing anything inside?"

"What?" Now just outside the door, Grey paused and snapped his gaze up from the porch floor. He glanced at Sirus, barely made eye contact, and then looked away, making Sirus wonder if he had the word MURDERER etched into his forehead.

"Help?" Sirus prompted. "Do you need some help bringing stuff in from your car?"

"Oh, no, that's all right. I have it." Grey buttoned up his leather jacket, a garment that wouldn't do a damn bit of good keeping him warm this high in the mountains at this time of year. "Thanks for the offer though. Umm, yeah, you do your thing and I'll do mine." Grey pointed in the general direction of the steps leading to the dirt path. "I'll be right back."

Sirus watched from a dozen feet away as Grey straightened, made a very precise turn, and moved down the stairs at an even pace. If Sirus didn't know any better, he would say the dude had a broomstick shoved all the way up his ass, right into his spine.

Well, hell. He could already tell Greyson Cole would be tons of fun.

Wonderful.

———

GREY STAYED HIDDEN IN HIS room for as long as he could. He took his time unpacking his bags, not seeing any point in living out of a suitcase and garment bag when he planned to be here for at least two weeks.

Truth was, Grey was damned tempted to take up residence in the mountain cabin. An epidemic of romance had broken out all around him down in Raleigh, going all the way back to when he'd made the decision to become celibate. He had reached a breaking point for other people's happiness when Kelsie and John had told him they were expecting their first child, due in June. It wasn't that Grey wasn't thrilled for them;

God knew it had taken them long enough to get together, and they were clearly meant for each other. But the thought of knowing he would only ever be "Uncle Grey" had Grey announcing he needed some time away from the business and that he planned to go out of town. Seeing the hurt in his sister's hazel eyes, so much a mirror of his own, *almost* had Grey relenting. Later that day one of his employees had burst into the offices and announced her engagement. At that point Grey made a quick phone call to his sister, told her he would stay in phone contact, and went home to pack his bags.

That was yesterday. Valentine's Day, for Christ's sake. How lovely this cabin had looked in Grey's mind, *yesterday*.

Today, he had a sexy-as-hell stranger sharing his one place of solitude, and sleeping with only one wall between them. *Fuck.* Grey wondered if Sirus slept in the nude. He just knew the man would radiate heat like a furnace and feel amazing to curl up against on a cold night. He bet Sirus would spoon a partner and blanket her with his big frame, probably wake up nuzzling against the fine hairs on the back of a person's neck too.

Oh, no, no, no. Grey did not like that kind of shit. It was great in a movie or a book, but in reality, a person needed his or her own space to breathe freely. It seemed all too often in Grey's real life, though, other men ridiculously tried to bare their soul on the first date, and became clingy and needy by the third. Grey shuddered just thinking about it. He couldn't imagine ever revealing his most personal secrets and fears, yet other people gave their own away like candy on Halloween. He didn't understand it one damn bit. And he was sick of dates or boyfriends trying to make him feel guilty, or manipulate him into cutting open a vein just so they could watch him bleed. Grey would never spill his guts for a partner. If that was what was required to go out on more than one date with a person these days, Grey went ahead and decided he didn't need to do it anymore. One-night stands didn't really suit him either, so that left a lot of yanking the one-eyed bandit on his own. There were worse things in the world.

A soft tap sounded at the door. "Grey?" Sirus's rich voice carried through the wood. "Are you hungry? I made dinner. There's more than enough for two."

Speaking of worse things... Grey could not get the visual of the almost-savage planes of Sirus's face out of his mind, most compelling of which were those deep slate eyes. The guy was built of steely muscle, but his eyes said he didn't spend all of his time thinking about his body and working out in a gym. Intelligence. That was a thousand times more dangerous than the perfection of Sirus Wilder's physique.

Shit. Shit. Shit.

Grey slumped and closed his eyes. "I'll be right there." He scrubbed the tiredness from his face. "Thank you."

"No problem." Heavy shoes made the hardwood flooring creak, telling Grey that Sirus had walked away. Taking a moment to remind himself that no business deal -- or man -- had bested him yet, Grey took a breath, gave himself a speech to be strong, and joined his temporary cabin mate for a meal.

———

SIRUS FIDDLED WITH THE LAST few bites of his chicken and steamed vegetables. Thick silence sat heavy in the air. From across the small table, Grey did a lot of staring at his now empty plate. No one had ever called Sirus a motor-mouth, but he could usually carry on a decent conversation, even with someone he didn't really know. This man, however, left him feeling tongue-tied. Sirus fucking didn't understand it.

Not giving himself any more time to think, Sirus blurted, "Can I ask you a dumb question?"

Snapping his focus up from his plate, Grey met Sirus's gaze. "Sure." His lips thinned and his jaw clenched. "Although now I'll feel like a fool if I can't answer it."

Grey didn't crack a smile as he made that comment, but Sirus did. "I'm gonna guess you rarely -- if ever -- have to worry about looking foolish."

"I like to be prepared," Grey replied. "That's just good business."

Sirus would bet money Greyson Cole made that his motto in *every* aspect of his life. Even sitting here at dinner, on vacation, his jeans and button-down shirt looked tailor-made for him. Shit. They probably were.

Taking a swig of his tea, Grey spoke from behind the rim of his glass. "What did you want to ask me?"

Sirus tried to hide his smile. "Actually, my question *is* about your business."

The rigidity in Grey didn't loosen one bit. "Then other than my partner, there isn't anyone more qualified to answer than me. Shoot."

So no joking or small talk. Check. "Well, I've met John on a couple of occasions now, and he has mentioned that you guys own a venture capitalist firm." His face heating, Sirus added, "I was just wondering exactly what that means. What is it you and John do?" He quickly held up a hand. "The stripped-down version will do fine."

"Stripped-down?" The tone of Grey's voice made it sound as if Sirus had insulted him. "Okay. Well, let's say you have a big idea, or even just a really good but maybe radical idea. You need help getting it past phase one, launching it into something big. You need capital; maybe more than a bank will give you based on just having a big concept. You come to us, you make a pitch, and if we think you have a good head on your shoulders and everything it takes to make your dream a success, *except* the money, then with investors John and I court, we'll get you the money and aid you in the steps to creating a profitable business. We've been very successful at reading people and knowing which risks to take. When the profits start rolling in, we reap some of that reward, as do the investors. Eventually most of the business owners buy our percentage out and go on to be very successful on their own, but some stay with us, whether because they feel they need the support we offer, or they know they want to keep growing and will need

more money down the line. That's what I do." Grey finally did
smile, and it was wry … and downright sexy. "*The stripped-
down version.*"

Sirus had the grace to blush. "Sorry about that."

"It's all right." Grey pushed back in his chair and stretched
out his legs, crossing them at the ankle. "What do you do?"

"I drive a truck." Sirus resisted the gut-level urge to apologize
for his blue-collar existence. "Not nearly so glamorous as what
you and John do, but I like it. I've been able to see a lot of the
country through driving, and I own my own rig so I make my
own hours. There isn't anybody I have to report to, so I can
come and go as I please and live on as much or little money
as suits me. In fact, I found my cabin by meeting someone
while on one of my routes. I came through these mountains a
couple towns over, broke down, and had to spend a few nights
with the locals. I met the woman who owned all four of these
cabins before she ever put them on the market. We were talking
about what we do over some burgers and fries. When she said
she owned a handful of cabins on the four corners of a lake, I
said, 'If you ever want to sell one, give me a call.' She laughed
and told me she was getting them ready for sale. She brought
me right up to look at them the next day, and I bought the one
across from this one. I saw the water and these mountains and
knew I'd come home."

"Where are you from originally?"

"Grew up in DC. Most of my family still lives there."

Grey settled in and crossed his arms against his chest. "Big family?"

"Big enough." Sirus smiled, but at the same time, his chest squeezed with old wounds. Better not to think about that. *You can't change her.* The smile stiffened on his lips, but he forced it to remain there. "Mom and Dad, four brothers, and one sister."

"Where did you go to school?"

"Didn't." Trying to fight it, Sirus couldn't stamp down the knee-jerk reaction to justify his lack of structured education. "I did fairly well in high school, but I always felt confined, as if I couldn't breathe. College didn't feel right for me, so I didn't go."

"I assume since you're the only one here that you're not married and don't have a wife stranded back at your cabin without water."

Sirus quirked his head to the side and studied Grey a little more intently. "Nope. Not married."

"Ever been?" Grey asked, barely letting a pause exist between a response and his next question. "Are you divorced?"

"Never been married."

"How about engaged?"

"Not even engaged." Sirus crossed his arms against his chest and drilled the man across from him with an unwavering stare. "Would you like to know my political affiliation next? Maybe how much I paid for my cabin? Or perhaps whether or not I claim a particular religion?" Grey sat across from Sirus and didn't so much as flinch at the dryness in Sirus's tone, let alone show a reaction on his face. "How many questions do you get before I get to ask another of you?"

Grey raised a brow, but other than that didn't respond.

Suddenly needing to move, feeling like this man could see straight through his clothes right into his soul, Sirus grabbed his plate and stood. He moved to the sink but paused before turning on the water. He looked over his shoulder back to the table where Grey still sat. "Are you trying to figure out if I'm going to fleece you in the dead of night while you sleep? What exactly are you hoping to find out about me with all those questions, Grey?"

Greyson Cole's poker face remained firmly in place. "Just trying to make conversation."

"Now why don't I believe that?"

Grey got up and moved to the sink to rinse his plate too. Standing so close, the guy somehow exuded dominating cool -- while at the same time made it hard for Sirus to find his breath. "You don't have to believe it." Grey's voice reeked of quiet command. "I don't owe you anything else."

Gritting his teeth, Sirus responded, "Ditto."

The air in the room was charged with electricity, creating tension Sirus could feel like a touch against his flesh.

Still standing so very close, Grey somehow managed to get the water running, rinse his plate and put it in the dishwasher, without ever giving up his position. "So then we understand each other," he finally said. "Good." With that, he walked away, leaving Sirus standing in the kitchen alone, stunned, and confused.

CHAPTER TWO

Hours later Grey rolled over in bed, cursing his inability to sleep. He fucking knew what was keeping him awake too; his behavior with Sirus after dinner. Damn it. Grey didn't know what the hell had gotten into him. Sirus was just trying to have a perfectly nice conversation, and Grey had to go turn it into the third degree. Grey might as well have shone a bright light on the man and read him his rights. If Grey had ever acted like that with one of his investors or clients he would be out millions of dollars or a potential moneymaking venture.

Sirus isn't business, asshole.

Grey growled in the dark as his cock stirred, reminding him just how little Sirus had to do with his life back home. Grey never let himself even think of his clients and investors as having any kind of life beyond business, let alone view them as sexual beings. Grey liked having a successful business and a roof over his head that said business provided, and he intended to keep his life prosperous for a very long time. The quickest way to kill that success would be to blur the lines and hit on clients, employees, or investors.

Sirus isn't any one of those things, idiot.

No, Sirus didn't have anything to do with Grey's business, so Grey didn't understand what in the hell had gotten into him to start grilling the man so hard in the kitchen. It had been clear the guy just wanted to talk and have a pleasant evening. Nevertheless, while sitting across from Sirus in the kitchen, Grey had felt deep-seated warning bells vibrate loudly through his insides. On instinct, he had turned the conversation around onto the asker. *Never give them anything real of you first.* Grey lived by that philosophy for most of his life, had been doing so as a teen before putting phrase to the thought, something that had eventually ingrained itself in his very being. He had achieved great success in high school, college, and business by staying true to those words.

Sirus didn't want to know your soul, you jerk. He made dinner conversation, and with one question, you went off the deep end.

One reason and one reason only stirred in Grey's mind to explain, although not justify, his behavior. *Three years without a date.* Fact was, Grey didn't know how to converse with people anymore when it didn't relate to the job. Other than his sister and John, everyone else in Grey's life had ties to his work. Hell, even John did, for that matter. Grey could turn on the work-schmooze on instinct. Until tonight, he hadn't realized just how rusty his social skills had become. He snorted at the thought. Maybe sharing a cabin with Sirus for a few days wouldn't be such a bad thing. He could practice banal, meaningless talk and sharpen his skills. He used to be pretty damn good at nonsense conversation. Had to be. If he didn't have a bunch of crap at the ready for when he went out on dates he would spill his guts just like everyone else in the world did.

Grey never spilled his guts. On top of that, Grey brutally chastised himself with a reminder that Sirus hadn't asked for any truly personal information. The man had zero interest in Grey's life beyond a thank you for giving him use of a room, and so Grey had no real reason to feel overly guilty for his behavior. Yet, still, Grey couldn't fall asleep, and so he reasoned that his insomnia must be related to something else entirely.

Maybe he was worried about being away from the business. He'd purchased this cabin five years ago, but the truth was he never made use of it. His sister stayed here more than he did. When buying the place, Grey had grand plans of taking regular long weekends to unwind, but when it came right down to it he always had pressing business that took priority over a vacation. He wasn't used to being away from work, yet today he had quickly, without any planning, taken himself out of his routine. That had to be why he couldn't sleep. Maybe if he just checked his email and skimmed a few proposals then he could satisfy himself that everything down in Raleigh was fine without him. Perhaps then he could let himself relax enough to get some much needed rest.

Crawling out of bed, Grey inhaled sharply as his bare feet met the hardwood flooring. The contact with the chilly surface drew out a shiver. Grey didn't tend to sleep in much more than a pair of sweats, but he might have to reconsider that routine while up here in the mountains. He moved into the hall quietly, not wanting to disturb his cabin mate. The guy had a fierceness to him, and while Grey's instinct was to puff up even bigger and intimidate with his presence and intelligence, the fact was Sirus Wilder could rearrange a person's face and internal organs with a few quick punches. Grey wasn't a stupid man, and he didn't discount that notion for one second.

Except when you acted like an asshole during dinner, inciting the man's anger without thinking twice.

Grey growled, commanding the jerk voice in his head to shut the hell up and go to sleep. He was in the process of cursing himself for making a noise and possibly bothering Sirus when the creak of a mattress spring drew Grey's attention to the very man's bedroom door -- and the fact that it was only half-closed. The squeaking sound came again, this time followed by a low, rumbling moan that rushed through Grey more potently than the most expensive whisky on the market. His cock stirred a tent in his sweats, forcing him to stifle down a moan of his own as he moved in the direction of Sirus's bedroom. Right before he reached the door, Grey edged back against the hallway wall, angled his shoulder into the plaster, and slid a sideways glance into Sirus's bedroom.

Jesus Holy Christ.

The man was nude, and goddamnit, he was stunning. No towel this time, Sirus lay tangled on top of his quilt in stark naked glory. Grey swallowed hard at the picture the man created. The blunt angles of Sirus's face appeared harsher, with deeper shadows filling in the rougher places. A thin line of light highlighted a sensuous mouth, half open with nearly silent, rapid breathing. A wide beam of moonlight highlighted Sirus's wide, muscular shoulders and chest, his cut, defined stomach, and long, lightly haired legs. The deep olive tone of his skin burnished with an almost bronze hue in the moon's natural light. Beyond that, though, what Grey kept darting his focus back time and again as he tried to mentally process every piece of Sirus Wilder, was Sirus's big hand stroking his even bigger, fully-erect cock.

Jesus Holy Christ.

The man really was huge all over. Grey couldn't even hazard a guess on girth and length, but fuck, Sirus's dick certainly matched his body, there could be no mistaking that. Grey's mouth watered as he watched, rapt, as the shiny head of Sirus's dick came in and out of view with every swipe of the man's hand. Damn it, Grey loved a mouth full of cock. He probably craved giving a blowjob just as much as he liked getting them. He missed the smooth heat of another man's dick pushing past his lips, of getting that first hint of salty precum on his tongue, or the slowly building slide of his partner pushing his length inside, filling Grey's mouth with every inch of his prick. Jesus, Grey would have to relax his throat and work hard to take all of Sirus, but his jaw dropped open a little bit right where he stood, imagining the pleasure in learning to take it.

Sirus suddenly started pumping his cock faster through the tight fist of his hand, and his body writhed all over the bed in that way a person only let happen when they know they are alone. Deep, needful noises escaped Sirus's lush, *fucking kissable* mouth, vibrating a frequency through the air that reached Grey in a sharp, palpable wave. Unable to walk away or even to turn his head, Grey pushed the front of his sweats down and freed his erection, taking it firmly in hand. Exquisite sensation rushed through Grey as he stroked his penis in time with Sirus's motions. He held himself in a painfully tight grip, imagining that Sirus would have a rough hand and would give a punishing handjob to a cock -- as it appeared he gave himself right now.

Mesmerized, Grey watched Sirus slide his hand up his body and stick two fingers in his mouth, wet them, and then rub them back and forth over his large nipples, tweaking the darker flesh until both tips stood out in pinpoints, making Grey want to nip them to see if Sirus would cry out with pleasure. Grey's cock jumped in his hand and his balls pulled heavy with cum, begging for a rough touch. Grey nearly groaned with need, and just then, Sirus dragged down on his length and kept right on going, reaching between his legs. He played with his nuts, alternating between rolling and pulling on his sac -- exactly what Grey needed too. Grey quickly followed suit, taking his weight with a good tug. Switching back and forth between his member and his balls until it wasn't enough, Grey then moved to using both hands, and he bit his lip as he fought the coiling need for release.

"Mmm … yeah…" Sirus's deep voice carried through the night. Even though he had his eyes closed and looked like he was a thousand miles away in fantasyland, it was as if Sirus took his cues from Grey's unspoken needs. Sirus two-handed his testicles and cock, spread his legs wide, dug his heels into the sheets, and thrust his hips in earnest with every move. Grey didn't think he had ever seen such masculine beauty as he witnessed in Sirus Wilder right now; Sirus's mouth was open, and his skin pulled taut over cutting cheekbones, perspiration glistened over every inch of his body, the sheen throwing every defined line of hard muscle into pure, shadowed perfection.

Grey's entire body buzzed with sensation, and he swore to God it felt like a thousand tongues licked his flesh all over, sending his nerve endings into a frenzy. With his stare locked on Sirus, Grey fisted his too-hard erection harder and faster, uncaring that he didn't have quite enough lubrication and it hurt a little bit. He ached all over with the need to come and he couldn't stop. Grey started thrusting his hips in counterpoint to Sirus's thrusts, imagining he had his cock buried deep in Sirus's ass, and that every time Sirus came down, Grey shoved up, taking the man's smooth channel to the hilt.

It had been so long since Grey had taken another man, in

any way, he almost whimpered with the imagined tight inferno of Sirus's snug hole smothering his cock with suffocating heat. Grey's hip thrusts turned jagged and off rhythm, and he began leaking more than enough precum to lubricate his length for the job. His balls squeezed and pulled up ultra-tight to his body so fast he didn't feel the endgame hit before it overtook him and shoved him right into orgasm.

"Ohhh fuuuuck…" Grey clamped his teeth together as he jerked and released, spraying cum with the hottest jolt of pleasure, not stopping until he spit a half-dozen milky lines onto the doorjamb and floor.

A hoarse, male shout yanked Grey's eyes open and straight onto the picture of Sirus's hips thrust up in the air as the man shot a load onto his chest and neck … with his eyes wide open, looking right at Grey as he did it. Desire, not revulsion, lived in his stare.

Oh shit.

Sirus was gay. Moreover, Grey could see it in the man's eyes; Sirus now knew Grey was too.

No, no, no. Grey didn't need this complication right now.

Grey pulled every discipline he had ever taught himself into play and didn't dart his gaze away from Sirus's. Instead, he stared the other man down without flinching or blinking, schooled his features to indifferent, stuffed his cock back into his sweats, and walked away.

Never let them see you sweat.

—

GREY ROLLED OVER IN BED and stretched his arms and legs, groaning as a beam of sunlight hit right on his face, blinding him enough to make him snap his eyes closed in protest. "Oh Christ Almighty." He dug the heels of his hands into his forehead, trying to suppress the dull ache already forming behind his skull. "Great way to start a vacation." He glanced at the digital clock on the nightstand, swearing at the early hour. Seven o'clock in the morning; he had gotten two whole hours of sleep. Great. He knew it was a miracle he had gotten that small amount and didn't bother burying his head under a pillow for more.

"Get up, get up, get up." His body protesting every move, Grey pushed himself to a sitting position and forced himself to stand. One of Grey's greatest secrets was how much he detested getting up in the morning. For the purposes of school, college, and work he had trained himself to do it, but at thirty-three years old he still had to give himself a pep talk every morning in order to get moving. He grabbed clothes but his feet dragged especially heavy today with the knowledge that he wouldn't be able to put off facing Sirus forever.

Holy fuck, Grey still could not believe what he'd let happen. He never should have invaded Sirus's privacy in the first place, but beyond that, he should have exhibited some personal control. He was not some goddamned ten-year-old pulling on his dick for the first time; he knew how to ignore and walk away from sexual excitement and arousal, and had been doing so for many years. He had never lied to himself about being gay but that didn't mean he jumped every man who showed an interest in him. Fuck, he'd just recently discreetly turned down an invitation from a hell of a sexy attorney who worked for one of his investors. Grey knew damn well how to walk away from the things he wanted.

He just didn't know why he hadn't been able to move away from Sirus's doorway last night.

"Doesn't matter why, damn it." His tone harsh, Grey locked the bathroom door and looked himself in the mirror. Speaking aloud always forced him to process the meaning behind his words in another way, helping to drive home the point. "Just make damn well sure it doesn't happen again." The picture of Sirus's beautiful body and the hard intensity of his face materialized like a specter in front of Grey's eyes, making him hunger for sweaty, entwined bodies and hot, open-mouthed kisses. Suddenly the image turned more graphic and Grey saw himself tangled on that quilt with Sirus. Only this time, Grey *felt* almost more than saw himself turn over, spread himself open, and beg Sirus for the fucking of his life.

Grey spun around, his heart pounding and legs shaking like a newborn colt.

What in the hell was wrong with him? Grey did not bottom. Ever.

CHAPTER THREE

"Oh, yeah, yeah…" Grey dug the side of his face into the mattress and thrust his ass up with every rough shove down of Sirus's cock. "Fuck me, man, fuck me hard!" In answer, Sirus grabbed Grey's hips and drove his huge length home, ripping Grey wide open and exposing his weakness in every way. "Ahh!" Grey jerked, suddenly scared to take it -- and nearly hacked his finger off when he snapped out of his fantasy and found himself standing in the kitchen trying to slice a tomato.

Cursing for real this time, Grey threw the knife in the sink and stuck his finger in his mouth, his sandwich forgotten. He glanced at his watch as he made his way to the bathroom for some antiseptic and gauze, stunned to see it was nearly six o'clock. He had started making that sandwich almost an hour ago, but like all day today, his thoughts kept returning to Sirus, pulling him into a daydream that felt a whole hell of a lot like a nightmare.

I don't take a fucking. Hell, Grey didn't even *give* them anymore.

Walking out of the shower this morning, Grey had psyched himself up to stare Sirus down and face what had happened earlier this morning. He refused to hide from the man just because they saw each other jerk off. Only, Grey came out of the bathroom, with a speech all prepared, and Sirus had been nowhere to be found. Grey figured on any one of a dozen possibilities as to why the man might be out, and he hadn't sweat having to put off the uncomfortable conversation. Now, nearly a dozen hours later with no sign of Sirus, Grey began to wonder if his Peeping Tom act hadn't run the guy out of the cabin for good.

Bandage secured around his index finger, Grey tore to Sirus's bedroom and pushed his way inside, pulling dresser drawers and closet doors open, searching for clothes, only to find empty space after empty space, where at least a sweater or a pair of jeans ought to be.

"Fuck." Grey turned in a circle, burying his hands in his hair. "I ran him off."

Great. The man would rather live in a cabin with no running water than risk Grey spying on him again. Perfect. Just perfect. His sister would kill him.

Grey rounded to the mirror and leaned in, bracing his hands on the dresser. "No, she won't," he talked to his reflection, "because you're going to go over to Sirus's cabin and fix this mess you started." Grey noted the wildness in his eyes and the disarray of his hair, and he quickly straightened, forcing himself to breathe normally. "Get control of the situation, Greyson." He combed his hair into order with his fingers. "Don't be a pussy. Do it now, before it gets out of hand."

Taking another few breaths to calm the chaos that often tried to edge its way into his world, Grey closed the closet and all of the drawers he'd opened, grabbed his coat off the hook by the front door, and went in search of his runaway roommate.

———

GREY KILLED THE MOTORBOAT'S ENGINE just before reaching Sirus's dock. At least, he hoped it was Sirus's dock. Sirus had said *"the cabin across the lake"* last night during Grey's dinner interrogation, so he hoped the guy hadn't actually been speaking in more general terms that might include the cabins on the east and west side of the water.

After tying off the boat, Grey hoisted himself onto the dock, shoved his hands into the pockets of his jeans, and trudged up the sloping land to a cabin that appeared slightly smaller than his did. As Grey got closer, the thrashing sounds of Guns-n-Roses *Welcome to the Jungle* hit his ears, drawing out a chuckle. Yeah, Grey figured he had the right place. Sirus Wilder just seemed like an old-school rock music kind of guy.

Taking the stairs two at a time, Grey rapped a sharp knock on the door and then leaned his weight back on his heels to wait. The music didn't die and nobody answered, so, after a minute, Grey gave it another go, and then one more, to no answer. He tried the doorknob, not terribly surprised to find it unlocked.

"Hello?" he called out, taking only a few steps inside. "Sirus? It's Grey."

Nothing but the continued music greeted him. G-n-R moved on to the next track on the CD, or possibly a tape or record. He doubted it was an iPod set up. Sirus struck Grey as a throwback in a lot of ways, although he didn't quite know why he put that label on the man.

"Sirus?" Not getting any response, Grey went ahead and shut the door behind him before more cold air swept inside. A living room sat to his left, done in warm mossy greens and deep midnight blues with touches of brown leather. A brick fireplace dominated the sidewall.

He followed the split-log wall to his right until he reached an opening, pausing to peek his head in what he knew would be the kitchen. Dark woods somehow made the area look cozy rather than dank or cave-like, and a multi-colored woven rug sat under a table with two chairs, brightening the small space.

Grey turned around. "Sirus? Are you here?" He made one final attempt to make his presence known, leaving nothing to chance as he cut across the living room to an opening on the backside of the cabin. He entered a short hallway with two doors, the first one leading to the bathroom, the second Sirus's bedroom. Averting his eyes as quickly as he could, Grey purposely noted nothing more than the tartan plaid blanket and a pile of pillows covered in snow-white fabric before whipping his head back out and making a beeline for the front door. He did not need to have a complete visual of where Sirus Wilder laid that stunning body of his to sleep every night.

The music continued to blast, so Grey loped down the steps and circled the cabin, following the wall until he reached the back. A large, open shed loomed some twenty-five feet away. Light shone through the thrown open double doors, and as Grey got close enough to peek inside, he changed his mind about his temporary roommate yet again.

A dozen mechanic's lights hung from various points in the ceiling, casting the entire area in warm yellow lighting. Perfectly aligned plank flooring and equally well-constructed walls and roof stepped this shed up a dozen levels from slipshod to a serious workspace.

In addition to a buzz saw, Grey noted that other power tools and machinery also filled a small portion of the area. Grey processed huge hunks of wood, stone, and sheets of metal lining the back wall. That all got a cursory glance from him. Then he shifted and took in the area at the far end of the right wall, and he gasped.

Holy fuck.

Three stunning pieces of sculpture took up the right back area of the workspace. Each sculpture combined abstract ideas with what was clearly the human form, each fashioned into works of stunning beauty. There were other more literal pieces as well, some life-size, others smaller. Various canvases and boards of carved wood leaned here and there, taking over the back portion of the large space.

Holy fuck.

Sirus wasn't building shelves in this workroom. The man was an artist.

And right now -- Grey shifted his focus again, and breathed through the vision standing before him -- that artist worked at a table in the center of the room, his back to the open doors, and no shirt in sight.

Holy fuck, again.

Grey curled his hands at his sides, itching to run his fingers over the thick ropes of muscle that tapered down to a snug pair of jeans encasing a tight ass and long, muscled legs. Dark hair clung to Sirus's neck, wet with sweat that ran in enticing rivulets down his back, where it dampened the waistband of his jeans. Without a belt, the waist of his pants rode low, making Grey's dick twitch as he imagined yanking them down, bending Sirus over his worktable, and plowing that firm ass until Sirus screamed with the need to come.

As he moved into the workspace, Grey spotted a drop of sweat starting right at the top of Sirus's spine. Grey zeroed in on it with the goal of lapping it up with his tongue before it disappeared inside Sirus's jeans. Then, since he would already be on his knees, Grey might just have to take a taste of what those tight ass cheeks kept hidden. *Yes.* Then he would turn Sirus around, smash his face into the guy's crotch, and get high on the musky smell of man he hadn't felt overtake his nostrils for far too long. Grey could practically taste the salty perspiration bathing his tongue.

Crash!

His mind fully on licking Sirus all over, Grey tripped over a wire cutting across the workroom and took a nosedive right for the floor, just thinking fast enough to throw his hands out and brace his fall. The heels of his hands took the impact, and he slid in a layer of sawdust and wood shavings, which sent his chin to the floor with a skull-jarring thud.

Shit.

"Shit." Sirus spun and dropped to the floor beside Grey. "You scared the hell out of me." He put his hands on Grey's shoulders, slid them along his arms, and then touched over his back, feeling him all over, and sending a shock of pure awareness through Grey that even two layers of clothing and a humiliating pratfall could not mask. "Are you all right?"

Heat burned a fast path up Grey's neck to his face. "Nothing disappearing into a hole forever wouldn't cure," he mumbled under his breath.

Sirus stretched his upper body and reached for the shelf under his worktable, pushing a button on a small tape deck that killed the rock music. Sudden, absolute silence took over the space, making Grey aware of just how loud the music had been. Right now, he wished for the pounding to his eardrums back in a flash.

Sirus slid back to Grey's side. "What did you say?" He put his hands under Grey's armpits and hauled Grey to his feet, as if Grey's six-feet, one hundred ninety-five pound frame were nothing. Sirus started dusting off Grey's jacket. "I'm sorry." He went down Grey's shoulders and arms and then turned Grey's hands over, palms face up. "I like the music loud while I work and I didn't hear what you said. Oh, here," he took Grey's elbow and guided him to a sink tucked in the front corner of the room, "your palms are a little raw. You should wash them off, just to be safe." Sirus turned the water on and then reached under the oversized tub, coming up with a thick, white bar of soap.

"Thanks." As Grey took the offered soap, he tried to control the rushing tingle as Sirus's callused fingers grazed his. "Uh, yeah, I didn't say anything of value before." He tore his attention away from this too-beautiful man and put it on washing his hands, careful to keep his wrapped finger dry. "Just cursing myself for tripping."

"Sorry about that." Sirus reached to his left, hooked a shirt in his fingers, and dragged it to his side. He untwisted the faded black material and put the shirt on but left it hanging open. He then crossed his arms and leaned back against the table next to the sink, the picture of masculine confidence and cool that Grey usually always possessed.

"It's okay." It grated on Grey's nerves that Sirus affected calm so easily while Grey couldn't seem to find it in himself when he was near this man.

Clearly unaware of the turmoil going on inside Grey, Sirus smiled and raised a brow. "It's just me working in here, and I'm to the point where I instinctually know where everything is so that I don't trip or step into anything. I didn't know you were there or I would have warned you about the extension wire."

Grey raised a brow right back. "I think I'll live." He turned off the water, dried his hands on a threadbare towel hanging on a hook above the basin, and then held out his palms in Sirus's direction. "See? They're not even scraped. Just a little bit red."

Sirus chuckled, the sound rumbling up from deep inside his body. "Glad to hear it." He gave Grey a half smile that somehow transformed the devastating hardness of his face. "I'd hate to have to explain to your sister that I'd caused you injury on your first vacation in years."

Grey snapped his stare off Sirus's smile and narrowed his gaze. "What in the hell do you mean by that?" His voice dropped into low, clipped territory as his mind started spinning. "Did you know I was coming here? Did Kelsie set me up?" Grey glanced down at the sink, and then pushed right into Sirus's space, bumping his chest against Sirus's crossed arms.

Storm clouds brewed in Sirus's eyes but Grey couldn't care and didn't dare back down. He leaned into Sirus until he had the bigger man bowed back over the table behind him. "You fucking have water. I just washed my hands. You obviously didn't need to stay at my place last night. What in the hell is going on here?"

The clouds erupted, and Sirus moved fast. He grabbed Grey's upper arms and spun them around so that *Grey's* spine dug into the workbench this time. "What the hell is going on here," Sirus's low, intimidating octave rivaled Grey's, "is that you just called me a liar." He grasped the table on either side of Grey's hips, trapping him in place. "You sure you want to do that, *friend?*"

Heat lightning charged the air around them, making the workroom feel like a sauna in the middle of snow. Every inch of Grey's skin hummed with vitality, something he hadn't felt consume him in forever. He didn't dare let his body shiver and give himself away. Drawing up all of his will, he looked Sirus in the eyes and didn't flinch. "You take a good hard look at me, Wilder," Grey breathed so heavily their chests touched with every intake of breath, "and you decide if you see anything close to a man who can be intimated living inside me."

"Maybe you're not intimidated by me --" Sirus broke eye contact and turned his focus down, perusing, just as Grey had challenged him to do. It felt like forever, and Grey had to work like the devil to control the shiver that wanted to work its way through him as he wondered if this man would find him lacking. Sirus finally put his full attention back on Grey's face, and deep charcoal swirled in the depths of his gray eyes. "-- but you damn well want something male living inside you." Cool confidence emanated from Sirus's very pores, and it didn't even look as if his heart pounded very fast. "I think we established that around five a.m. this morning."

Grey never played from a position of defense. That was a losing strategy. Emotions long unused spiraled nearly out of control in him, though, and he attacked before thinking, before assessing, before predicting the response he would get from his opponent. "And maybe you want it just as much," he taunted, "which is why you tucked tail and ran home."

White hot fire flared in Sirus's eyes, and Grey knew he had misread his opponent.

A fatal mistake.

CHAPTER FOUR

Sirus assessed the arrogance surrounding Greyson Cole like a full-body cloak, and he wanted to punch the bastard.

"You fucking smug suit," he said, his voice whisper soft, but deadly. He fumed inside and had no idea how he managed to keep his outward appearance so still and calm. "You set your sister up with your best friend for a week in your cabin, and you automatically think she's gonna turn around and do the same thing to you?" Awareness flared in Grey's eyes, and Sirus chalked up one point for the home team. "That's right, Kelsie is my friend, and she did tell me how she and John ended up together. And while *she* might want to return the favor one day, what in the hell makes you think for one second I would agree to do it? I never even saw your face before yesterday afternoon.

Maybe you go around fucking everything with a tight ass that likes cock, but that isn't me." Sirus let his gaze drop and linger over the fine lines of Grey's body, beauty that no amount of winter clothing could hide, and he cursed under his breath at the waste of such a thing of perfection attached to such an asshole of a person. "I actually like to know the person I'm screwing, and I like to think they *don't*," his gaze came back up and locked right on Grey's eyes, "believe I'm a liar when we're doing it."

Grey shoved in to Sirus, and suddenly they were toe-to-toe, circling and pushing into each other's space. Grey's hazel eyes darkened to almost green, and an arrogant smile twisted his hard lips. "You flatter yourself, Wilder, if you think I would ever bend over for you."

Sirus snorted in Grey's face. "You think I'm insulted by that statement, *Cole*? All I have to do is look at you to know you wouldn't spread yourself open for anybody." God, Sirus fought the urge to shove Grey onto the floor and penetrate his ass just to prove how much the man would love a fucking between them. Sirus's cock stirred to do that very thing but he ignored it for the purely physical response it was. "Don't pretend your refusal has anything to do with me."

"I'm not pretending one goddamn thing." Grey snarled and pushed as if Sirus had just accused him of murder. "You're the one who has water," he reached back, opened the spray, and waved his arm across the basin in a sarcastic sweeping gesture, "when you told me yesterday that you didn't."

"And in my house," Sirus spoke each world very deliberately, "I still don't." He shoved Grey's arm aside and shut off the water. A rich bastard like Grey might not care, but Sirus didn't waste money just to prove a point. Curling his hands into tight fists, he bared his teeth right back at Grey. "You want to go take a shit or a shower in my bathroom and find out?" He grabbed Grey's arm and hauled him out of his workspace toward the cabin. "The water that runs in the shed doesn't have anything to do with the pipes in my cabin, so yeah, I can have water down there and still not have it in my home."

Grey struggled against Sirus's rough hold but Sirus couldn't stop walking or make his hand release the hard, toned muscles that strained under his digging fingers.

"Which attack from you should I defend next, huh?" Sirus threw the words out over his shoulder. "That I knew you hadn't taken a vacation in a long time? Guess what, asshole? I already told you that your sister and I are friends. She loves you, so she talks about you, and that's how I knew. There is no vast conspiracy to get me into your cabin and your bed, so get the hell over yourself. You want to be alone, then be alone. Nobody gives a shit."

Grey yanked his arm out of Sirus's grasp with a surprising burst of strength, growling as he did it. He spun Sirus around and jammed him against the cabin wall with a palm pressed flat against his chest. His fingers curled and dug into Sirus's pecs, and his face seemed to become a creation of all hard lines and angles, with mossy coldness in his eyes, and lips that thinned down to little more than a slash. "You don't know anything about my life or why I'm alone." Grey flinched as he spoke those words; Sirus saw it. He watched as the man shook off the tell and regrouped. "But don't you dare say nobody gives a shit about me. Kelsie cares. John cares. I have people." His chest heaved, and his voice cracked. "I do."

Sirus stared at the man before him, at a hard shell straining on all four corners, struggling to contain whatever volatile emotions lived inside him. Sirus's chest squeezed, and he slumped against the wall at his back, all the strung-tight tension melting right out of him. "Okay," he said softly, uncertain about speaking loudly in Grey's presence right now. "I believe you. I apologize. You implied I was a liar, and it pissed me off. I retaliated. You can call me a lot of harsh names, and some of them will even be true, but I'm not a liar, and I won't just stand quietly when someone implies that I am."

Grey let go of his hold on Sirus and shoved his hands into his pockets. "And maybe it just seemed like too many coincidences, so I put pieces together and drew a conclusion that wasn't fair." Puffs of clouds swirled in front of Grey's face, proving just how hot the man was inside when matched against the frigid air outside "But you have to understand, I came up to my cabin to get away from everybody and everything, and instead I found an almost naked man in my living room. Within less than twenty-four hours, I find out he's gay too. I wouldn't put it past my sister to think it very clever to set me up in the same way I helped John do with her. If you really do know her as well as you say you do then you know that's true."

Sirus thought about tattooed, pink-haired, fireball Kelsie, and chuckled. "Yeah, I suppose you would think that."

Rocking back on the heels of thick-soled boots, Grey let his gaze drift to the right, to across the lake. "Pair that with the fact that you were gone this morning when I woke up, and didn't return once all day, and I wasn't sure what to think. I came here to apologize for running you off, only to find you do have some water running, and I began to question --"

"Wait." Sirus reached out and touched Grey's forearm, drawing the man's attention back to the two of them. "Run me off?" His brow furrowed. "What are you talking about? I probably lost track of time, but I really don't have water. I was -- am -- coming back."

Grey pointed in the direction of his cabin, confusion mapping his face. "But there's nothing of yours left at my place."

"Yeah, I know." Sirus bit his cheek, determined not to laugh. He somehow didn't think Greyson Cole had a very big sense of humor about himself, or liked to admit he had jumped to *very* wrong conclusions so *very* quickly. He seemed more well thought out than that. "I've been at your place for three days already. I brought my dirty stuff home and traded it for clean. My shaving kit is still there."

"I guess I didn't see that." Shifting his stance again, Grey took his hands out of his pockets, crossed his arms against his chest, and looked Sirus straight in the eyes. "Look, I figured when you saw me watching you jerk off, and then were gone all day, I'd freaked you out and you ran. I came here with the intent to apologize, but then you so casually knew I hadn't taken a vacation in a long time, and you had the water in the shed, and my plan went to shit. So I apologize for that too, on top of pulling my dick out while watching you masturbate. That was what I really came over here to say. When I heard you this morning, and then saw that your door wasn't entirely closed, I should have just walked away."

Sirus wasn't so sure he wished the same. He had gotten ten times harder this morning when he'd realized he had an audience. That *Grey* was his audience. "I wondered if you would admit you got off on watching me or would act like it had never happened."

"Hey," Grey dropped his arms and moved in on Sirus again, "I know I'm an asshole sometimes, but I'm not a liar either. I came here wanting to make my behavior right, and to tell you that you can use the extra bedroom for as long as you need it. Anything beyond that, and I'm not interested. You might have one fucking insane body," Grey leaned in and inhaled, but abruptly stepped back, "but I am not in the market for a partner. Not right now. Not ever. I just want to make that clear."

In that moment Sirus forced himself to conjure the crushing pain that had consumed him at the end of his relationship with Paul, and automatically thought about the permanent evidence inked into his chest he still bore as a result of his blindness.

The hard-on threatening to emerge right this moment for Grey disappeared. "Then we're on the same page," Sirus said. Fuck, why couldn't he be one of those one-night-stand kind of guys? "That makes everything a whole lot easier."

"Excellent." Grey's lip flattened, and he nodded. "Then I'll see you back at the cabin in a bit." He looked up at the sky as he started walking backward toward the lake. "It's getting dark fast. Feels like rain is coming too. You might not want to wait much longer."

A shiver rolled through Sirus, and he suddenly realized he stood outside in an unbuttoned flannel shirt. "I won't." He wrapped the two halves of material around his middle. "See you in a while."

"Okay." Grey stopped and turned back around. The man stood more than half in shadows, and Sirus could only see one eye, sharp cheek, and the back edge of Grey's jaw line. "One more thing," Grey added.

What now? "Go ahead."

Grey's jaw ticked visibly, and when he spoke, his voice was full of grit. "You're an amazingly talented artist, and I'd buy your work for my home any day of the week." Grey looked down and shrugged. "Just wanted to say that. 'Night."

Sirus stood locked in place, watching as Grey climbed back in his boat and sped away across the water. A tremble rocked through Sirus again. This time, Sirus knew it didn't have anything to do with the cold.

———

Rain blasted in a thundering sheet against the front of the cabin, stamping a relentless beat into the windows and wood. The power had gone out long ago. A blazing fire roared in the fireplace, but Sirus could not settle down. He knew why too.

Greyson Cole.

The man sat on the couch with his laptop in hand, an external battery allowing him to go right on working without a pause. The fire and a half-dozen kerosene lanterns cast the entire living room in a soft glow, cast *Grey* in a soft glow, and Sirus couldn't keep his cock down to save his life. He stood by the window, forced himself to watch the rainstorm putting on a show outside, and tried to ignore the silhouette of Grey he could see from the corner of his eye.

Fuck, though, the guy was so damn sexy, and Sirus hadn't been with a man in over two years. He'd done a lot of yanking on his dick during that time, and he had a handful of toys for when he craved feeling something inside him. Playing with himself satisfied the physical need for release but it didn't stop the craving for companionship ... or for something more. Sirus had learned how to cope with the wanting and he even understood it had its place. He also knew he had a tendency to pick men who would not stand up and be with him out in the open. After his last break-up, he swore he would never again pursue someone who wouldn't be out and equal with him. Sirus had a damn good feeling that included Greyson Cole.

Sirus was an adult and he knew how to control his physical needs and desires. As attractive as Grey was, Sirus could easily share a cabin with him and not be overly tempted. That was until Grey had to go let that slip of vulnerability show through earlier today and mess with Sirus's head. How could Sirus have complete disdain for someone so clearly alone that he almost attacked in his need to prove he had people who cared about him? And beyond that, to then stop himself and compliment Sirus's art, when he so clearly wanted to get the hell off Sirus's side of the lake, showed admirable character too. Both of those things burrowed their way under Sirus's skin and wouldn't let him go.

Sirus's attention strayed Grey's way again. He latched his gaze onto the solid frame of the man, watching Grey as he focused so intently on whatever project he had open on his laptop. Grey had his feet kicked up on the coffee table, his legs stretched out, covered in dark denim, and his feet bare. The man looked sexy when he worked. Sirus rubbed one of his own bare feet against the other, his toes curling at the curious intimacy of them both, together, without shoes and socks. It made Sirus think he had every right to walk over to Grey, extricate the laptop from his hands, and sink into a deep, distracting kiss. He would settle on Grey's lap, straddle him, lean in close, and rub his ass against Grey's dick. Sirus would tease the hard ridge of flesh until they tore each other's jeans down and, with a cry, Sirus would impale himself on Grey's cock. Sirus bit down a moan, almost able to feel the claiming right where he stood.

Stop it, goddamnit!

As he snapped out of his fantasy, Sirus's heart slammed with fear. He looked to Grey, searching for some kind of awareness in the man, as if he might be able to read Sirus's thoughts. Grey went on, unaware, typing away on his keyboard. Immediately Sirus slipped again as he imagined the damage those fingers could do in his ass.

Fuck. Sirus's channel clenched, begging for attention, for a complete filling. His gaze drifted Grey's way again. He took a step forward even as he knew this guy was so, so wrong for him. A picture of Paul flashed before Sirus's eyes right then and stopped him dead in his tracks. Sandy blond hair and blue eyes seemed to look right into Sirus's soul, suffocating him, forcing him to relive the last time he had taken a chance on someone that deep down he knew wasn't right for him. Still, as Sirus stood there and experienced the brutal break-up again, his body ached for a man, and he took another step closer to Grey.

No! That scream of denial woke Sirus up, resonating in his head. He turned, rushing to the door. *I have to get out of this place.*

Now.

Sirus threw open the door and a blast of wind and rain soaked his front before he took one step outside. He forged into the frigid display of nature, letting the cold wash over him and cool his insides. Sirus made it halfway down the steps, almost to freedom, when a ruthless grip locked on his arm and jerked him against the step railing.

Sirus looked up, and with the light from the fire and lanterns inside the cabin helping to cut through the darkness, he witnessed rage in Grey's face.

"What in the hell do you think you're doing?" Grey looked as if he shouted, but it barely registered as such above the noise of the pounding rain. "It's goddamned pouring."

Looking up into the darkened night, Sirus welcomed the torrent of rain beating down on his face. For the first time in what seemed like forever, he felt alive, and he forced himself to believe it was because of the harsh elements and not this man's bruising hold.

"Come on!" Grey shook Sirus again and tried to tug him up the stairs. "Get inside!"

Sirus pulled back, digging his feet into the wood. "No, it's just rain. It won't hurt me." He could not -- COULD NOT -- go back in that cabin with Grey.

"You'll get sick as a dog," Grey argued. Rain plastered his hair to his head in a skullcap and poured down his face. "Of course it can hurt you." His lips pulled with hard lines, and all Sirus could think about was kissing Grey breathless and shoving his tongue into the warmth of his mouth.

Stifling a groan, Sirus pushed past Grey and down the steps. He called over his shoulder, not daring to look back, "If I get sick, I'll deal with it." His feet squished in the mud the dirt path had become. The cold no barrier, a painful erection raged in his jeans. "You go inside. I want to be out here."

Grey shouted a curse and then slammed into Sirus from

behind, locking his arms around Sirus's arms and chest. "You're not running around in the rain and the dark! Fucking stop, damn it!" As Grey struggled to take Sirus to the ground, his muscles contorted wildly against Sirus's back and arms, surprising Sirus with his strength. Sirus had the extra height and the bulk, though, and he ripped Grey off his body to then whirl on him, his emotions playing too close to the surface to fully conceal.

Sirus laid his stare on the hard set of Grey's face, and his body heaved with labored breathing. Grey's soaked shirt clung to his chest, exposing hard pecs and tight nipples, the tips jutting with the cold. Sirus looked; their gazes clashed, the heat so intense Sirus jerked with it. A rough noise escaped Grey right then, and that was when Sirus glanced down. *Shit.* A thick bulge thrust hard against Grey's pants, giving him away.

Grey stared right back at Sirus's cock and figured him out too.

"I don't want this," Sirus uttered, his voice stripped bare.

"Me either." Grey sounded as if he were in agony.

Swearing, they flew at each other in a furious kiss.

CHAPTER FIVE

G rey kissed Sirus with brutal force, and Sirus welcomed it with an internal shout of pleasure. Sirus's mouth was pried open with a rough clamp of Grey's hand on his jaw, and Grey pushed his way inside to a frantic meeting of tongues. Sirus whimpered, his cock straining for release, aching for something he knew he couldn't have.

Greyson's ass.

Sirus moaned as his dick pushed against his jeans, pounding painfully with a rush of blood.

Grey slid a hand down Sirus's back to grab his ass; he held it and ground his prick against Sirus's bulge. "I want your cock," Grey murmured against Sirus's mouth, biting Sirus's lower lip just before he spoke. "I want to see it; I want to taste it; I want it in my mouth."

Oh holy hell. Sirus jerked and went shaky in the knees. He had a man in front of him enthusiastic about blowjobs. Giving them. Very few things in life were better than that. Sirus grabbed Grey's other hand and forced it between their bodies, digging past his stomach until he got Grey's palm on his prick through his jeans. Grey immediately clutched Sirus's length in a snug hold and began to rock him in between his grip on Sirus's cock and ass, making Sirus vibrate with the pleasure of it.

Leaning in, Grey scraped his mouth across Sirus's, the touch pulling on his lower lip. "Take off your shirt." Grey squeezed Sirus's length, drawing a hiss. "Now."

Unused to taking orders -- in anything -- Sirus burned with a retort. At the same time, his cock was harder than he'd ever experienced, and he had a man willing to go down on him to take care of it. Those two factors had Sirus pumping his hips into Grey's hold and tearing at the plackets of his shirt in unison, ripping off buttons in order to comply.

"Yours too," Sirus said. As soon as his own shirt hit the muddy ground, Sirus yanked Grey's shirt out of his waistband before the man could say a word. He pushed the fabric up to Grey's neck, and there was enough light from the cabin for Sirus to revel in the sight of a stunning, fit chest. Sirus paused for a moment, taking his fill of the display of masculine lines before him. "Damn it, I could study you for days."

Grey let go of Sirus and shrugged out of his shirt while Sirus ran his hands all over Grey's chest and stomach, feeling every indent and groove, and he already started to visualize his hands chiseling pieces of granite away from a block until something resembling Greyson Cole's torso remained. Sirus rubbed the pads of his thumbs over tiny brown nipples and immediately brought the tips to twisted points once more. In response, Grey drew in a quick breath, and his belly trembled. Sirus loved Grey's visible reaction, and he brushed his fingers over the raised skin again.

"Jesus." Grey's voice was rough as he watched Sirus play with him. "You're making me so fucking hard."

Emboldened, Sirus twisted Grey's aroused nipples and tugged, tormenting the sensitized flesh. Grey moaned, pushing into Sirus's touch as he made a grab for Sirus's belt. Jerking the leather out of the loop, Grey leaned in and fused his mouth to Sirus's again, invading with a voracious, deep kiss. Sirus thrust his tongue into Grey's mouth and took over the mating of tongues, mimicking every stab he wanted to take at Grey's ass with his cock. At the same time, he shoved his hands down and tangled his fingers with Grey's, eager to get his pants down and his dick free. Sirus's erection pulsed with blood, hot to feel a mouth on it again.

Zipper and fly finally undone, Sirus winced when the snug, wet denim pulled at the hairs on his thighs as the fabric moved down his legs, tormenting his body in yet another way. His erection sprung heavy, the cold rain bearing down on them no match for the heat coursing through his body. Sirus would have been happy leaving his jeans around his ankles, but Grey dropped to his knees and took them the rest of the way off, leaving Sirus standing nude, soaked in the torrential rain -- and hard as a rock.

Grey looked up, and Sirus somehow found the man's eyes through the storm. The men connected visually, and they began to breathe in tandem, as if they had already become one. Sirus trembled, and it had nothing to do with the cold. Grey's face was so close to Sirus's erection that the warmth of every breath he exhaled washed over Sirus's dick in a wave, sending more shivers through his body. Hunger shone in Grey's changing hazel eyes, and Sirus had never wanted to be another person's meal more.

"Feed me your cock." Grey put his hands on Sirus's hips, clutching the flesh there, and opened his mouth.

Holy Mother. Sirus's legs weakened, and he didn't know how he kept from coming right on the spot. With hands that shook, he wrapped one around the base of his penis, buried the other in Grey's wet hair, and guided his dick past Grey's lips.

Grey immediately closed around Sirus and sucked on his thick cockhead, teasing the already leaking slit, and sent Sirus up in flames.

"Oh God, yeah." Roughness coated Sirus's words as he pushed more length into Grey's mouth. Every nerve ending in his shaft started singing with joy at its temporary home. Wet, suctioning warmth enveloped Sirus's cock with steadying degrees, and Grey accepted Sirus inch by inch until half his dick took over Grey's mouth and his tip touched Grey's throat.

"Fuck, man," Sirus squeezed the base of his cock as he stared down at Grey blowing him, "you're so good."

Grey looked up, mesmerizing Sirus with his intriguing eyes. As much as Sirus wanted to close his own and succumb to pure sensation, he couldn't look away from the picture Grey made. The man had his lips stretched unbearably wide around Sirus's thickness, and he sucked Sirus's penis in a slow, sensual back and forth motion, as if he had all the time in the world. Sirus couldn't see it, but God, he could he *feel* the magic of Grey's tongue against his supersensitized skin. Grey swirled his tongue around Sirus's embedded length and did amazing things to every bit of straining flesh he flicked or licked. The damn man was so fucking thorough Sirus couldn't stay still; he started pumping his hips in to Grey's face, fucking his mouth in shallow, faster strokes, needful of a quicker movement to match the nerve endings popping to crazy life over every inch of his body. Sirus kept his fist locked tight around the root of his cock, bumping his hand into Grey's mouth with every thrust, always aware not to give too much and make Grey choke. Sirus knew he was big but he wouldn't overpower a partner for the world.

Grey made throaty, murmuring noises of appreciation. He bobbed up and down on Sirus with a twisting motion and a rougher, suctioning pull, making Sirus's ass throb with just as much excitement as his dick did, his chute begging for equal attention. *Goddamnit, yeah.* Sirus gritted his teeth in response to just thinking about Grey sticking a few fingers in his asshole and fucking him hard.

Right then, Grey slid his hands around Sirus's hips and grabbed his ass in a bruising hold, splitting his cheeks wide open. As Grey dragged with insane, suctioning force down the length of Sirus's dick, he slipped the tip of one finger over Sirus's exposed hole and sent Sirus's bud into a frantic flutter of need. *Fuck.* Usually able to withstand a whole hell of a lot more foreplay than this, Sirus dug his fingers into Grey's scalp. He pulled away in the nick of time, roaring above the thunder of the storm as orgasm hit him full force. "Ohhh, oh God…" He jerked his cock with one painful pump from his fist and then unloaded his seed, shooting on Grey's neck, shoulders, and chest.

Almost manic, in a way he had never experienced before, Sirus shoved Grey onto his back and fell to his knees, straddling the man's stomach. Lines of pleasure still shot through Sirus's body, and his cock remained more than half-hard. "Oh fuck. I'm still there and can come again. Gimme, gimme." Sirus grabbed Grey's hand and shoved two fingers into his mouth, not waiting for Grey to agree. Sirus laved Grey's digits up good with saliva, his cock already getting stiffer again with just that small move. His rectum squeezed, knowing what would come next. Giving one more good lick all around the webbing of Grey's surprisingly rough fingers, Sirus rose up on his knees and shoved Grey's hand in between his legs, aiming for his pucker. "Help me…" He wiggled his ass down, grunting at the wonderful pressure pushing against his snapped-shut hole.

"Fuck, I want you inside me."

Fingers suddenly grasped Sirus's chin, and Sirus dropped his focus to the man beneath him. With their stares locked on each other, Grey said, "Breathe for me," and took over probing at Sirus's entrance. He pushed up, Sirus bore down, and, with one flash of pain, Sirus's hole gave up the fight and let Grey's fingers inside.

Sirus's ass burned with the invasion but it immediately clamped down on Grey's fingers and dragged them deeper into his channel. "Mmm, yeah." Sirus braced his hands on Grey's chest and pushed down, forcing more of the other man's long fingers inside his body. "Fuck me, fuck me." Clenching his teeth against the pure, unadulterated delight his squeezing tunnel and Grey's embedded fingers created together, Sirus rolled his hips down onto each spearing his passage took and reached for more. His prick grew to full arousal once again, and his balls tingled and drew tight against his body, shoving him once again to the breaking point.

"Take it, Wilder, take it." Grey's voice was harsh and forceful as he plunged and scissored his fingers with great enthusiasm in Sirus's quivering channel, stretching him with almost savage aggression. "Feel every goddamn inch of me playing in your ass."

"Uh-huh ... fuck." Sirus pulled his lower lip between this teeth and bit, drawing blood as he tried to stave off release. He couldn't control the panting and writhing, though, and his knees slipped wider apart in the mud, pushing his ass down even harder and trapping Grey's hand against his stomach. Sirus didn't care and couldn't stop gyrating his ass against Grey's fingers. His thighs shook, his arms felt weaker than a kitten, and just when Sirus didn't think he could take even one more sensation, Grey crooked his buried fingers and stroked right on Sirus's sweet spot, tipping him headfirst over the edge.

Crying out as the second release hit him, stronger and sharper than the first, Sirus sank his fingers at least half an inch into Grey's chest muscles, searching for a toehold with which to cling. His entire body convulsed, his ass closed in a vise on Grey's fingers, and he swore he felt cum race through his bowel and belly before finally letting it go and shooting a stream of hot semen on Grey's forearm and chest.

Grey locked his gaze on Sirus's, and it was frightening in its depth. The man looked pained. Sirus scrambled backward, letting Grey's fingers slip free of his body, and he positioned his ass over the other man's crotch. Grey's jeans acted as little to no barrier, and Sirus ground his buttocks into the bulge. His crease split and his asshole found the ridge of Grey's cock, and Sirus immediately began rocking over the connection in a frenzy. "I'm still open … ah, yeah…" Sirus groaned and bucked as Grey knifed up into his loosened hole. "Fuck me and let me feel you come."

Grey growled and latched onto Sirus's waist, holding him down as he thrust up repeatedly, taking with aggression, as if there were no clothing between them at all. Sirus rode the shape of Grey's cock with piston-fast sweeps along his crack, knowing he had never done anything like this in his life. He felt like a teenager in the backseat of a car doing something fast and without finesse because it was forbidden and he didn't want to get caught.

"Ohh … ohh…" Moaning, Grey strained under Sirus and then quickly stiffened, his body arching in a bow. "Coming…" His mouth fell open, his eyes squeezed shut, and his fingers bruised a punishing hold on Sirus's waist. "Damn it, damn it…" Grey's entire body shuddered and then the heat of ejaculate warmed Sirus's buttocks, even through underwear and jeans, as Grey succumbed to release.

Eventually, the tension eased from Grey's body and he lowered back to the ground. Just as he opened his eyes, the rain broke, turning from a downpour to a light mist, as if Mother Nature took its cue from the severity of Sirus and Grey's coupling. Sirus couldn't move as he absorbed what had happened, the heat of the moment so intense he couldn't walk away, even as he accepted he'd just done something incredibly intimate with a man he didn't know very well at all.

With someone whom less than twenty-four hours ago he wasn't even sure he liked.

Damn it. Scrubbing his face, Sirus exhaled slowly and tried to figure out what the hell to do next.

Fucking A. Grey had a naked man sitting on him, he'd just come in his jeans like a preteen discovering his cock, and, for the first time in his adult life, he didn't have any clue what to say, how to behave, or have a plan of attack in place.

It's not a big deal, Greyson; people have little moments like this all the time. Pull your shit together and act like an adult.

Grey cleared his throat, and Sirus jolted on top of him, giving Grey his full attention. Slate-colored eyes pierced right through Grey, and once again made Grey's breath catch. Stole the coherency of his thoughts too.

"Ah, if you could," Grey's focus dropped to his stomach and landed right on Sirus's cock, "you know…" Fuck, Grey's ass throbbed as he stared at Sirus's prick, and he flashed on an image of Sirus rolling him over and filling his hole. *No, you don't open yourself up for anybody, Greyson.* Grey tore his gaze off Sirus's dick, and he took a deep breath, gathering himself again. When he felt back in control, he looked at Sirus and spoke in an even, cool tone. "If you wouldn't mind getting up, we could go back inside where it's dry and warm."

"Oh!" Sirus shot off Grey's lap, and Grey tried not to notice the immediate sense of loss. Snatching his muddy clothes off the ground, Sirus looked at them, shook his head, and went ahead and left them hanging at his side. "Sorry."

"Not a problem." With Sirus's weight gone, the clammy chill of the mud beneath Grey's back sank in with penetrating cold. He got to his feet, shaking off the rain and muddy earth clinging to his back as best he could. "It's late. Let's just go inside." He took a stiff step toward the porch.

"Wait!" Sirus grabbed Grey's wrist in a manacle hold.

Grey's eyes fell closed, and his heart plummeted to his

stomach. "Yes?" Grey spoke the word with command, but in his head, it was little more than a weak whisper. He didn't feel any stability under his feet; the sense of uncertainty took him back to his childhood -- where he *so* did not need to be right now. Ever, really. *Please, I can't deal with drama or overwrought emotions right now.* He forced himself to turn around and face Sirus with a calmness that belied the racing in his heart. "What is it?"

Sirus shifted his weight and twisted his soaking clothes in his big hands. "What we just did," his attention dropped for a second to the ground where they'd both just lain, "I need you to know I don't do that kind of thing regularly or casually." Sirus took a step forward, his savage face earnest. "Which is not to say I'm declaring love here or anything, but I need you to tell me something you wouldn't tell someone you weren't intimate with. Give me something personal so I don't feel like I just did what I did with an almost stranger."

Grey searched Sirus's face and demeanor, looking for even the slightest sign of deception. He found none. "Just one thing?"

Nodding, Sirus clutched his clothes to his belly. "Yes." He didn't look away and he didn't waver.

"And you'll give me something in return?" Grey pushed, needing something more.

Sirus nodded again sharply. "Agreed."

Oh fuck, don't do it. "I haven't shared a bed with anyone in three years, and I fucking hate sleeping alone." Grey rushed through the confession he could not believe came out of his mouth. "Now you."

"It has been two years for me," Sirus confessed, spilling his words in just as fast a tumble as Grey had done. "And I hate it just as much as you do. I don't normally do this, and I don't have any expectations," Sirus pulled Grey to him with one gentle tug, "but with what you just said, and what I admitted as well, you have to know I don't want to sleep in that guest room tonight."

Sirus's body heat shimmered off him in tangible waves, making Grey realize how cold he was inside. How cold his bed was too. *No expectations.* Grey couldn't stop thinking about that, and he couldn't take his eyes off the stunning piece of man standing before him, someone his sister knew, and more importantly, trusted.

Against every rule he had ever set for himself, and every promise he'd made to himself three years ago, Grey said, "So don't." His blood rushed so fast he felt a little dizzy. He said the rest anyway. "Share the master bedroom with me."

Chapter Six

Grey's request hung heavy in the air, standing between him and the man before him like a ghost in the dark night. Stunned disbelief didn't even begin to describe the expression on Sirus's face, and frissons of extreme discomfort crawled under Grey's skin, attaching doubt to his one act of selfish need.

Suddenly amazingly uncomfortable, Grey shrugged with indifference. "It was just a suggestion. Suit yourself." He hardened the hint of vulnerability that had leaked out of him and schooled himself not to show he cared. "I'm going inside."

"Were you serious?" The quiet of Sirus's voice cut across the small amount of space between them, stroking the sliver of needy weakness inside Grey before he could completely cauterize it. Sirus looked at Grey with that stormy gaze of his and tugged at Grey's long-buried need to be something more than a solo act. "Do you really want me to share your bed?"

Grey opened his mouth and, "I can't remember when I've ever wanted anything more," *almost* came out. Panic swirled in his chest, though, suffocating him, and instead he coolly delivered, "Look, it's late, and we're both exhausted. I don't know about you, but I'm about thirty seconds away from freezing my balls off. I plan to go inside, have a hot shower, and go to bed. We can double up, or we can go it alone. It's up to you." Grey looked right at Sirus and did not show so much as a shiver. "Either way, I'm not standing here and discussing it any further."

Sirus penetrated Grey with a brief, intense stare that left Grey feeling touched from top to bottom. Then Sirus leaned down, scooped up Grey's shirt, and thrust it against Grey's chest. Grey grabbed it before it could fall, and when he did, Sirus slid his hand down Grey's stomach, past his cock, and cupped his balls through his jeans. Sirus's face was only inches from Grey's, and Grey was caught, trapped, and unable to breathe. "Can't have these falling off," Sirus answered, and flashed a fast, wicked smile. He squeezed Grey's nuts and gave them a placating pat. Then, holy shit, he winked. "Let's get you into a hot bath." Sirus's hand trailed over Grey's thigh and around his hip as he moved up the steps, setting Grey's body to roaring with renewed life. "Coming?" he called out, and kept right on going, the view of his tight, oh-so-enticing bare ass luring Grey with every step he took.

Lord knew, Grey acknowledged, he should walk to his car and drive straight down the mountain. His legs wouldn't obey. Against his better judgment, Grey followed.

———

"OH FUCK, THIS WAS A good idea." Grey moaned, his body spiking with pinpricks as his chilled skin came into contact with steaming hot water. He sank all the way into the bath and leaned back against Sirus's chest. The man's long, lightly haired legs encased Grey on both sides, and his cock hit right at the cleft of Grey's ass. The hot water felt so damn good, though, Grey didn't sexually respond.

Aside from wanting to get warm, Grey had spent the walk from outside to the bathroom reminding himself that in his business life he dealt with billionaires on a regular basis -- and did it without ever breaking a sweat. He reasoned if he could do that then he could certainly deal with a simple sexual attraction to one good-looking man. He knew the pitfalls to avoid, he knew how much to share, and most importantly, he knew in two weeks time he would walk away refreshed, reenergized, and ready to get back to work. Of course, success depended on Grey being completely open about his position and feelings, and Sirus agreeing to a brief affair.

With that realization, Grey belatedly figured he probably should have planned something more neutral to that kind of discussion than a damned romantic lantern and candlelit bath.

Fuck.

Just then, Sirus ran his hands up Grey's arms and curled them around his shoulders. He dipped down and spoke at Grey's ear. "Your body just went from comfortable and relaxed to tighter than the strings on a guitar in less than five seconds." Sirus dug his fingers into Grey's muscles and began to give him a massage. "Just because I don't normally accept blowjobs and invitations to share a bath and bed from men I hardly know doesn't mean I'm looking for a marriage proposal. It is unusual for me, but you don't have to worry that I'm going to think we're a couple or anything."

"It wasn't that." Grey scrambled, his mind racing for cover. He hated that Sirus had picked up on the tension in his body, and worse, that he'd so easily pinpointed why it had happened. People did not read Greyson Cole. Business associates and ex-boyfriends alike told him his poker face had no match. "I was thinking about outside." Jesus, Grey could still feel the thickness and heat of Sirus's cock taking over his mouth. His dick twitched a little bit as he recalled the man's tight, scorching ass clenching around his buried fingers too. "You pulled away before you came. Is there something I need to know about you?"

"I'm clean," Sirus said. He ran his hands down Grey's chest and settled their upper bodies into one another more comfortably. "You didn't know that, though, and I didn't want to presume something you might not have wanted."

Grey closed his eyes, trembling as he imagined warm spits of Sirus's cum coating his tongue and throat. Christ, how he missed blowjobs. "I wanted." He reached up and fiddled with Sirus's fingers where they rested on his chest. "But thank you for being clearheaded enough in the moment to think for both of us. Normally I know more about my sexual partners, not to mention we've been tested together so we each know the other is clean." Even then, Grey always wore a condom when he had sex. He hadn't brought any condoms with him on this trip though. Hadn't needed any in a very long time. "This is a unique circumstance, and I guess we need to discuss our histories and expectations a little bit so we can decide how best to proceed."

Sirus nuzzled his lips against Grey's temple and squeezed him with his legs. "You're very precise in everything you say. That's cute."

Grumbling, Grey felt his face heat. "Being smart and well thought out is not cute. It's…" He looked around the softly lit bathroom, searching for the right word. "It's…"

"Smart?" Sirus helped, chuckling.

Discomfort burned Grey's already warm cheeks to a blaze. "Okay, fine." He did not allow people to laugh at him when he was trying to be serious. Bracing his hand on the lip of the tub, he rose to his feet. "Maybe you think your health is a joke, but I don't."

Sirus snaked his arms around Grey's knees and held him firmly in place. "Get back down here." He looked up at Grey as he tugged, and like a man without his own will, Grey lowered himself to his knees between Sirus's thighs. Sirus touched Grey's face, held it, but then curled his hands into fists and let them drop into the bathwater. His slate eyes hardened to granite, and Grey's heart lurched and raced.

"What?" The steam and candlelight in the room pillowed Grey's voice, softening the anxiety twisting in his gut. "Is there something wrong after all?"

"No, I'm good," Sirus said, washing relief over Grey in a flooding torrent. Christ, he couldn't believe how much he already cared that nothing bad ever befall this man. "I take my personal safety and health very seriously," Sirus continued, clearly unaware of the turmoil going on inside Grey. "As seriously as I'm sure you do. Even though I always used protection with the last man I was with -- all of the men I've been with, of which there have been four -- I have in the last two years been tested numerous times for every goddamned thing in the book, as my last relationship ended in part because the man was married."

Grey's jaw dropped right into the water.

Crap crap crap. Sirus stared at Grey's obvious shock -- or possible horror -- and wondered what in the hell had made him share that information about Paul. The stupidest thing in the world a guy can do is talk about his former lover to his current one. Of course, Grey wasn't really Sirus's lover, at least, not in the *relationship* sense. *Not quite in the literal sense yet either*, he thought with dry humor. Now, maybe Grey never would become a lover. Damn it, Sirus had screwed this up nicely, and so very quickly too. Had to be a new record for him.

"Forget I said that." Sirus rubbed his hand over his chest, knowing the goddamned tattoo was still there. Kelsie had counseled him to think hard before getting it but Sirus had believed so deeply in Paul he hadn't listened. "We're not going to be doing anything for long enough that we need to know specifics about each other's pasts. You wanted to know if I'm safe, and my point was just to assure you I am. Many times over."

Grey shifted, the motion awkward in the space available, and drew his knees up to his chest to wrap his arms around them. "Did you know the guy was married?" he asked, it seemed cautiously. "I don't know you very well, but I only ask because with what little I do know, you don't strike me as the kind of man who would engage in that kind of behavior."

Sirus's hackles rose and a rumble vibrated in his throat. "What kind of behavior is that?"

"The kind where innocent people get hurt," Grey answered, his voice calm in a way that nothing inside Sirus was. "Like that man's wife."

Grey's generous thought constricted Sirus's chest. "You're right," Sirus admitted. God, he did not want this man thinking he condoned adultery. "I didn't know Paul was married when we met, but by the time I did find out I was in so deep I couldn't make myself walk away. Paul promised me the marriage had not been an intimate one for a very long time, and he said he was in the process of separating and ultimately divorcing. He lived in Texas. I wasn't there all the time to check up on him, so I accepted him at his word." Sirus chuckled, the sound laced with cynicism -- directed squarely at himself. "Hell, who am I kidding? I wanted to believe him, and I jumped at the chance to do it. Then one day when we hooked up I believed him a little less, and then a little less the next time, until I went all stalker on him and saw him with his wife." The sense of wanting to be sick at the sight he had witnessed that day still sat sour in Sirus's stomach. "She was very pregnant."

"Shit." Grey stared, rapt, as if Sirus told him a bogeyman story by a campfire. "You sure it was her?"

Sirus grimaced. "Saw her picture in his wallet once. It was her. He obviously never stopped having sex with her. When I figured that out, the floodgates burst open, and I imagined he probably hadn't been any more faithful to me than he had been to her. He promised me there weren't any other men, and he just hadn't figured out a way to break from his wife and tell his family about us, but by then I couldn't believe anything he said, and I broke it off. That was two years ago. In fact, it was shortly after I saw your sister and assured her Paul was worth it and that we would be together forever." Sirus closed his eyes for a moment and breathed, fighting through the anger and rage that wanted to resurface. He brutally reminded himself he hadn't lost anything; Paul had never been the man he'd pretended to be while with Sirus. All Sirus had lost was a lie; a fantasy of what he'd wanted Paul to be.

Pushing away the hardness that always wanted to show

itself lately, Sirus opened his eyes and looked at Grey once again. "Anyway, that is why you should believe me when I say I'm not interested in a relationship right now. It has been a while since I had sex, though, and I won't lie, I miss it like hell."

Eyebrows rising, Grey laughed. "Believe me, I know the feeling."

Grey's easy laugh startled Sirus into a fast smile. *No, no, no. Don't start liking him; that is not what he wants. It's not what you want.* "So," Sirus quickly turned the tables, "what about you? Tit for tat here. You said you hadn't been with anyone in a long time either. Why did things end with your ex?"

"Certainly nothing as dramatic as what happened with you." Grey's voice sounded natural and he didn't flinch or dart his attention away from Sirus. At the same time, he scraped a fingernail through a bar of soap on the tub's ledge. For some reason Sirus couldn't explain, that one little motion canceled out the ease in other two. "He just wanted something I couldn't give him."

"Which was?"

The amber flecks in Grey's eyes flattened to a dull, one-note hazel. "He wanted me to love him, and I couldn't." Grey shrugged. "Simple as that."

A shiver went through Sirus, and the bathroom suddenly felt as chilled as the biting weather outside.

"Still sure you want to sleep with me?" Grey asked, his voice the same as when he'd asked Sirus if he wanted more tea last night at dinner. "It won't be any different with you."

Couldn't love him. Not that he didn't or wouldn't, but that he couldn't. Those words of Grey's sat heavy in Sirus's gut, the finality of them so certain. A frisson of fear skittered across his heart at the upfront coldness in Grey's proposal. At the same time, after being lied to by Paul so completely, and for such a long time, Sirus respected that Grey didn't pretend in order to get what he wanted.

He looked at Grey, into eyes that didn't dare care, and the only answer he wanted to give escaped his lips. "I'm sure." Sirus reached out, curled his arm around Grey's neck, and dragged him to a meeting point between their bodies. "Now hold your breath," he brushed his lips achingly slowly across Grey's, thrilling at the little catch of breath he felt from the other man, "because I'm going to wash your hair." With that, he turned the tap and sent hot rain pouring down on them both.

———

SIRUS RIFLED THROUGH THE FRESH changes of clothes in his duffel bag, searching for something he could use as pajamas. The power still hadn't come back on but plenty of moonlight streamed in through the window and allowed him to search without any problem. He had a too sexy man waiting for him one room over, but he didn't think he would get a wink of sleep if he slept in the buff as he normally did. It was one thing to say they wanted to share a bed, or do what they had done outside, or even to say they wanted to have sex; it was another to follow the guy into his bedroom and pounce. Especially since Sirus knew he couldn't take Grey the way his body so desperately wanted to do. After their bath, Sirus had needed a few minutes alone to catch his breath and steel himself to the fact that he wouldn't be fucking Grey, and so had used the lame excuse that it would be cold tonight and he needed to get some sweats to wear to bed.

Finding a black pair, Sirus slipped into them quickly, cursing only a bit at their snug fit. Fuck, he hardly ever wore them. It was only because he hadn't had much left clean that he'd thrown them in his bag in the first place. He found a navy blue T-shirt and put that on, then paused to look at himself in the mirror and comb down his damp hair with his fingers. That done, he rushed to the door, nervous excitement coursing all the way through him.

He just managed to slow down his fast stride in the hallway and talk down his case of the jitters. He finally stepped into Grey's room with relative cool -- and found the object of his latest fantasies buried under the covers already fast asleep.

God, he's so fucking handsome. The room, bathed with light from the moon, highlighted Grey's stark face, not softening his cheekbones or jaw one bit, even in sleep. Brown hair lay perfectly across his forehead, as if he had artfully arranged it with styling products before getting into bed. Sirus knew better. Grey was just that damned perfect -- physically anyway. Inside, Sirus figured the man had a few scars.

Ones he didn't want anyone to see.

Couldn't love him. Grey's declaration echoed in Sirus's head again, sobering him as he made his way to bed and crawled under the covers. He rolled onto his side and studied this intelligent, determined man, and didn't think him incapable of doing anything he truly wanted to do. "Maybe not so much *couldn't*, as *wouldn't*," Sirus whispered.

A rumble vibrated through Grey, as if he challenged Sirus's opinion.

"Don't worry, tough guy." Sirus smoothed a hand over Grey's damp hair, and then pressed a gentle kiss to his forehead. "I don't need you to love me, so we're going to do just fine."

Grey rolled over and snuggled into Sirus's side right then, settling in as if his body were made especially for Sirus's nooks and crannies.

As Sirus lay there holding Grey in his arms, he wondered if he was lying to Grey, or himself.

CHAPTER SEVEN

Twinkles of light played over Grey's face, pushing through his closed eyes and forcing him from sleep. *Gonna have to start closing the damn curtain on that window.* He rolled over and stretched his arms and legs, cursing when his knuckles hit the headboard and shot tingles up his arm.

Scrubbing his face and scratching through the stubble, Grey pushed up in bed and smacked at his cheeks. "Wake up, wake up, wake up." Familiar lethargy made his arms and legs heavy, but he was used to it; he blinked the sleep from his eyes and forced himself to face the day head-on. "Time to wake up."

"You have a little wake up ritual." Sirus's voice snapped Grey's eyes fully open. Sirus stood at the door, all tall and big, dressed in jeans, boots, and another one of his flannel shirts, this time a charcoal gray in color that perfectly matched his eyes. "That's cute," Sirus added, and brought a steaming mug to his mouth. He made a vibrating noise of pleasure as he swallowed, and Grey's cock responded as if that sound had been hummed right against his flesh.

Fuck. Grey didn't need a hot beverage to warm him up. He had only woken up once during the night, but damn, he could still feel Sirus's body heat surrounding him as the man slept deeply, his wide chest rising and falling with every silent breath he took. A man who didn't snore. Christ, as if Sirus needed anything more to sell himself beyond his incredible art and insane body.

Maybe this sharing a bed thing wasn't such a good idea. The sex, yes, but the same bed before and after perhaps needed reevaluation. They were going to learn too many little intimate details about each other by sharing a bed, probably things neither one of them wanted anyone else to know. Such as Sirus catching Grey waking himself up with a pep talk, as he'd just done. Grey didn't want anyone to know he talked to himself out loud.

Lectured himself.

Chastised himself.

Right then, steam tickled his nose, and the decadent smell of rich coffee made Grey's mouth water. He shook his head, pulled himself back into the moment, and found Sirus sitting on the edge of the bed, his coffee cup waving under Grey's nose.

Sirus smiled, and his eyes twinkled as brightly as the morning sun breaking through the windowpane. "I thought that might wake you back up." He took another sip of coffee and then set the mug on the nightstand. "You drifted there for a minute."

"You should have woken me up." Grey glanced longingly at the mug of coffee but instead noticed the digital clock radio behind it. It was literally sunrise. "I see the power is back on. Damn, you're up early."

"I have a lot to do today." Sirus pushed himself upright and made his way back to the doorway, but then he paused before turning down the hallway. "And I would have woken you up, but you're on vacation, so I wasn't sure you'd appreciate it. I was just coming in to check if you were stirring before I left. When I saw that you were, I thought I'd share the coffee." He pointed to the steaming cup. "That's for you."

"Thanks. Have a good day." Grey picked up the mug and discreetly turned it, keeping his head down as he put it to his mouth exactly where Sirus's had been. He swore his lips tingled with the placement, and hot cinnamon-tinged coffee burst over his taste buds and rolled down his throat, leaving a hot path of bitter warmth in its wake.

"Shit." Sirus threw a few other curse words out into the air as he strode across the bedroom in three steps and then lifted the cup of coffee right out of Grey's hands. "You think I didn't see you do that?" Grey opened his mouth to protest, but Sirus swooped down on him and crushed their lips together. Moaning, Grey relented and opened up, accepting the immediate thrust of Sirus's tongue. Sirus slid one knee on the bed, and at the same time tunneled his hand in Grey's hair. He jerked Grey's head back and slanted his mouth, devouring Grey in a fast, eating, kiss, mingling their shared cup of coffee in a different way.

Fuck, yes, please. Sirus gave Grey a moment to breathe, and Grey fucking sighed and trembled like a favorite animal who'd just been lovingly stroked.

Sirus bit at Grey's lips once more, making them even more sensitive than they already were, but then pulled back, the mercury fire in his gaze burning strong. "You make me hot without hardly doing a damn thing," Sirus said, his voice full of gravel. "Damn it." He dipped down and scraped their lips again, clinging and speaking against Grey's mouth. "I have to go." Sirus's mint and coffee breath fanned hot over Grey's face. He stared intently, although Grey couldn't imagine what he thought to find. Sirus bruised one more hard kiss on Grey's lips, cursed and bit again, but this time did pull away and walk backward to the door, leaving Grey a puddle. "God, I want to crawl right back in bed with you, but I can't." He braced his hand on the doorframe. "Noah will be wondering where the hell I am."

Any sleepiness or jittery stomach remaining in Grey disappeared in a shot. "Noah?" *Who the hell is Noah?* Grey kept his voice carefully modulated. "Is that a friend?"

"A friend who happens to be my plumber," Sirus answered,

and Grey just barely stopped himself from slumping against the headboard in relief. He managed to keep the anger at himself for reacting so strongly hidden too. "He's going to get started on the repairs today. I want to be there just in case there are any problems. I also want to get back to the piece I was working on yesterday when you stopped by. Plus, Ginny is going to drive up to take a look at my completed projects to see if there are any she thinks she can sell."

Grey sat up straight, this time not caring to hide. "I didn't know you had an art dealer." A weird bubble of pride Grey could not control burst in his chest. "You should give me her card."

A charming as all get-out half smile transformed Sirus's face into something breathtakingly handsome. He laughed, the sound full-bodied, and completed the picture. "Ginny will love to hear herself referred to as an art dealer." He shook his head, his mirth clear. "She runs a craft store over in Clarkson. She showcases a dozen or so locals from the surrounding area in one section of her store. She usually takes a few pieces of mine at a time, and I make an okay buck every now and again." Sirus's focus drifted to the clock on the nightstand, and he stood up straight. "Okay, I really need to go. I'll be back in time for dinner. Bye." He waved, and didn't wait for Grey to answer before disappearing down the hall.

Picking up his coffee again, Grey smiled against the rim as he took another sip, hardly noticing it had turned lukewarm. He leaned against the headboard and stared out the window, listening as Sirus shut the front door and then started his truck. Grey watched the pretty day start to unfold, but in his mind he saw three or four key pieces of art that had so captured his interest while in Sirus's studio. "Damn, I should have taken some pictures with my cell."

Coffee in hand, Grey got up, not tired anymore in the slightest, and went in search of his phone to make a call.

———

"Now how would I know you were going to be at the cabin this week, let alone that Sirus would have problems at his place?" Kelsie grumbled through the phone. "You never even go to the damn place. I swear, Grey, you have become a very suspicious man." Grey could practically see his twin glaring at him through the phone. "Maybe it has something to do with your own guilty actions of the past?"

"All right, all right, all right," Grey relented. "It was just a surprise to see a stranger in my cabin when I got here, that's all. Besides," Grey wrapped one hand around his neck and started pacing the length of the cabin, the phone at his ear, "it's not like you didn't end up getting something great out of my machinations, so don't go getting some convenient memory about your husband now." Grey thought about Kelsie's pregnancy and suddenly forgot anything other than brotherly concern. "How are you feeling lately? Getting sick yet or anything?"

"I feel pretty fantastic, actually," Kelsie answered with a

laugh. "You could call your best friend and tell him to ease up on the worrying though. He's getting a little out of hand."

Yeah, Grey could imagine John jumping to attention and wanting to call 911 with the smallest sneeze out of Kelsie. "Afraid I can't help with that. John loves you and nothing is going to change that. You can handle him. God knows you always have."

"Yeah, I'm not handing the keys to The Sweetest Tattoo over to someone else, even temporarily, until the time I deliver the baby, I can tell you that." The Sweetest Tattoo was his sister's tattoo parlor. "Hey," Kelsie's voice perked up, "speaking of tattoos, how's my buddy with the sexy mustang on his chest doing? Does he have an ETA on the repairs to his cabin?"

"Not sure. He mentioned his plumber is starting the work today." Grey spoke carefully and tried like hell not to look at the front door -- for the fifth time since calling his sister. Fuck, though, Sirus would return soon, and Grey ached like hell to finish what they had started last night. "I guess he'll get an estimate on the timeline today."

"And how are you doing with sharing?" Kelsie asked, making Grey sound like a ten-year-old who didn't want to share his Star Wars toys. "You're not exactly used to bumping into another person every time you turn around."

"I'm managing, sis." Damn, if Sirus would just open that front door they could start bumping into each other a whole hell of a lot more than they had thus far. *Thump thump thump.* Shit, was that Sirus coming up the porch steps? Grey's hands started sweating just thinking it might be his temporary bedmate.

Jesus, what in the hell was wrong with him?

"Listen," the front door opened, and Grey immediately dropped his voice to a whisper, "I just called to check in to see how you were doing. Say hi to John for me, and I'll talk to you soon. Bye."

"Say hi to Sirus for me!" his sister shouted before Grey ended the call.

Sirus walked in, a cell attached to his ear as well. He waved when he found Grey, but continued his phone conversation. "I'm not pretending anything for her," he said, his voice rising. "I don't have to. She won't acknowledge it anyway, so what does it matter?" Sirus stopped talking, but nodded, as if the other person could see him. "Okay, okay, fine." He sounded like a mixture of exasperated and mildly pissed. "I've been warned. But just so you know, it's not as if you have to do it. I don't have gay porn sitting all over the place or pictures of well-hung naked men gracing my walls. You might come for a visit and find that out for yourself." Using one hand, Sirus shrugged out of one arm of his heavy coat, switched the phone to his other ear, and slipped out of the other, catching it by the collar and draping it over the back of the couch before it hit the floor. "Yeah, I know you are. I love you too, jackass. Bye." Sirus flipped the phone closed and tossed it on the coffee table, a rumble working in his throat as he shoved his hands through his hair, leaving tunnels in their wake.

The man looked a little feral, and Grey stepped forward without thinking, itching to calm the metaphorical hairs standing on end. "Everything okay?"

Shaking his head, Sirus looked at Grey, took a visible breath, and his hackles seemed to settle. "Yeah, I'm fine." He blew out another slow breath and linked his hands behind his neck. "That was one of my brothers; Nic. He was giving me the heads up that my mom will be gracing me with her presence sometime in the next few days. She'll be working nearby and wants to check in on me to see if I'm dating anyone."

"Oh." Well, hell, that was inconvenient.

"A woman." Sirus grimaced, his face hardening as he shared. The air went right out of Grey. "Oh."

"No, not that kind of 'oh'." Sirus practically snarled the word. "My mother knows I'm gay. I'm not faking anything. All of my immediate family knows, and some of my extended ones do as well. My mom just acts like I never said it and goes about her business, occasionally trying to get me to come home to visit in order to set me up. I swear she thinks if I just get a look at the right woman then I'll go straight."

"I wasn't judging you," Grey quickly explained. "You're welcome to do or not do whatever the hell you want. I don't ever lie to anyone myself, but that also doesn't mean I tell everyone I meet that I'm gay either. My business is my business, and I tend to keep my work separate from my personal life. That just makes good sense all around."

Silver sparked in Sirus's eyes, and his lips hitched at one

edge. "Three years of celibacy should make that pretty easy for you to achieve."

"Right." Grey quickly sidestepped the talk turning toward him and put the conversation back on track. "You just seem so comfortable with yourself that it would have shocked me to hear your family didn't know."

"They know. And when my mother visits, I will be clear with her. Again. My brother says she's driving over and is going to stop overnight to visit with an old friend who lives outside of Charlotte before she makes her way to me. Listen," Sirus flexed his arms over his head and then pulled the edges of his shirt and T-shirt from the waistband of his jeans, moaning with that end-of-day joy as he did it, "I'd just assume we change the subject to something else entirely." He pulled the snaps open on his shirt and scratched his chest through his white T-shirt. "How does that sound to you?"

"Fine with me." Learning about each other's families wasn't part of their bargain anyway. It didn't matter that Grey itched to ask more questions about Sirus's parents and siblings. He ignored the fact that he was strangely fascinated to find out where this man came from and where he fit in that other world. Grey wouldn't share the same information in return, so it wouldn't be fair to ask.

"Good." Sirus circled the coffee table as he removed his watch, pausing by the fireplace to put the timepiece on the mantel. He rubbed his wrist, and Grey's penis started to push against his jeans.

"Did you fare any better with Noah?" Grey asked, staring, unable not to. He studied every inch of Sirus's stunningly fit body and had difficulty swallowing past the sudden dryness in his throat. Sirus looked a little rough from his day, but not overly so. "Did he get a lot of work done at your cabin today?"

"Fair amount." Sirus spoke and all Grey could imagine were the scrapes of strong, callused hands running all over his skin. Standing half a dozen feet away, Sirus raked his gaze the length of Grey's body, and the silver in his eyes deepened to putty. "Says he'll be done in another day, two at the most, and then I can move back in."

Two days. *Fuck fuck fuck.* Grey had a feeling he would need at least a dozen to get this man out of his system. Of course, that depended on him getting Sirus Wilder *into* his system first.

Forty-eight hours flashed in Grey's head, the numbers ticking down like a clock on a bomb. Grey growled, the sound coming from deep within. Christ, they were wasting time. He fucking needed to get inside Sirus, and they had far too much distance between them right now to achieve his goal.

Something raw and primal took over inside Grey. He planted his boot right in the center of the coffee table, taking the most direct route to his target.

"Grey?" Sirus looked up, and as Grey loomed taller on the table for a moment, his attention latched onto Sirus's Adam's apple, the little bump bobbing as he swallowed. Jesus, Grey's dick twitched as he imagined himself sucking on that enticing protrusion for hours.

Grey stepped off the table into Sirus's space, letting barely a sliver of air exist between them. "I made food." Leaning up, Grey kept his gaze riveted to Sirus's, watching as he captured Sirus's lower lip between this teeth, and then tugging before letting it go. "Do you want to eat?" He reached down and stroked the length of Sirus's already straining cock.

Sirus pushed into Grey's touch, and a funny noise choked in his throat. "I could wait." His eyes closed to half-mast, his lips parted, and every fast little breath he took fed Grey's desire and pulsed more blood straight to his erection.

Tripping Sirus up, Grey circled his arms around the man and helped cushion their tumble to the floor. "I need to fuck you." Grey ground his ridge against Sirus's through their clothes, and leaned down to steal another aggressive kiss. "Right now." He dug between their bodies and started to work open Sirus's belt.

"I brought lube from home." Sirus leaned up to help keep their mouths fused together with fast kisses. "It's in my coat pocket. Ahh," he hissed as Grey spread his legs and pushed up against his balls, "that's feels so good." Sirus pulled back, the haze in his eyes clearing as he looked at Grey. "I don't have any condoms. Do you?"

That jerked Grey to a standstill. "No." He hummed all over and wanted nothing more than to get inside Sirus's tight ass. He had Sirus's zipper halfway undone, but his fingers sat frozen in place. "I don't want to stop what we've started." Grey stilled on the outside, but his blood raced like mad on the inside. He didn't move, though, and stared right into Sirus's eyes as he said, "But we can halt things right now. It's up to you."

CHAPTER EIGHT

S ex without a condom.

Sex with *Grey* without a condom.

Oh fuck. Sirus looked into Grey's eyes, saw the amber chips within nearly taking over the hazel, and his chest thumped faster with every second he stared. His skin felt tight and hot, and his ass pulsed in time with his heartbeat, his body begging him to say yes.

Sirus reached up and brushed his fingers over Grey's cheek, stunned when the man trembled in response. *Hell, he wants this just as much as I do.* "You trust me at my word?" He ran his hand down to Grey's chest and worked open the first button on his shirt. "I should have thought to go buy --"

Grey clamped his hand over Sirus's mouth. "I didn't go buy

any either."

Sirus pushed open Grey's shirt and scraped his fingers down the man's smooth chest and hard belly, making Grey hiss, stopping only when he hit the waistband of Grey's jeans.

Grey closed his eyes, and his lips parted as he rocked himself into the V of Sirus's legs. "Christ, I don't want to stop and go buy any right now either." He opened his eyes and set his focus, hot and full of wanting, on Sirus. "I want inside, and I want it bare."

Oh double fuck. It was a damn good thing Sirus was already lying down. "Me too." Sirus clutched Grey's face, keeping him close. "Me too," he whispered again. Their gazes held for a moment, their bodies in limbo as heat lightning flared between them. Then, in the blink of an eye, they both went at each other with savagery -- tongues dueling and teeth clinking into one another, licking and biting over entire faces and even up into hair and scalps, tongues thrusting into ears as they clutched each other's heads in a bruising hold for more.

Grey's complete abandon, and even his violence, hit Sirus's blood like the most potent drug. This wasn't anything like what he'd expected out of this careful, precise man. The intense passion went right to Sirus's head ... and his cock. Sirus forced Grey's jaw apart and swept his tongue inside, needing to get deep and taste as much as he could. He scraped his tongue over Grey's teeth and the roof of his mouth, and pushed his hips up against Grey at the same time, grinding their cocks together through their jeans.

With his fingers digging into Sirus's cheeks, Grey bore down with his weight and pushed them both to the floor, dominating with his position. He thrust his groin against Sirus, putting exquisite pressure on Sirus's balls and erection. Sirus gasped as his nuts drew up and tightened, quickly signaling the end -- proving just how hot he had been all day while thinking about Greyson Cole.

Jeter, Rodriguez, Longoria... In his mind, Sirus quickly started listing the names of the sexiest players on the 2008 AL All Star team. Just as he did, Grey reached down and yanked Sirus's hips up as he knifed down. Grey sank his tongue all the way into Sirus's mouth, licking voraciously, and pushed Sirus over the edge with two minor league moves.

Sirus groaned into Grey's mouth, the sound muffled as orgasm overtook him. With his cock still tucked in his jeans, his lower body jerked viciously. Release shook through Sirus as deeply as if he had his length buried balls deep inside Grey's snug ass. Ejaculate warmed Sirus's lower belly and crept out of his waistband. He knew it seeped through his jeans and that Grey could feel it too.

God, what is the matter with me? Sirus had no control around this man. "Sorry about that."

"Don't be." Grey let go of Sirus's hip and burrowed his hand between their bodies, touching his fingers over Sirus's spent cock through his damp jeans. Grey looked up, found Sirus's stare, and a cheeky smile graced his kiss-tinged lips. "I know you'll be hard again in a minute." He finished working

Sirus's zipper down and stuck his hand inside Sirus's jeans and underwear, stroking his sticky length, and making Sirus whimper with renewed need. "I saw you do it last night." Grey milked Sirus's penis and, sure enough, the tingle in Sirus's spine started all over again and he began to harden in Grey's hand.

Shifting up to his knees, Grey lowered Sirus's underwear down in the front and unearthed his rapidly thickening prick. Sirus's cock reared up toward his stomach, his tip nearly touching his belly button. "Damn," Grey whistled as he jerked Sirus off, "that is amazing."

Sirus bit his lip, refusing to admit this was the first time his body had reacted in quite this way with so little provocation or control. He knew Grey didn't want to hear anything that might hint at something special between them, and Sirus had a bad habit of wanting to see more in his sexual partners than was really there. This short-term "acquaintances with benefits" Sirus had going with Grey was the perfect opportunity to prove he could have a fling without turning the relationship into something more. With that knowledge, Sirus throbbed with need all over and had to sate some of that lust right now. He pushed his shirt up and took his own nipples between his thumbs and forefingers, twisting the aching points of flesh and pulling on that invisible line between his chest, belly, and cock.

"Yeah, I like to see that." Grey's voice was thick and full of heat. He gave up his agonizingly wonderful chokehold on Sirus's cock and pecked a line of kisses up Sirus's stomach, making Sirus's flesh quiver with every light touch. "Get this the rest of the way off so I can see more." He pushed his hands under Sirus's T-shirt and eased it off over his head, taking the unbuttoned flannel shirt with him.

Pulling up onto his knees again, Grey took off his own shirt, never taking his eyes off Sirus as he did it. "Jesus." He worked the button and zipper on his jeans, pushed them down past his hips, and sprung his hard cock free. Grey looked Sirus up and down, his eyes darkening with desire with every inch of Sirus he openly studied. "I don't think I could ever get bored looking at you."

Heat seared Sirus's flesh, setting him aflame with just Grey's stare. Sirus took good care of himself and it was nice to look into the eyes of someone who appreciated it. Sirus's breathing turned erratic quickly, making every deep breath a nearly painful task.

The desire for connection overwhelmed Sirus. He reared up, snaked his arm around Grey's neck, and yanked the man to him until their foreheads touched. So close like this, their chests met with every deep breath they took, scraping sensitized nipples over firm flesh. "I don't mind looking at you either," Sirus stated, his voice low. Their gazes clashed, challenged, and Sirus obliterated the scant distance between them, delivering Grey an openmouthed, hot kiss.

Moaning as Grey sank in to a licking of tongues, Sirus slid his arms around Grey's back and drew the other man down on top of him, loving how Grey's weight pressed him into the nubby rug. Sirus touched all over Grey's back, his palms scorching on hot, solid ropes of muscle that flexed and rolled under his hands. Wanting more, Sirus slid his hands down and clutched Grey's ass, squishing their cocks together in between their stomachs. Sirus kneaded Grey's buttocks with every rock of his hips, and his fingers slipped into Grey's crease.

Grey suddenly jolted and tore his mouth away, panting heavily, his eyes swirls of amber and green. "Clothes," he said, the one word a rough bark. "I want the rest of your clothes gone." He strong-armed into a one-armed push up stance and dragged his own jeans down his legs. "Mine too. I want the nakedness I didn't get outside last night."

His mind still in a fog of lust, Sirus toed off his shoes and socks, and then wiggled out of his pants. All the while, he watched Grey as his mind tried to catch up to the man's withdrawal. Sirus shook his head, trying to clear some of the blood from his cock to send it back to the other crucial parts of his body -- mainly his brain. Opening his mouth to ask what had prompted the flash of shadows in Grey's eyes, Sirus snapped his lips closed again as Grey dipped down and licked right up the underside of Sirus's cock and shot Sirus straight back into drugging pleasure. Questions forgotten, Sirus bowed his back off the floor, his prick quickly leaking precum like brand new one more time. Grey swirled the tip of his tongue around the head of Sirus's dick, teasing him into shaking. Then he flattened his tongue and did a reverse lick down Sirus's erection, and dragged Sirus into a sensual haze where nothing but sex mattered.

Sirus looked down the length of his torso but could barely see clearly through the need clouding his gaze. Grey buried his face in Sirus's thatch of dark pubic hair, and a wonderful hum buzzed against Sirus's balls, excitement making them weighty with seed again.

"I love the way you smell," Grey murmured, his mouth right on Sirus's testicles. "It's pure sex and man." He drew one of Sirus's balls into his mouth and suckled it like a babe at his mother's teat, and Sirus swore he could feel his response all the way down into his toes. Pushing Sirus's thighs open wider, Grey worked Sirus's full sac into his mouth and rolled it around in the heavenly wet warmth, only to release him and lick at Sirus's sensitive perineum, pushing at Sirus's sweet spot from outside his body.

"Ohh God, yeah." Sirus moaned and humped his hips into Grey's face, begging for more.

Grey took Sirus's thrusts with a quiet murmur, and he pushed Sirus's legs farther apart, splitting his crack. Grey's fingertips dug into the backs of Sirus's thighs, flattening flesh and revealing his pucker. "Damn it, Wilder," Grey's nostrils flared, and his fingers flexed around Sirus's legs, "you look good enough to eat all over." With that, he rolled Sirus's lower body right off the rug and stuck his face in Sirus's crease, his tongue going right for Sirus's asshole.

Sirus jerked, his muscles seizing as he struggled to accept the pleasure Grey delivered him. "Oh, oh, oh God…" Gritting his teeth, Sirus could barely breathe through the first intimate laps and licks. Grey nibbled and probed at Sirus's bud, and the nerve-rich skin rippled with delight. It felt perfect and right, and at the same time terribly wrong to be doing this so quickly, yet Sirus never wanted it to end. He hooked his arms around his knees and held himself open for more of Grey's tormenting ministrations. Grey added the pressure of his thumb to the mix, and Sirus bit the inside of his cheek, drawing blood as he fought to stave off a second orgasm. God, he hadn't had a guy rim him in a half-dozen years, and it was so goddamned good he didn't know how much he could take.

Straining his neck, Sirus watched Grey work his entrance with complete and total focus, as if nothing else in the world existed or mattered. The rough pad of Grey's thumb brushed over Sirus's tight ring again. In immediate response, Sirus's inner passage contracted, his cock throbbed, and he pushed out more early seed. Grey pressed against Sirus's snug muscle, enticing it to open with alternating flicks from his tongue and pressure with his thumb. "Come on, honey," Grey's softly spoken words caressed Sirus's most intimate flesh right along with his thumb and mouth, "give it up for me."

As if it had a mind of its own and could be sweet-talked, Sirus's asshole gave way right then. Grey's thumb slipped inside, immediately pushing all-in and taking over Sirus's ass. Grey didn't give Sirus time to adjust. As soon as he worked Sirus open a little bit, he pulled out and slipped two fingers inside, massaging Sirus's clenching channel in a deep in and out corkscrew motion, stretching Sirus's flaming ring with every turn. As Sirus stared, his belly tightened and his cock twitched. He could not tear his gaze away as Grey's fingers disappeared into his rectum again and again. Grey grazed Sirus's prostate with every stroke, and then pushed a third finger in and widened Sirus's passage even more with agonizingly painful pleasure, killing Sirus with the need for something longer, harder, and thicker to penetrate his ass to the hilt.

Sirus's walls shivered all around the invasion, clutching with a strong squeeze.

"Jesus." Grey looked up and made eye contact with Sirus. As he eased his fingers in as far as he could get them, and then slowly pulled them back out, driving Sirus's backside crazy for more, he stared with an intensity that made it hard for Sirus to breathe. "You have an incredibly responsive ass."

Sirus wanted Grey so goddamned badly right now his body hurt with it. "Fuck it then. Take me, Grey, please." Sirus heard the plea for connection in his voice, and hated it. He growled, covering the slip of weakness with naked rawness that lacked any hint of intimacy. "Fuck my ass. Hard." He pushed up, jamming his stretched ring into Grey's hand. He *could not* let this be anything more than sex. Sirus screamed those words in his mind, above the lust and passion, and didn't quiet the voice until the message hardened in his heart. "Do it," he commanded, his voice harsh. "Give me your fucking cock deep, right now." He demanded it, and didn't back down.

Jesus. Fucking. Christ. Grey had never been harder in his life.

His prick reared against his belly in reaction to Sirus's tone, smearing a line of precum onto his skin. He had his fingers invading Sirus's ass to the second knuckle, with Sirus's burning channel clamped tight and quivering around the penetration. The visual swelled Grey's balls, making them weighty and achy, and he knew his response would be a thousand times more mind-blowing when it was his cock encased in the suffocating home of Sirus's ass.

No, don't think like that. Panic constricted Grey's chest in a painful band. *Sirus's body is not your home.*

On instinct, Grey withdrew his fingers from Sirus's asshole and smacked his hip, gaining the man's full attention. "Roll over." His voice was full of grit, but that, Grey could not hide or control. He forced himself to study Sirus's stunning form as purely something of physical perfection and tried not to think about the man who made beautiful pieces of art, kissed like he needed the act in order to breathe, and who didn't snore. Grey looked at the male body and edged out the *man* he was accidentally getting to know. He looked down and teased his finger into Sirus's open entrance again, focusing back on just the sexual. "On your hands and knees." He eased his finger out of Sirus's channel just as quickly as he had poked in, and then reached over to the couch to grab the hem of Sirus's coat. "I want a nice view of my cock taking your sweet ass."

Grey's hand trembled as he felt around in Sirus's pockets for the lube, but he refused to shy away from the intensity heating Sirus's stare to charcoal. As he waited for the man to roll over,

Grey watched, unwavering, challenging the fire burning hot in Sirus's gaze.

Sirus lifted up to his elbows but didn't make any effort to shift his position. In fact, he looked downright defiant, and Grey's pulse started to race.

Never let them see you bested; never let them see you sweat. Remembering his words to live by, Grey palmed the bottle of lube and got right back between Sirus's spread thighs. On his knees, he looked into Sirus's eyes and didn't blink. "You want me to flip you over and hold you down, fuck you that way?" Grey squeezed out a dollop of lube, dropped the bottle, and slipped his middle finger into Sirus's ass again, pushing through the tight, moist tunnel until he hit the kill zone he wanted. He held his finger right on Sirus's sweet spot, denying the man the pressure Grey knew his body so desperately needed. With every miniscule pump of motion Grey made in Sirus's ass, Sirus gasped, and his cock released a steady stream of early semen. "Yeah, you want it." Christ, how Grey's dick cried in anticipation of filling Sirus's ass. He teased Sirus's channel with one lonely finger some more. "But is it the fucking that has you leaking so damn hard, or is it the thought of force?"

On the heels of that taunt, Sirus knocked Grey's finger out of his hole, and then quickly reared upright. He shifted to his knees, putting their fronts in full contact with each other. He looked right into Grey's eyes while he reached down and stroked the full length of Grey's rigid penis. "Don't try to overtake me," Sirus bit Grey's lower lip and tugged, letting it pull through his teeth until it released, "unless you're ready to be the one who ends up on the bottom, with my cock buried in your ass." He planted a hard kiss on Grey, bruising in its force, but then abruptly pulled away, turned around, and rubbed his ass against Grey's erection. "Remember that."

Grey wasn't sure Sirus's words were a threat, a challenge, or a promise. Right now, with his dick slipping into Sirus's crease, riding his crack and sending every nerve ending on Grey's cock into a frenzy, Grey couldn't think clearly enough to care. He wrapped his hand around Sirus's throat, yanked the man's head back, and took his mouth in a hard, thrusting kiss, going deep with enough aggression to make Sirus jerk and go compliant. An almost silent whimper escaped the man, begging without words for more. Knowing he was fully in charge once again, Grey reached between their bodies, positioned the head of his cock to Sirus's ring, and drove his length home.

Shit. Grey shuddered through the insane pleasure.

"Ahh ... fuck, fuck." With the first piercing, Sirus dropped down to his hands and pushed his weight back against Grey's cock, forcing Grey's erection deeper inside. "Fuck me, Grey." Sirus started helping himself by pumping his hips back and sliding his channel along Grey's embedded cock. "Fuck me."

The wrongness of that *home* word slipped into Grey's consciousness for a second time in nearly as many minutes, nagging him to correct his thought process. But this time, Jesus Christ, this time, Grey had his unsheathed dick lodged inside another man's tight, hot ass, and his brain could not process anything as more important or relevant than that. Grey looked down and watched his cock push into Sirus's stretched hole, invading the man's very body, with nothing in between them. Sirus moaned as Grey filled his channel, the sound coming from deep inside him, and Grey was pulled completely into the undertow of sex with this man.

He fell on top of Sirus and fused their bodies together in another way, covering him like an animal in heat; then he withdrew and knifed his length through Sirus's clenching rectum, jamming his cockhead into a second interior barrier that wouldn't budge. Grey nudged, and Sirus grunted. Sirus's knees slipped a little farther apart, and the slight motion pushed them both a few inches down toward the floor. Grey nudged again, but still didn't get what he wanted, what he ached for with every fiber of his being.

Full penetration in Sirus ass.

Grey licked Sirus's neck and bit his shoulder. "Give me the rest," he said, his voice rough and hard. Grey probed his tongue into Sirus's ear at the same time he pulled out and sank his prick back into Sirus's ass, taking as much as Sirus gave. "I want it all."

Sirus breathed heavily beneath Grey. Sweat poured off his body too, making them slick like seals at play. "Take it." He shoved back into every pump of Grey's cock, seemingly as desperate for more as Grey was. "I want it." His legs fell open wider, and he slipped to his elbows, his forehead digging into the floor. "Make me yours."

When Sirus gave that raw permission, Grey lost what little control he had left. He bore down and shoved Sirus all the way to the floor, collapsing the man's arms and legs as he thrust his hips against Sirus's ass. He rammed his cock in with driving power, breaking that second ring of muscle and invading Sirus to the hilt.

Sirus cried out with the deeper fucking, but the man's snug passage felt so damn good that Grey couldn't stop taking Sirus's ass with fast, full strokes. He planted his hands on either side of Sirus's shoulders, and he pulled almost all the way out, only to push his way back inside that suffocating, tight heat, until the base of his cock kissed Sirus's stretched ring. Grey held himself up with straight arms and a rigid upper body, but everything below his waist moved in a frantic pumping motion; his balls slapped into Sirus with every slam in, the sound mingling with his own heavy breathing and Sirus's low moans and gasps for breath.

Grey shook his head, working like the devil to clear the drugging, wonderful pleasure wreaking havoc in his body. He needed to be able to think about the man taking the punishing blows of his ardor. "Okay?" Grey's lips parted as he choked and willed his body not to move. "You ... oh fuck, so tight ... okay?"

Sirus reached back and scraped his fingers across Grey's buttocks, grabbing for purchase. "Don't stop." His voice was rusty and breathless. "Oh God, I feel so fucking full with you." He bumped his ass up into Grey's dick, providing delicious friction that got Grey growling with pleasure and pounding away again. "That's it, that's it…" Sirus looked back at Grey and his gaze was slate-colored with his lust. "Fucking let me feel you come."

Sirus's face, voice, and Jesus God, those expressive eyes of his slammed Grey right into a brick wall. Grey let go of his toehold and dropped down, burying his hand in Sirus's hair and twisting his head at an unnatural angle, needing the man's mouth. Grey bit and got his tongue inside.

Sirus whispered, "I want you…" brushing the sentiment over Grey's lips, stilling Grey in place, their bodies locked in an intimate puzzle, "…to give it to me," Sirus went on, his voice a whisper and a command at the same time. He pulled back an inch, and their gazes locked, once more slipping this to something more complicated than sex. "Now."

Grey could not look away, and he could not control his body. With his cock tucked deep in the tight confines of Sirus's flaming ass, his balls drew up and his spine raced with that familiar tingle. No time to get away, Grey squeezed his eyes shut as he drove his cock deep, orgasm overtaking him. He jerked and spilled inside Sirus's body, shuddering with every drop of seed he gave.

Just when Grey thought he might feel far too naked to ever look at Sirus again, the other man shuddered beneath him, and his ass channel contracted in tight spasms around Grey's still embedded, amazingly sensitive cock. Grey opened his eyes, found Sirus's face pulled taut, his eyes half closed, his teeth gritting, and knew without a doubt the man had just ejaculated and stained the rug with cum.

Goddamnit, Sirus is something to behold when he comes.

Grey didn't know how it happened, but he found himself getting hotter than hell to go at it all over again.

The trembles in both men eventually subsided. Sirus opened his eyes, the shine in them punching Grey right in the heart.

"Holy shit," Sirus's voice held a smile, "we are good at this." He rolled over, dislodging Grey from his body as he shifted to his back and put one hand under his head, using it as a pillow. Darting up fast, he nipped Grey's lips with a quick kiss and then pecked his cheek too. "That fuck deserved an award." Every word Sirus spoke put lightness into the air, sweeping the intensity of the sex they'd just had from the room. "We ought to look into that online or something. A fucking championship. What do you think?"

Grey's stomach chose right then to rumble in a very unsexy way. "I guess I want food." He chuckled, and he could have hugged Sirus for so naturally infusing needed levity into the moment. *If I hugged people, that is*, Grey amended silently. "I did make something earlier. It should be fine if we reheat it. Are you hungry?"

Sirus groaned, but did pull himself to a sitting position. "I could probably make it to the kitchen and eat something." He actually shifted to his hands and knees and started to crawl. Grey's gaze dropped right to the man's red, raw ass, his focus zeroing in on the semen already starting to leak from within.

Stopping about halfway to his destination, Sirus looked over his shoulder and forced Grey's attention to his face. "You coming?" he asked, his tone as deep, flirty, and sultry as anything Grey had ever heard. "It is your meal, after all."

Groaning as his dick tried to thicken, Grey looked Sirus over from top to bottom, and he knew the man understood exactly what he'd implied. *Son of a bitch wants it just as much as I do.*

"Hell yeah, it's my meal," Grey threatened. He jumped to his feet and took two fast strides toward his goal, watching Sirus's eyes widen in response. "And I'm going to fuck you right through the table if you don't start running."

Sirus shouted, and he managed to get to his feet fast enough to allow chase, but he didn't put up much of an effort. Grey caught him and wrestled him right up onto the sturdy kitchen table, making a damn fine meal out of Sirus Wilder before he ever touched a bite of food.

Chapter Nine

Grey shoved Sirus into the back of the couch and plunged his cock into the man's tight, scorching ass, slamming his length to the hilt.

Sirus cried out at first full penetration, bracing his hands on the sofa as he pushed his backside against Grey, demanding more without words.

Jesus, he has the finest, tightest body I've ever seen. Or fucked. Running his hands all up and down Sirus's exquisitely muscled back, Grey stared down at his prick disappearing into Sirus's entrance time and again, and he slipped to a place of pure, physical desire. "Take it. Oh fuck…" He pulled all the way out, left Sirus gaping for a moment, and then filled his begging hole again. "Take my cock."

"Give it to me." Sirus squeezed his anal muscles in a vise around Grey's invading prick, driving Grey insane with pleasure. "Give it to me hard." Sirus bucked and grunted as Grey pierced his channel with vigorous, full thrusts, giving Sirus what he said he wanted. "Oh, yeah, fucking ... just ... like ... that."

Animalistic aggression Grey usually kept banked deep inside emerged, and he mounted Sirus like a stallion on a mare. He bit into Sirus's thick shoulder as he covered the man completely and started a series of piston-fast pumps of his shaft into Sirus's body, humping him in the most rudimentary of ways.

Sirus moaned and pushed back into the mating. He looked over his shoulder, and his eyes flashed silver light in the charcoal depths. "So goo -- ahh!" Sirus shouted hoarsely as Grey drove particularly deep and ground his pubes into Sirus's stretched ring.

Unable to help himself, Grey forced his way inside Sirus somehow even deeper, needing every goddamned inch of the man he could steal.

Just as quickly, Sirus reached back and grabbed on to Grey's hips, pulling them together. He pressed his forehead into the couch, hiding his face once again. "So ... good." Shortness of breath guided Sirus's words. "Fuck me; fuck me. Don't stop."

"No." Sweat poured down Grey's naked body, and his skin felt like it was stretched tight and on fire. "Can't." Grey wrapped his arms around Sirus's torso and dug into his chest with the blunt tips of his fingers. Holding on tight, without gentleness, Grey rammed Sirus forward, doubling the other man's upper body over the back of the couch with the force of his fucking.

Sirus let go of Grey and planted his hands on the cushions of the sofa, making himself stationary once again. "Jerk my cock." Sirus tried to reach down with one hand and do it himself. He made contact with a hiss. "Hurts ... so hard."

Grey knocked Sirus's fingers away and wrapped the man's burning erection up tightly in his hand, giving the thick length a rough tug. Sirus groaned and pushed into the milking of his dick. At the same time, his snug passage rippled all around Grey's cock and squeezed, killing Grey with unfathomable pleasure.

"Oh shit..." Grey's nuts quickly sucked up nearly into his body, making him grunt and grit his teeth as he fought to hold off release. He frantically jerked and pulled on Sirus's velvety-hard prick, trying to get the guy to orgasm faster than the tingling already coiling in his own belly and racing up his spine. "Coming... Too fast." Grey curled his fingertips around the thick head of Sirus's dick and teased the wide slit, smearing slickness all over the cap. Sirus shuddered, and his ass contracted in a suffocating hold around Grey's embedded cock, tormenting Grey into giving up the battle.

"Ahhh!" Grey speared his penis into the deepest reaches of Sirus's body, lifting Sirus all the way onto the tips of his toes as release overtook him. Semen shot through Grey and raced to his cock; his shaft pulsed inside Sirus's rectum, beating in time with every spit of hot cum he dumped in Sirus's ass. Grey buried his fingers into Sirus's hard chest, kept a fist clamped around his member, and stuck his face into Sirus's damp hair, barely holding onto sanity through the fiercely pleasurable ride.

Wet heat emptied out of Grey, filling Sirus's hole. Through the hazy, sex-filled blur of coming, Grey dragged his hand up the length of Sirus's erection and pinched the tip. Hard. Sirus groaned, the low rumble vibrating all through his body, almost like an animal in pain. Right on top of that, his cock jumped in Grey's snug hold, swelled, and then the waterfall-loud sound of ejaculate hitting the floor filled Grey's ears. Sirus seemed to come forever, almost motionless and silent as he did.

Grey stayed still and quiet for a moment afterward, slipping to a place of ease he had never felt in his life. Everything about the steady rise and fall of Sirus's body beneath him -- that Grey's body naturally found and mimicked -- dragged Grey into its spell, intoxicating him with the touch, smell, and taste of Sirus, lulling Grey into never wanting to let this man out of his arms.

Ever.

Grey jerked, feeling as if freezing lake water had splashed over his heated flesh. *No, huh-uh, not forever. Absolutely not. I don't do long-term. I don't even know this man. Not really.* His heart racing for an entirely different reason than fucking, Grey let go of Sirus and withdrew his cock, stifling a moan at the last sliver of pleasure.

Sirus straightened, and Grey slapped the guy's ass, forcing humor into his voice. "That'll teach you to beat me in a foot race." They'd started out this morning going for a perfectly innocent hike. During the course of conversation, and playing around, competitive spirits had risen to the surface, resulting in Grey challenging Sirus to a race back to the cabin. Sirus had taken him up on the taunt, eagerly.

Shaking himself back into the moment, Grey flipped Sirus over the back of the couch onto the cushions and then hopped over on top of him, sitting on his stomach. "If it happens again, I might not get us inside the cabin before I retaliate. I could end up fucking you right outside on the porch steps."

His eyes twinkling, Sirus rubbed Grey's thighs while flashing a naughty grin. "Mmm, remind me to call my brothers and thank them for cramming competition down my throat when I was a kid. If this is how you punish me," Sirus's hands inched closer to Grey's dwindled cock, "I'll happily continue beating you. Allow me to introduce you to wrestling."

In a flash, Sirus wrapped his hands under Grey's legs and flipped him to the other end of the couch. Grey landed on his back, with Sirus on top of him, pinning his straining arms to the sofa.

Gnashing his teeth and pushing against Sirus's hold with all of his might, Grey muttered, "Not gonna win twice, Wilder." He immediately wrapped his legs around Sirus's body, and with every muscle in him working overtime, he forced Sirus off him and onto his side. Sirus pushed back with equal power, his hands still manacled to Grey's forearms, and his legs struggling to overtake Grey's.

They tangled back and forth with their legs, rolling from one side to the other as they each gained and lost the upper hand. Sirus's hands slipped with every move he made. Eventually their palms touched and their fingers entwined, but the push of strength didn't allow Grey to mistake it for holding hands. Sirus's face was pulled taut, his eyes shone with his determination, and his muscles flexed with every shift, each line highlighted by a sheen of sweat.

Grey fought like a dog protecting his only T-bone, but his spent cock wanted like hell to stir, and he licked his lips. "Christ, man," he locked his leg around Sirus's knee, pressing their dicks together in the battle, "you're so fucking sexy."

"Oh boy." A burst of laughter escaped Sirus, and he threw his head back against the armrest. "My brothers never said *that* to me when we wrestled."

As he laughed, Sirus's hold relaxed, and Grey moved in fast. He shoved Sirus the rest of the way onto his back, held his hands prisoner, and wrapped the other man's legs up in a tight hold.

Grey looked down, his heart lurching at the sight of Sirus's deep breathing and the lightness brightening his eyes. "Got you," Grey said, his tone ridiculously ragged.

Sirus looked up, open in every sense, and Grey almost couldn't breathe. "Yep. You win." Sirus's voice was soft, and his eyes even more so. "What are you going to do about it?"

His gaze held captive, Grey dipped his head, needing a piece of this man's confidence and peace. *I want you so damn much; I don't know how to stop.* Grey stilled mere centimeters from Sirus's mouth, panicked by the turn of his out-of-control thoughts. Instead of going for Sirus's lips, Grey pecked a fast kiss on his cheek and pulled away. "How about I give you a few minutes reprieve while I catch my breath." He let go of Sirus's hands, released his legs, and pushed himself to lean against the other armrest, adrenaline making his movements rigid and jerky. "You and your brothers must have played hard as kids. If you hadn't gotten distracted by laughing, I'd be suffering defeat once again."

His forehead scrunching, studying Grey for an excruciatingly long moment, Sirus eventually shifted and sat up too. "I didn't always win with my brothers," a fast smile returned to his face, "but I learned how to at least be respectable in a fight."

"You said you have four brothers, right?" Grey winced as soon as the question left his lips. He hated this tangible desire in him to know more about this enchanting man.

"Yep," Sirus answered. "Nic -- the one who called to warn me about my mom visiting -- is the oldest. I'm the youngest, of the brothers anyway. After Nic there's Richard, Matthew, Thomas, then me, and finally Diana."

Grey could completely picture Sirus surrounded by a brood of siblings and family. Something about him screamed of a tight family bond. "How old are you?"

"Thirty-one." Sirus looked Grey up and down; his focus, *interest*, rubbed at Grey's instinct to shield himself from probing stares. "You?"

"Thirty-three." Scratching his hand through his hair, Grey scanned his internal information about Sirus, searching for something banal -- something safe. His chest burned and he wanted to get up and move -- anything to redirect these innocent questions away from himself.

Innocent always leads to intimate.

Grey finally found something, and the tightness banding his middle released. "I've been meaning to ask about your rig. You said you're a truck driver but I didn't see your vehicle at your cabin."

"When I'm not driving, I park it at a garage in town." Sirus's answer came as easily as Grey found it difficult to share. "The owner and I worked out a little rental fee for the space. Since I set my own schedule, and I don't require a whole lot of money to live a life that is comfortable for me, I can sometimes go a month without driving it, if the mood strikes me." Another lingering look from Sirus had Grey squirming; this time he fought down the sense of being caressed by big, callused hands. "The desire for a break struck me a couple of weeks ago. Seems to have been nice timing so far."

Grey adjusted his dick, and cleared his throat. *Stay down.* "It must be nice to allot yourself such big chunks of time to work on your second career."

Sirus tilted his head. "What?"

"Your art?"

"Oh," Sirus relaxed back into the armrest, shaking his head, "that's not a career. That's something I do for the joy of it. Giving stuff to Ginny is just for fun. I get a charge out of discovering a new craft or medium and seeing if I can figure it out. I don't have any interest in turning it into a job."

Modest too. Of course Sirus wouldn't just be sexy, sharp, and know how to take a fucking like no man Grey had ever met. He had to be humble about his talents too. "You probably could turn your art into a career."

Shrugging, Sirus said, "If I were so inclined to pursue it, but I'm not. How about you?" He nudged Grey's hip with his bare foot. "How did you and John decide that pairing people with money to start a business was what you wanted to do with your life?"

"John had the entrance into a circle of people with large amounts of disposable income." Grey breathed easier; he knew his work inside out and was used to discussing it with people. "John convinced me I was a good enough talker to get just about anybody to part with anything, including money. We were both always good with numbers; we like them. We liked the thought of being part of discovering innovative new businesses too. When we were in high school we took a course together that challenged the students to play the stock market with monopoly money; we realized with the proper amount of research we had a really good ability to predict what would do well. It seemed to work well when we worked a stock together -- when we could talk the pros and cons out with each other. Conversely, we didn't have as much success when we tried it on our own." Grey chuckled. "We really liked when we did well and beat out every other team, not only in our class, but in the entire school. That was heady and addictive." Grey suddenly stopped, stricken. *What in the hell was that?* Telling people about playing stocks in high school wasn't his and John's standard "about us" company line. Always, whenever asked, they discussed business courses in college, their credentials, and their myriad of successes. They never talked about playing stock market in school and catching a fever for making money, even if at the time the money wasn't real.

Sirus snapped his fingers, the sound cracking through the silent living room. "Grey, you all right?"

Grey shook himself and forced a placid expression to his face. "Yeah, fine. Sorry." *Get back to the standard company information, Greyson.* "Anyway, going through college, and taking lots of business courses, we saw how damn hard it is to start and succeed as a new business in this country. We figured with the strengths we each brought individually, along with how well we worked as a team, we could fill a niche in the market and do very well for ourselves at the same time. That's what we did."

"Must have been nice going into something where you had complete trust in your partner," Sirus said with gentleness in his voice. "John's more than a friend and a business associate; he's like a brother to you, right?"

A picture of John sitting at Grey's grandmother's dinner table virtually every night from the moment he, John, and Kelsie had met when they were ten years old flashed through

Grey's mind. "You could say that. He was around enough that we considered him family."

"But in reality it's just you and Kelsie." Slate eyes looked straight at Grey, uncomfortably direct. "You don't have any other siblings, right?"

"Nope." Hairs on the back of Grey's neck stood on end. The disquieting sensation quickly raced down his arms, leaving him chilled. "Listen, I need water after our marathon run and fuck." He slid his legs off the couch and stood, making only fleeting eye contact. "You want something?"

"Sure," Sirus murmured. "Thanks."

Grey circled the couch and grabbed his pants. *Gotta get away for a minute and breathe.* "Be right back."

Damn it.

Sirus pushed upright and discreetly watched Grey disappear into the kitchen, the man's back ramrod straight. Sirus told himself not to stare, not to develop an attachment beyond the act of fucking, but he couldn't shift his focus from the strict lines that ruled Grey's stance or stop the ache to know more. A knot grew in Sirus's belly, filling him with failure. He had given Grey a little bit of information about his family without even thinking twice about doing it. Only, when Sirus maneuvered and tried to get something in return, Grey had clammed up tighter than an oyster.

The man is not capable of sharing. He has already intimated that; believe him.

Still, something in Sirus's gut, while watching Grey so closely, said that Grey had been on the cusp of revealing personal information. Perhaps already had. That would explain why he'd gone from being laid back to coiled like a striking snake in almost one blink of his eyes. The man's guard was slipping a little bit and that clearly made him uncomfortable.

Sirus couldn't help wanting to know more about Grey; he wanted to figure how to keep Grey talking each time those instincts kicked in and told Grey to close his mouth. Sirus had watched Grey shut himself down just a moment ago, and it hadn't been the first time that had happened since they'd begun sharing this cabin. Something in Grey's eyes spoke of secrets and loneliness, and it tugged at Sirus's heart. This man made Sirus want to work on getting him to open up, to show him there could be trust and companionship with someone other than John and Kelsie; perhaps something as deep and abiding as what John and Kelsie shared together.

Stop it. You're doing it again. You're trying to create a relationship and feelings where they don't exist. Grey only wants to fuck you for two weeks. He could not have been clearer about that.

Strictly fucking, that's what Grey had said. Sirus's head told him to accept those terms, and if he couldn't, then he needed to walk away right now. And maybe Sirus could accept those words, that is, if he hadn't already experienced the desperation in the way Grey made love, or hadn't witness these intense passing glances and touches that spoke of longing for a deeper connection. Sirus swore he saw hints of a man living inside

Grey who *wanted* to talk about all kinds of things, not just weather, work, and sports. Small pieces of that man slipped out every once in a while, Sirus *knew* it. His gut knew it. His head knew it. And his heart knew it too.

He just didn't know what the hell it would take, or if it was even possible, to coax the *complete* Grey out into the open. Or if he would get smacked out of this little part of Grey's world for trying to do it.

Stop it, Sirus; stop it right now. You can't force someone into a change they aren't ready to make. Look at what you hoped for with Paul, and the reality that slapped you in the face.

Sirus's heart started pounding like a son of a bitch, and his hands went numb. Danger lay in pushing a regimented man like Grey out of his comfort zone. Potential destruction and total heartache too. Sirus wanted to know more about Grey but he couldn't ignore the risk to his own wellbeing either. He'd left himself open to heartbreak before and he just didn't know if he would recover from another man stomping on his soul.

Sirus's fingers tingled with returning sensation, and his pulse settled too. Just as fast, he jumped as warmth caressed his penis, stirring the shaft with new life.

Blinking, Sirus came back to reality and looked down. His gaze collided with Grey's.

"You ready for round two?" Grey kneeled between Sirus's spread legs, his hand wrapped firmly around Sirus's cock. Sirus peripherally registered the glass of water sitting on the coffee table.

Grey stroked Sirus's dick with one full drag, and Sirus's length shot up to almost full salute. "You feel like you'll be rock-hard with one good suck," Grey said. He swirled his tongue around the sensitized rim of Sirus's dick and then pressed a chaste kiss to the equally nerve-rich tip, his gaze lifted to Sirus the entire time. "I want my jaw aching by the time you come again."

Those hazel eyes of Grey's, studded with flecks of gold, held Sirus locked in a sensual hold, tying him up in a frightening mixture of needs, wants, and pure desire. Unable to walk away, no matter the foolish risk, Sirus pushed Grey's head to his cock and forced the man's hot mouth down on his length, succumbing to the physical bond between them that neither one of them could deny.

CHAPTER TEN

"Come on, son, it'll be fun." Grey's father stood beside the aboveground pool in their backyard, the collected rainwater within frigid and littered with tree branches and dead leaves. Jeremiah Cole's clothes hung loosely from his tall, lanky body, and his overlong hair brushed past his shoulders in thick, dark strands. "Help your sister in and splash around to get clean. Here." Jeremiah tossed a multi-colored beach ball over the width of the water, forcing Grey to jump in order to catch it. "Make it into a game and you'll be done before you know it."

Kelsie stood beside Grey, a brisk autumn breeze lifting her long hair and blowing it in his face. His sister had already started to shiver, her nose ran with the beginnings of another cold, and she hadn't even removed her clothes. Grey could see the purple tinge taking over Kelsie's lips and noticed the way she clung to her stuffed dog, fearful of getting into the cold water.

Grey looked at his sister and then the water again, and a familiar knot of hatred he couldn't control churned in his stomach and grew into a ball that felt bigger than the inflated beach one he held.

"Go on then, kids." Jeremiah smiled at his children as he waded through the dried out, over-tall grass to the backdoor of their house. "Mommy will be out with some towels in a few minutes."

"Dad!" Grey's voice was striking, sharper than any nine-year-olds' should be. His father spun, and their stares found each other from across twenty feet. Grey's heart once again raced, this time charged with a tinge of fear, knowing that his father was a man and thus much bigger than Grey.

"Please," Grey pleaded, the sting gone from his tone. "Kelsie…" He slipped his sister's hand in his, absorbing the chill in her fingers. "She's not feeling too good. Let's go to a motel and have a hot shower and sleep with a heater running." They didn't have any water or electricity in their small home right now. They rarely did. "Just for the night."

For a second, Jeremiah's gaze narrowed, and a real sliver of uncertainty iced its way down Grey's spine, colder than the water he knew waited for him in their makeshift bathtub. "Don't tell me how to take care of my family, boy," his father whispered, pointing his finger in Grey's direction. "Now get your sister in there and get yourselves clean. I don't want to hear any more about it." With a blink of his eyes, Jeremiah was back to his smiling self. "Now have fun! Your mom and I will be out in a bit to check on you."

Jeremiah disappeared into the house. As Grey stood there staring at the vacated doorway, his insides grew incredibly hot. His skin felt like it would burst into flames, and he wished with every fiber of his being that he could shoot a ball of fire into this awful house where they never had any water or electricity, where they could never have a friend visit, and where they didn't even eat every single day. Grey wished the home would burn to the ground, or a bulldozer would come in and knock it over, or that the God his mother always talked about would strike a giant bolt of lightning right down on it, or send a tornado crashing through it --

Kelsie went into a fit of coughing right then and pulled Grey out of his destructive thoughts. His sister was pale and skinnier than he knew she should be, and he knew from what he'd learned about nutrition in school that how little she ate made her immune system weak. Grey tried to give her some of his food when he could, but portions were doled out by the size of the person in their house, so he didn't get a whole lot more than she did most of the time. The way they lived, in a way that sometimes seemed worse than animals, wasn't right. Grey didn't even have to go to school to know that much.

Another brisk gust of air swept through their open lot of

a backyard, and Kelsie shook and coughed again. Where heat had previously filled Grey's blood, ice quickly replaced the burn. Grey knew he was smart. Every teacher he ever had told him so. He went to the school library whenever he could and was always reading tons of books. His teacher, Mr. Meacham, said he was so good at his work because he was a thinker and good at solving puzzles.

"Grey," Kelsie whispered, her hazel eyes wide, "I don't want to get into the pool." She squeezed her dog against her chest. "I'm too cold."

Looking around, taking stock of what he had available to him, Grey ran across the yard and snagged one of his T-shirts and a ratty quilt off the wash line. "Here, take this." He thrust them at Kelsie and then raced across the yard to a pile of junk to fish out a big plastic container. It was discolored but no dirtier than the pool itself. Grey dragged that to his sister's side, grabbed a smaller bucket, and started filling the plastic tub with rainwater from the pool. When he'd filled it about halfway, he took the quilt from Kelsie. "Okay," he moved behind her, "use my T-shirt as a washcloth. Just clean up with the water in the little tub. I'll hold this up," with two corners of the quilt in his hands, Grey reached his arms up as high and wide as he could, creating a fabric wall, "and you can be private." Not that they had any neighbors close by, but still, they were nine years old now. "Hopefully you won't be so cold."

"'Kay." Kelsie's high voice reached Grey through the fabric. "I think this will be better. Thank you, Grey."

"No problem." He knew his arms would get tired before too long. "Just hurry it up."

Today, Grey would get into the pool and take a bath in collected rainwater. He didn't have a choice. Tonight, he and Kelsie would both freeze under their covers when the sun went down. Grey wouldn't have any say so in that matter either.

But soon, things would change. Grey was smart. He knew Kelsie would only get sicker as the season changed to winter. Between her allergies and colds, she hardly ever stopped blowing her nose. As Grey stood there holding up that quilt, listening to his sister's teeth chatter as she cleaned herself, Grey thought about how smart his teachers always told him he was. Right then, in the backyard, Grey came to the realization that he *had* to be smart. He had to be smart enough to outthink his mom and dad and somehow still keep him and his sister together. He had to get Kelsie -- much more than himself -- out of this house for good.

Grey stood there in the cold and started to think...

———

...In bed, Grey jerked and shook his head, fighting the dream, even while still asleep. A small part of his brain tried to force logic and consciousness into his slumbering mind and body, telling him to calm himself and that the past couldn't hurt him anymore. Grey settled, forcing the childhood memory out of his head. Nevertheless, the night held on to him, and he slipped back in time again...

—

…Grey closed his eyes and stuck his face into his boyfriend's pillow, all the while mentally chanting to himself, *you're gay; you want this; just do it; it's part of what you do when you're with a guy*. Grey breathed, and logically reminded himself that he'd accepted Joe's finger in his ass okay, and even got a little hard with it. A cock wouldn't be all that different.

Then why was his heart racing so fast? Why was his chest squeezing so hard he thought he would either throw up or pass out? Why did he want to get off this bed and swear he would never spread himself for another man ever again?

"Found one." Joe's voice broke through Grey's frantic thoughts, and it seemed like only a second later the bed dipped under his weight. "I knew I had a box in the bathroom."

Joe crawled between Grey's legs. The hair on his legs scraped against Grey's inner thighs and ratcheted Grey's uncertainty up about a thousand notches. A tearing sound ricocheted in Grey's ears as if it was in stereo, and he knew Joe opened the condom packet and sheathed his cock in a layer of latex. A few seconds later, Joe's weight covered Grey and something pushed at his entrance, and, *oh shit*, Joe pushed more lube into his hole.

Grey winced at the pulling on his ring. Joe smacked Grey's buttocks with his other hand and muttered, "Damn, you have nice ass, Cole." He withdrew his finger; something bigger replaced it and immediately applied pressure. "Can't wait to fuck it."

Before the next frisson of second thoughts could ripple all the way down Grey's spine, Joe took Grey's hips in a tight grip, yanked him almost off his knees, and knifed his dick all the way into Grey's ass in one jamming thrust, engulfing Grey in fiery pain and stealing the breath from his body. Grey could barely swallow through the blinding hot discomfort of Joe's first lancing of his channel but he bit his lip clean through and let Joe go at him, allowing Joe to saw his length in and out of Grey's virgin ass with increasingly rougher strokes.

Grey crouched on the bed on his hands and knees, taking it up the ass in a way he had always imagined he would love, all the while willing himself not to cry out and show weakness in front of this other boy. He would make up an excuse in a week or so and they would break up, but no one would ever know it was because Grey had discovered that he *could not* do this again. He would never roll over and give someone the power to cause him pain, not even temporarily, not even to fuck.

Especially not to fuck.

Oh Christ. Grey choked as Joe pulled all the way out, sending Grey's ass into a strange series of spasms and clenching. Then, Joe forced Grey's passage all the way open as he pushed his dick in again. *It fucking hurts so badly.* Grey didn't dare beg Joe to stop, but damn it -- he sucked blood from his cut lip -- he knew it would be better if Joe would just slow down a little bit and let Grey's body adjust…

———

... "Roll over, baby," a deep voice -- not Joe's -- snuck into Grey's head, saying, "I'm gonna give you exactly what you want."

Sirus. Oh, yes, Sirus would make it better.

Wait. Grey jerked, half in and half out of his dream, confusion making him panicky. *I didn't know Sirus in college. Joe didn't turn into another man while in that bed. I let him finish, and then I walked away as if nothing were wrong. I never let him see me sweat. He never knew why I ended our relationship.*

"He doesn't matter anymore." Sirus's voice whispered in Grey's ear -- in his mind -- once again. "I know how to take care of you." Sirus pressed a line of kisses up Grey's spine, ending with his mouth at Grey's ear. "Now roll over," he lifted up and gave Grey the space to move, "and I'll show you how much you'll crave having me in your ass."

Grey trembled as he turned over, his mind and body hovering somewhere between excited need and abject fear. He settled comfortably on his back, breathing deeply before he looked up ... right into Sirus's eyes. Sirus kneeled between Grey's thighs, his hard face somehow handsome, and his smile somehow soothing and sexy at the very same time. Grey studied Sirus's body, letting his attention wander until it landed on Sirus's cock. Thick and long, Sirus's member stuck out straight and rigid from his patch of dark hair, and it pointed right in the direction of Grey's asshole.

Grey's *exposed*, rosy asshole ... because Grey suddenly had his elbows hooked under his knees and his legs spread high and wide on either side of his chest, *giving* himself to Sirus. Grey's pucker clenched visibly and his channel contracted in a strong spasm.

"Oh yeah." Sirus made a clicking noise of appreciation, his eyes locked on Grey's entrance. "Look at your sweet body begging me to fill you up." Grey didn't know how it happened, but Sirus's erection somehow grew even bigger, not stopping until the cum-covered head touched Grey's ring.

No! Grey opened his mouth and tried to say he didn't want it and that he never begged but the words wouldn't move past his throat. Instead, his voice raw, he looked into Sirus's eyes and ordered, "Fuck me, Sirus. Fuck me goo --"

Sirus didn't let Grey get that final word past his lips. He threw his head back and roared, spearing his massive cock into Grey's ass, ripping him open with sweet pain...

...Grey convulsed with a start, suffering the dizzying sensation of falling as he jerked out of sleep. His eyes popped open on the end of the powerfully real dream, his breathing choppy as he struggled to erase it from his mind. He blinked repeatedly, careless of the bright light that streaked in through the window and hurt his eyes, only wanting the remnants of the strange dream -- the nightmare -- to get out of his head.

Why would he dream about the pool he and Kelsie had bathed in as kids? Shortly after that moment, Grey had researched his mother's family on the computer at the local library and found the phone number for a grandmother he could barely remember seeing more than four or five times in his young life. Grey had called her, told her about what was going on in that house, and about how sick Kelsie was all the time. His estranged grandmother had come and taken them to her apartment right away, where they lived with her from that day forward. It had scared the shit out of him to do it, but Grey had taken control of his and his sister's lives out of the hands of their parents and had made their circumstances a million times better.

Grey had resolved the situation with his college boyfriend Joe in much the same manner. Grey knew he was gay. He could not stop being gay; he was attracted to and wanted men. That encounter with Joe, however, had taught Grey a valuable lesson. He would never be submissive, no matter how minor the part, with a partner. Grey surmised that any relationship he even *thought* about starting after that, he would have to set the rules and parameters of what he would and would not do. After Joe, Grey had sought bottoms for partners and had once again found success in taking control of his life. At least until the guys had started wanting to share families and histories. As a result of that, Grey had also found success by ending those partnerships, until he'd eventually taken a sabbatical from dating entirely.

So then why now, less than a week into knowing this new man, did his mind keep twisting the role Sirus would play in this vacation tryst? Grey didn't want the entanglement of knowing personal information about Sirus, so he couldn't understand why in the hell he kept asking Sirus questions about his work and family. And *why, why, why* in the hell did he keep dreaming about Sirus Wilder fucking him? Grey didn't bottom.

Did. Not.

Grey knew how much the receiving end of screwing hurt. As far as he was concerned, he might as well be tied up with chains, cuffs, or ropes as let someone as big as Sirus hold him down and invade his body. Grey jerked, and his brow broke out into a sweat, but goddamnit, his cock stiffened with excitement in his sweats too. His ass clenched, as if reaching for an invasion from Sirus. Grey cursed, angry with himself for allowing this kind of confusion into his thoughts and dreams.

"Did you win?" Sirus murmured, making Grey jump again.

Shit. Grey's heart beat hard and fast enough to make him sweat a little more. *I still haven't adjusted to having another person sharing my bed.* Grey glanced over his shoulder, found Sirus's scrutiny more than he was ready to handle, and shifted back to stare at the wall again. "What did you say?" he asked, his voice still thick from sleep and the intensity of his dream.

Sirus shifted closer to Grey and slipped his arm around Grey's waist. He rested his head right behind Grey's, and his breathing fanned enticingly over the back of Grey's neck. "I asked if you won," Sirus said again. "It looked like you were having quite a struggle in your sleep, so I wondered if you beat whoever you were fighting in your dream."

Grey's heart started hammering even harder. He knew

Sirus must be able to feel it through the hand he had on Grey's stomach but he could not slow it down. "Not a fight." Their previous conversation about lying tied Grey up in knots and wouldn't let him out-and-out fabricate a story. "Just a … weird dream. Confusing. Disturbing."

"Want to talk about it?" Sirus rubbed his fingers in a soothing pattern on Grey's abdomen and pressed a chaste kiss behind his ear. "You can, you know."

"No thank you." Grey shivered just with thinking about sharing anything too personal with another person, let alone this man he kept dreaming about, in ways he had never dreamed about another human being before. He burrowed under the covers and hoped Sirus would believe he was just cold. "I'd rather forget about it entirely and start the day off on a more pleasant note."

"Well," Sirus tickled Grey's stomach and nipped at his nape, "if you take your death stare off the wall and shift it to the window, the pretty view there ought to make you smile. Look," he took Grey's head and angled it for him, "it's snowing."

Through the window, white blanketed the ground and capped the tree-covered mountain as far as the eye could see, turning the land into a scene from a movie. "Oh wow." Awe hushed Grey's voice to a near whisper. Up here, where there weren't any cars or pedestrians to trample the snow, the sun shone down on a pristine layer of white, creating such sparkles of light it hurt the eye to look at it.

"Beautiful, isn't it?" Sirus whispered.

Grey covered Sirus's hand on his stomach and settled back against his wide chest. "Yeah." Everything that had been bubbling inside Grey slowed down, and he swore it felt as if he and Sirus were the only two people in the world. He stared out the window to the purity of nature and let himself enjoy the moment. "It is amazing. It's a living photograph."

Sirus pressed on Grey's belly and edged him onto his back, where he then crawled on top of Grey and settled his lower body between Grey's legs. With his arms bracketing Grey's head, Sirus looked into Grey's eyes; the warmth lighting Sirus's stare from within stole right into Grey's locked heart.

"It's nearly as breathtaking as you are," Sirus said. He dipped down as he made that declaration and captured Grey's mouth in a slow, easy kiss.

Jesus. Grey moaned at the first touch of their lips, and his entire body went lax, welcoming Sirus's wonderful weight. He scratched his fingers up Sirus's bare back. The man's skin was so damn hot and his shoulders were so fucking wide Grey wanted to touch and taste until he could recreate every square inch of muscle by memory alone. Grey kept right on going until he had his fingers tangled in Sirus's hair, holding on with a touch he knew had to sting. Grey twisted his hands in Sirus's thick locks and pulled, drawing a jerk and a nip from Sirus as the man pulled back a few inches, breaking their kiss. His mouth open, breathing heavily, Sirus studied Grey with questions in his eyes.

Heat filled Grey's face, but it didn't stamp down his ardor

one bit. "Sorry." He lifted up and darted out his tongue, letting his tip graze Sirus's skin. "You make me feel a little aggressive sometimes." He dipped his tongue out and touched it to Sirus's again, pulled back, and then connected a third time. Forcing his fingers to obey, Grey unlocked them from Sirus's hair. "I'll ease up."

Sirus clamped his hand over Grey's mouth. "Don't." His voice rough, he looked at Grey, piercing right through to his soul. "Don't ever censor yourself with me." Sirus tore his hand away and shoved his tongue inside Grey's mouth, kissing him with the same roughness that drenched his voice. Grey's mouth felt raw and ravaged, and with every thrust, sweep, or bite from Sirus, Grey's cock grew harder and pushed against his sweats, stabbing the unwavering wall of muscle covering Sirus's belly. Grey's balls ached, heavy with cum, needful of release. He whipped his groin back and forth over Sirus's stomach, searching for any kind of friction that would help him come.

Sirus reached down and grabbed Grey's sac through his sweatpants, tugging him hard enough to make Grey wince with a quick stab of pain. "Hold on." Sirus bit Grey's chin as he eased away from Grey's mouth. "Don't lose it yet." He issued that order as he licked his way down the column of Grey's throat, sucking the notch of his Adam's apple along the way. "I'm going to let you go." The snug hold on Grey's nuts disappeared, and Grey bit his lip, struggling with everything in him to force down his orgasm. "But don't you dare shoot until I get my mouth on your cock."

Oh holy hell. Grey blinked rapidly, and he mentally started to account for every penny of money he and John had invested so far this year. He visualized columns of numbers in his head, working like the very devil himself to focus on sums and figures as Sirus slowly moved down his body, tasting every inch of skin his mouth crossed. The man let his wicked hands drift ahead and push their way inside Grey's sweats, digging his fingers into Grey's hips as he eased the fabric down and freed Grey's rearing, sticky cock. The head wept a steady line of precum, and it reached for his stomach, the shaft so swollen and sensitive Grey thought it might burst a fire hose worth of seed on Sirus's chest at any moment. Sirus took his goddamned time, though, swirling his tongue around Grey's already stiff and pointing nipples, worrying them into such tight buds Grey thought he might scratch them off his own body just to get some relief.

Grey squirmed all over the bed, unable to keep still. Sirus moved lower, but not fast enough to suit Grey's needs. With every hot breath Sirus exhaled against Grey's flesh, Grey shook as if he felt it sink into his pores and invade his blood. By the time Sirus reached Grey's belly button and sank his tongue into the little dip, Grey was spread-eagle on the bed, humping his hips and ready to scream.

"My cock, man." Grey's voice was barely a scrape of sound. "Take care of my cock." He reached up and wrapped his hands around the headboard so that he didn't shove Sirus's head down to his straining dick. "Suck me." Grey would never beg, but he had also never gotten closer to outright pleading for what he needed than he did right now. "Now."

Sirus looked up, his eyes pale as the moon. "Thought you'd never ask." He engulfed Grey's dick in one fast swoop, surrounding the length in suctioning, wet heat, and pulled until he took Grey's tip to his throat.

Then, Sirus swallowed, and he mastered Grey's prick with one simple move.

Grey threw his head back, shouting hoarsely, "Ahh ... fuck ... fuck!" He bucked wildly, shoving his cockhead farther down Sirus's throat as release overwhelmed him and he came. No time to feel it in his belly or core, Grey just let loose and spewed, his dick swelling and jerking with every jet of semen he unloaded down Sirus's throat. Grey's eyes practically went crossed as he felt the ripple of Sirus's throat on his tip, knowing each time he felt it that Sirus swallowed down every drop of his cum.

Still breathing heavily in the afterglow, Grey watched through slitted eyes as Sirus reared up, tore Grey's sweats the rest of the way down his legs, then yanked his own off, springing his raging cock out of hiding. The first coil of awareness and comprehension hit Grey just as Sirus said, "God, baby, I'm so hard." Sirus licked his fingers on one hand and stroked his erection with the other. "I need to fuck you right now." He spread Grey's thighs with the stance of his own and slipped his slick fingers through Grey's crease, teasing right on Grey's hole.

Grey inhaled sharply, and he grabbed Sirus's fingers, clamping a chokehold around them just as they pushed at his pucker.

So close.

Grey's heart sat right in his throat. "No, you can't."

Sirus snapped his gaze up, his hand still holding his dick, and agony mapping his face. Where only seconds ago Grey had felt wonderful, his stomach now churned with nausea. A twisted desire to let go of Sirus's fingers and scream *"Yes, fuck me,"* pounded like a second heartbeat in Grey's core, but years of answering to his personal code finished his comment on automatic. "I told you, I don't bend over for anybody, and I meant it."

Angry storm clouds swirled in Sirus's eyes, darkening the color so deeply a chill trickled down Grey's spine. Pure unadulterated need sat visibly on Sirus's striking face. For a moment, Grey feared Sirus would overpower him and take what he so clearly wanted.

"Let me suck yo --" Grey started. The cold in Sirus's gaze shut down Grey's offer more effectively than the loudest shout ever could.

Sirus stumbled out of bed and turned away from Grey, barely making it to the foot of the bed, where he stopped and braced his hand against the footboard. Half bent over, Sirus jerked himself off without a sound, the tension in his back and legs speaking volumes above the most intimate of moans. Grey knew he shouldn't look, but as much as he knew he'd caused this, and that Sirus would not want him to witness this personal act, Grey couldn't turn away. A dozen fast jerks of

Sirus's fist up and down his cock later and the tiniest intake of audible breath reached Grey's ears. Then, the splash of semen hitting the floor sounded like a pressure washer hitting siding as Sirus succumbed to orgasm.

One long minute that felt like an eternity hung heavy in the air between them, but, eventually, Sirus turned and grabbed his sweats from the end of the bed. He lifted his head and looked Grey in the eyes, and Grey knew he sat in the presence of a better man. "I hate like hell you saw that," Sirus said, his voice hard and distant. "If I could have made it even to just the hallway, I would have."

"I know." Shame blanketed Grey, even though he had been honest with Sirus about his position regarding sex from the start. "I'm sorry if you got the impression I was going to change my mind about letting you fuck me. I won't. I don't bend over. For you, or anybody."

Sirus slipped on his pants and adjusted his cock. "You're scared," he said, not looking away even for a second. "Literally and figuratively."

"Why?" Grey snorted, covering the fact that his hackles rose to full alert. "Because I don't want someone to fuck me? That makes me scared?" He stacked his hands behind his head and stared right back. "It's not possible for you to believe I just don't want it? Some men don't, you know."

"Some men, yeah." Sirus didn't back down or skip a beat. "But not you. I could feel it in every line of your body this morning, Greyson. You want me inside you. Maybe you're scared of what it will feel like or if it will hurt." Looking Grey up and down, Sirus raised a brow and said, "My money says you're scared to give up control of your body and put your pleasure in someone else's hands."

Grey rolled his eyes. "Don't make me into a romance novel cliché, Wilder."

"If the pages fit..." Sirus shrugged and turned away; two steps into leaving he turned back around and leaned right into Grey's space. "You know what? I'm not one of your little boyfriends back home. I don't give a shit about your job, or your money, or what I'm sure must be one hell of an apartment. I don't want anything from you, so I don't have anything invested in shutting my mouth and rolling over every time you want to plug my hole, rather than speaking up and saying that I want to fuck you too. I think you already know that, and I think it terrifies the shit out of you that you already treat me differently than one of your regular, easy, forgettable lays."

Sirus leaned in even closer and braced his hand on the headboard, right beside Grey's face. "I want inside you," he said, making the hairs on the back of Grey's neck stand up on end. "I want to work like hell to give you pleasure before I take you, if that's what is required. I'm not gonna say I never want you to fuck me again, because the fact is I like feeling your weight on me, and your cock in me. I like it so much I want to do the same to you, and I won't pretend I don't just to keep you happy for two weeks while you're on a vacation from your life. I don't need any man's cock that much. Not even yours."

Grey sat stock still, unable to move, even just to breathe. After a few ticks, Sirus cursed and pushed away from the bed. "I have to go. I need some air." He waved his hand without looking back. "Maybe I'll see you later."

The door slammed seconds later and Grey knew Sirus had left the cabin, probably without grabbing more than his coat that hung by the front door.

Grey sat in the middle of his big bed feeling empty inside.

Feeling damned unworthy of even having a fling with a man like Sirus.

Thinking, thinking, thinking, but seeing no solution to solving this puzzle, Grey slammed his fist into the headboard, and then did it again, and again, until his knuckles hurt like a son of a bitch.

He deserved it.

CHAPTER ELEVEN

Hours later, Sirus slashed another charcoal line across the page of packing paper as he worked to release the cauldron of emotion still seething inside him. *Greyson Cole.* The damn bastard wouldn't even give up his hold on Sirus long enough to let him focus on his sculpture.

It's not Grey's fault you can't concentrate, you pussy, it's yours. You're the one who won't stop thinking about the harsh words you exchanged this morning.

Sirus growled and swept another defining line across the paper, angry with himself even more than he was with Grey. Sirus didn't have to like it one damn bit but Grey had been honest about what he expected out of this vacation fling. Sirus thought the man was lying to himself about why he didn't want to let a partner fuck him, but at the same time, Grey had never pretended he was open to receiving another man's cock in his ass. It was *Sirus* who couldn't control his goddamn *wanting* and had pushed an issue he had no right to press.

You know why you did it too. You don't want to just fuck Grey; you want to know him in a deeper way. You're starting to fall for him, just like you always do.

"No." Sirus threw the piece of charcoal on his worktable, and shot to his feet, knocking his stool over in his haste to stand. He strode to his current project and put his hands on the partially chiseled slab of stone, willing his vision for this piece to return to his head and hands. A picture of Grey standing half-naked in the rain filled Sirus's mind, and the cool material under his palms started to warm with life. "No." Sirus withdrew his hands and spun away, looking for something to hit. "Not you."

"Afraid it is me." A familiar voice broke into Sirus's workspace. "But I have good news."

Sirus whipped his head up, still caught in a maelstrom of hostility … and lust. "Noah." His plumber. Pursing his lips, Sirus rubbed his hand over his face, wiping away the hardness he knew must show there, and forced a smile. "Hi. Ah, sorry about that; I wasn't talking to you. Just fiddling, trying to figure something out."

Noah moved a few steps into Sirus's shed, his hands tucked in his pockets. "I can see that." He stopped at Sirus's worktable and looked down; he then immediately jerked his gaze away and darted it around the area. "I didn't know you did sketches. I thought you did … I don't know," he shrugged, "sculpting, I guess you call it."

Moving in closer, Sirus wrinkled his brow as he took in Noah's obvious discomfort. Sirus's focus caught the edge of his drawing, and he slumped, closing his eyes at the picture his hands had formed with the charcoal. *Shit.* He'd drawn a picture of Grey in bed. He hadn't even realized what his hand was putting to paper. The image of Grey's face, forever frozen on paper in that stark, hard place of release, stared up at Sirus and Noah. With his muscles tense and bulging, in the picture, another man had his hand wrapped around Grey's erect cock. Sirus's hand. *Well then.* Sirus didn't deny his homosexuality to anyone in town who dared question him about it, but he also didn't have any interest in making someone uncomfortable with what he desired. As he'd told his brother, he didn't have pictures of naked men lying around for anyone and everyone who visited him to see.

At least, not until now.

Sirus pulled a drop cloth over the sketch. "I apologize if that made you uncomfortable," he said, tracking Noah's gaze until it stopped and met his. "Not that I drew it, but just that I didn't give you a head's up that it was out on my table."

"No, it's fine." Noah waved his hand in a negligent gesture, his attention briefly dropping back to the covered paper. "It just surprised me for a minute, that's all. It's not the kind of stuff you usually give Ginny to sell."

That got Sirus standing up straighter. "You've seen my stuff?" *Huh*. He wouldn't have expected such information from a rough guy like Noah Maitland.

"Janice likes to go into Ginny's store," Noah explained, mentioning his wife. "Sometimes you have to kill an hour or two in one of those craft places when the wife wants to grab a few things, you know?" The man momentarily looked pained, as if he relived one of his trips to Ginny's shop. "A guy tends to wander off from the scrapbook section every now and again. I saw a good number of your pieces over the last, what, six years?"

Sirus nodded. "Give or take."

"I think they're pretty nice." Noah attempted a smile. "Your art ... things, I mean. Whatever." A dull crimson crept up Noah's neck and into his hairline. "You understand what I'm saying."

"I do. Thank you." Sirus dipped his head. "That's very kind of you to say." His chest swelled and he started to feel excited and human again. "Let me know if you ever see something you think you might want. It's yours, free of charge."

"Oh, no, I couldn't do that." Noah backed up and lifted his hands, shaking his head. "It's your art." He ran his hands through his blond hair, as if his attempt to push the short length off his forehead made any difference. "It has too much value to just give away."

"Creating these pieces is not my job; it's my hobby, and it gives me joy to share it with friends. I drive my truck to earn a living. I do this," Sirus turned in a circle, letting every inch of the excitement this workspace brought him catch fire in his heart again, "because it brings me peace and pleasure. You and Janice come up whenever you want and pick something out. Or, if you like, I can create something special for you both."

"No, you can't." Noah stilled, and his face became a mask. "Janice and I aren't living together anymore." His brown eyes dulled to mud. "We've separated and are filing for a divorce."

"Oh, I didn't know." Sympathy filled Sirus's voice, and his chest hurt over a long marriage ending. He didn't know Noah or Janice well but he figured they had to have twenty years of marriage on them. They had two teenage kids. "I'm so sorry."

"Thank you." It looked like it hurt Noah to swallow as he spoke. "It's not easy, but it's for the best." More dark shadows crossed his gaze before he banked the pain completely. Abruptly, he crossed his arms against his chest. "I've been staying at a motel. I was thinking about biting the bullet and renting a place but I just heard the other day that the McClusky's are selling their house and moving to New Mexico to be closer to their grandkids." Noah mentioned the retired couple who owned the cabin on the east side of the lake. "It's a big step, but I'm thinking about buying it."

"I hate like hell the reason it's happening," Sirus replied, "but I'd love to have you as a neighbor. I'm biased and love this land. If you're looking for a place where you can just stop and breathe for a while then I can't think of a better place than this mountain."

Noah's attention drifted to the open shed door, staring, as if he could see through Sirus's cabin to the lake beyond. "Yeah, that's what I thought too." His voice waned, and then he seemed to turn inside himself, slowly altering from loose to stiff once again.

Sirus moved closer to Noah and touched his arm. "You okay?"

Noah jerked and shook his head. "Sorry. I'm fine." His focus cleared and he became all business once more. "I apologize for unloading on you. I actually just came to tell you that you are good to move back into your home. I finished installing your new piping. Everything that was damaged has been replaced and is as good as new. I turned your water back on too. You can move back in," Noah's attention fell to the covered sketch of Grey again, "uh … whenever you want."

Shit. Shit. Shit. Noah knew Sirus had been staying at Grey's cabin during these repairs. The man must have seen Grey in town at some point; he clearly recognized the drawing as a real person and not some random art model. Damn it. Sirus could not predict how Grey would react to someone seeing a sketch of him in the nude, let alone what the image implied. Sirus shifted from one leg to the other, suddenly wildly uncomfortable with what to say next. "Listen."

Noah lifted a hand as he moved to the open door. "Don't even worry about it. I'm about to go through a divorce. Believe me when I say I have no interest in slinging other people's private business to the gossips down in town." His face took on a haunted quality that weighed down the air around them in a blanket of loneliness. Sirus recognized the features; he had looked much the same when he'd walked away from Paul after realizing his former lover would never be the man Sirus needed him to be.

"Thank you for your discretion." Sirus leaned against the doorjamb and studied Noah, a man obviously struggling with his life. The dark circles and deeper grooves in the lines of Noah's face made so much more sense to Sirus now than when he'd noticed them a few days ago. "I'm here if you need me," Sirus offered. "I know we're not best friends or anything but I'm serious about that."

A hint of naked need slipped into Noah's gaze. "I might just take you up on that one day." He blinked then and the flash of vulnerability was gone. "I'll send you a bill for the work." He didn't wait for Sirus to reply before walking away. He called back, "Have a good night."

"Bye." Sirus hung at the door until Noah drove away, his heart heavy with the strange conversation. As he stood there, not yet ready to face the picture he'd drawn of Grey, Sirus realized he'd just had a more open, revealing conversation with his plumber than he'd ever had with Greyson Cole.

A man he had let fuck him. Multiple times.

Something wasn't right about that.

———

AS GREY SAT AT A TABLE in the local diner and waited for his take-out meal of a burger and fries, he fiddled with his cup of coffee. He slipped his cell phone out of his pocket and pulled up the selection of photos again, stopping on the ones he had discreetly taken at Ginny's Crafty Delights a short while ago. Ginny had two of Sirus's pieces on consignment: one in ash wood that loosely resembled a male torso in a turned, reaching position, and a freeform piece made from woven bands of metal. Grey could not believe the paltry price tags being asked for Sirus's artwork, and he would have purchased them both himself if his gut didn't say doing so would look damned suspicious.

Christ. Grey had not seen nor heard from Sirus all day long, and he had no expectation the man would return to the cabin tonight. The plumbing work on Sirus's home had already gone one day over schedule, so there was no way Grey could expect another day of delays would force Sirus back to the cabin for one more night. Nope. Grey figured he'd had about as much ass as he was going to get on this vacation and he might as well be satisfied he'd even gotten that.

No more kissing, fucking … *sleeping* with Sirus Wilder. Sweet, sexy, strong Sirus Wilder. All because Grey wouldn't bend over and give up his own ass.

Damn it. Grey's cock pressed against his jeans as he thought about being naked in bed with Sirus. His length pushed against his zipper where he sat, protesting the prospect of renewed celibacy. His chest squeezed tightly as well, as it had done all day every time Sirus's name popped into his head. Worst of all, though, his ass throbbed a steady, aching staccato as a fast vision of Sirus penetrating him and stuffing his channel with exquisite, slow tenderness filled Grey's head. Grey gasped as his heart rate increased and his erection grew, shocking him with the intensity of his physical response *while in a public place.*

Grey sat in a booth where the table concealed his crotch. Thank God. All the same, he scanned the diner's patrons and prayed like hell it took at least a few more minutes to complete his order. He could not stand up right now. With his attention subtly touching on nearly every customer in the diner -- none of whom paid him a damn bit of attention -- Grey started to breathe a sigh of relief. Then his gaze clashed with a brown one that stared right at him, no blinking or backing off when Grey caught him in the act.

What the fuck?

From one booth away the blond man continued to stare. The feral business tycoon inside Grey stirred to life, putting an immediate cockblock on his hard-on. Grey regularly shat the remnants of millionaires and billionaires who thought they could intimate him; he sure as hell wouldn't tuck tail and run over a small town local eyeballing him -- no matter that the man looked like he could knock Grey unconscious with one punch.

His erection no longer an issue, Grey slid his phone back into his pocket, grabbed his cup of coffee, and moved to the other man's table. "Mind if I join you?" Grey asked, but didn't wait to get an answer before sitting down. He put his cup on the table and wrapped his hands around it, letting the warmth of the liquid inside seep into his palms. Not that he needed it. Grey tended to get damned hot under the collar when another alpha dog tried to hold him down and piss on his fur. Grey felt like this man sitting across from him attempted to do just that with one cold, unwavering look.

Grey settled into the cushion of the booth seat and bared his teeth. He doubted the guy mistook it for a smile. "You got a problem with me, *friend*?"

"Not right now," the man answered. His deep voice scratched like sandpaper and he didn't look like he so much as twitched under Grey's cool delivery. "Just looking you over, though, and trying to figure out if I will before you leave this mountain."

Grudging respect for this man's balls had Grey retracting his fangs. "That seems unlikely," he studied the guy's roughly handsome face, searching for familiarity, "seeing as I don't know who in the hell you are."

"Noah Maitland." Noah did not reach across the table for a handshake.

Noah Maitland. Noah. Maitland. Noah. *Noah*. Oh. *This is Noah*. "Noah Maitland." Grey maintained a sense of ease in how he sat but he couldn't help but think about his immediate response when Sirus had mentioned the man's name the other morning. Right here, Grey's skin got as hot under the surface as it had back then. Grey breathed and kept the evidence of his reaction at bay. "You would be Sirus's plumber."

"I know how to do one or two other things, and I work for a few other people as well." Noah sat across from Grey with quiet authority, and Grey knew, just on experience from dealing with entrepreneurs every day for over ten years, that Noah was a financial success in his business. This man was no pauper, and nobody's bitch. "But yes," Noah added, "most recently I did work up at Sirus's cabin."

Grey's gut instinct hit him on another level -- a personal one -- and jealousy grew in his belly. He glanced down at Noah's hand and noticed a wedding band on his finger. Even with that, Grey wondered if Sirus knew Noah Maitland was gay. And if he didn't, but discovered it, would Sirus's interest in this man exceed home repair?

You can't have him sat right in Grey's throat, choking him with its ferocity. *Not right now. Not ever.*

A buzzing clouded Grey's hearing. Noah Maitland -- with his way too sexy rugged man vibe -- blurred before Grey's eyes, covering his vision in a film of red.

No. Get control of yourself, man. Don't you dare let this guy see you lose your cool. You're a possessive person; anger is a natural reaction to seeing someone else crush on the man you're fucking. You don't like to share. Anything. It doesn't mean you care.

Grey muzzled the monologue looping in his head, locked his inner dog in another room, and affected a mildly interested arched brow. "What is it exactly you think you know that has you so concerned, Maitland?"

"I don't know anything," Noah replied. "Just saw something

that allowed me to draw a conclusion on my own."

"That's not much to go on to make a snap judgment about a man."

"No, sitting here watching you," Noah sliced panic through Grey with his never-ending, assessing stare, "I think I figured the situation out exactly right."

Right then, an earsplitting whistle cut across the diner. Everyone turned toward the pass-through window behind the lunch counter, and owner Ruthie Costa pointed at Grey with her spatula. "Order's ready, honey," she said, losing the interest of all the other diners with those words. "Nice and hot. Be out with it in just a second."

"Thank you." Grey dipped his head; he made to slide out of the booth but a strong hand wrapped itself around his wrist and locked him to the table. Grey's attention slid down to the fingers holding his arm in a bruising vise. He blinked and brought his focus back up to Noah's face. "You're going to want to take your hand off me." Grey's tone dripped colder than the polar icecaps. "Right now."

Noah released Grey's wrist. "I apologize," he said, but again, looked Grey right in the eyes without cowering. "Let me just say one thing before you go." The color in Noah's eyes softened even as his hand curled into a fist on the tabletop. "Sirus is a nice man. Kind. Generous. A lot of people in this area care about him and do not want to see him hurt again."

Again? Did these people know about Sirus's relationship with Paul? Or had there been someone else? Jesus. The desire for knowledge about Sirus clutched at the inquisitive nature of Grey's personality, at his need to know every little detail about any situation in which he was involved. At the same time -- *fucking shit* -- he couldn't ask without becoming one hell of a hypocrite. There wasn't any damn way he would exchange equal information about himself with Sirus just to get some answers.

"If you're a good man," Noah continued, pulling Grey out of his private thoughts, "and you think there's even the possibility you're going to cause him pain, maybe you need to think about walking away right now."

Grey fought down an unnatural wave of violence, and he just resisted hauling this pretender to his feet and shoving him against the wall. "And give you room to step in?" Grey hissed, keeping his voice low out of a respect he wasn't sure this man deserved.

Noah flinched and his pupils flared. "I didn't say that."

"No," Grey bit down and took some of the rancor out of his tone, "but you're thinking it."

"Just don't hurt him." Noah's gaze touched over every other patron in the diner and then came back to Grey. "Trust me when I say it would be more than me who cared."

A young waitress passed by the table right then, a brown bag in her hands. "I have your food, Mr. Cole." She smiled at both men shyly. "I'll be waiting at the register whenever you're ready."

"Be right there," Grey answered.

"Think about what I said." Noah's voice and stare were still quietly threatening.

The dog within Grey slipped out and for just the blink of an eye morphed into a wolf. "I'll think about your fucking motives too," he said, his voice cutting. He blinked again and everything slipped right back to cool. "You have a good night."

Grey walked away and paid for his meal, smiling and making friendly chitchat to the server and the couple who'd also stepped in to pay their bill. On the inside, though, Grey saw the snarling teeth of a brown haired beast shredding to pieces a golden haired wolf.

To the victor went the prize.

Sirus Wilder.

———

IN THE DEAD OF NIGHT, FREEZING cold, Grey banged on Sirus's door. A little porch light offered the only illumination. He'd gone home after his showdown at the diner but he'd had no appetite for the burger and fries. He'd tried to wipe the conversation with Noah from his mind but he kept hearing the words *"don't hurt him again"* in his mind. More than that, Grey couldn't shake the absolute *caring* in that damn warning, as well as a very real concern that Grey had the power to hurt Sirus.

Grey had spent the better part of the evening telling himself that Sirus's going home to his own cabin was for the best. All through his shower, though, and through masturbating while in that shower -- with Sirus on his mind -- Grey had reiterated that things were better this way. He didn't want complications in his life, and spending too much more time around Sirus would undoubtedly become messier with every day added to their brief hook-up. Grey had even crawled into bed and tossed and turned for at least two hours, surrounded by the scent of the very man in question embedded into the sheets and comforter, torturing Grey with how fucking big the bed was without an even bigger man sharing it. Then Grey had rolled over and turned toward the window, and his attention had snagged on a navy blue T-shirt. Sirus's shirt.

Grey had found himself out of bed, the T-shirt in hand, and behind the wheel of his car before he'd even processed that he'd pushed back the covers and gotten up. He didn't know why he was here now, or what he wanted to say, what he should do, or if he should mention his conversation with Noah.

The door swung open right then and stole away any attempt Grey had to throw together a late plan. Sirus stood in the open doorway, a soft light behind him casting him in near shadows. He wore nothing but a pair of white briefs.

"It's late." Sirus appeared scruffy and rough, but he didn't look any sleepier than Grey did. "What do you want?"

"We had an agreement." Grey's voice was stripped and harsh, more than he wanted to show. "We share a bed while we're up here together. That was what we said." Grey snaked his hand around Sirus's neck and pulled his head down. He looked right into Sirus's eyes, internal nakedness swirling and surely showing through from his own. "Don't break our deal." Christ, how Grey wanted this man. "Please," he added, and crushed his mouth on Sirus's in a raw, openmouthed kiss.

CHAPTER TWELVE

Oh God, he's so stunningly beautiful.

Sirus couldn't stamp down that destructive thought about Greyson Cole just a split second before the man grabbed him and took his mouth with a deep, wildly aggressive kiss.

Wanting to resist, knowing for his own protection that he should, Sirus melted on the *"please"* from Grey. He sank into Grey's burning hot frame and let Grey's body heat shield him from the gust of bitter cold wind. Sirus knew he would never get secrets and confessions from a man like Grey, but the fact that he had said that one word in such a guttural way shattered every protest Sirus knew he should speak. It stopped his hands from pushing Grey away and slammed a lid on every valid reason Sirus had mentally listed as to why he should never sleep with Grey again.

That damn *"please"* reached deep inside Sirus and latched on to an aching need to know more, and it had him throwing himself into the kiss, groaning as Grey ate at his mouth.

Eventually, Grey broke the kiss and came up for air. "Invite me inside," his hazel eyes were full of shards of fiery amber, "or I swear I will fuck you right on this porch." He angled Sirus's head and stole another kiss, tangling tongues between gasps for air. "Jesus," Grey licked Sirus's lips, "it feels like forever since I've been in your ass. Tell me I can have you."

Don't. Don't weaken and give him all the power. "I --"

His eyes glittering with arousal, Grey whispered roughly, "I want you so fucking much." He grabbed Sirus's hand and shoved it down over his cock, grinding it against the hard ridge of flesh. "Feel it ... Ahh yeah," he hissed when Sirus squeezed his prick, "and let me inside."

Oh God, I shouldn't. I shouldn't... Sirus looked at Grey, taking in every inch of his face in one fast second, and swore he saw agonized longing living in every stark line. He let go of Grey's erection and touched his fingers over the unforgiving angle of Grey's jaw; the man jerked and shivered, and Sirus had his answer.

"Yes." Ignoring every warning bell of common sense, Sirus dragged Grey over the threshold into his home and then shut the door behind them. He tore at Grey's jacket and ripped open the buttons on his shirt, dragging him toward the couch, certain that his pure need was open and visible for Grey to witness. "Oh God, yes," Sirus said again, and yanked Grey to him, fusing their fronts together from mouth to cock.

"Thank you." Raw need edged Grey's voice; he grazed his palms across Sirus's abdomen with tormenting brushes of contact. "Thank you." Grey scraped his mouth across Sirus's, teasing the seam with darting licks from the tip of his tongue.

Every light brush of lips accompanied a few steps toward the living room; with their arms entangled and their legs getting crossed over one another, it might have looked like they were slow dancing to anyone who saw the pair. Sirus pushed Grey's coat and shirt off and let them float to the floor, glorying in the feast of fit body revealed to his eyes. He slid his hands around Grey's back and slipped his fingers inside the waistband of his jeans, tugging him close. Their chests rose and fell in uneven falls with every shared breath they took, and their cocks strained as their kiss turned deeper and became more desperate, proving to each man that this was a tango meant only for the eyes of two.

They kept moving until they bumped into the arm of a cushioned chair, at which point Grey reached between their bodies and pushed his hand down the front of Sirus's underwear. "Damn it," he wrapped his fingers around Sirus's stiff length and gave it a hard jerk, "you feel good." Grey stuck his tongue into Sirus's mouth as he pulled on Sirus's dick again, and Sirus thrust his hips into the heavenly, rough touch. His cock leaked precum over Grey's palm and his asshole fluttered at what it knew would soon come.

"Yeah, that's it." Grey teased Sirus's slit with the blunt edge of his fingernail, snaking a shiver of delight through Sirus's body. "Show me more of that excitement." He pressed a line of kisses across Sirus's cheek up to his ear, flicking his tongue over Sirus's flesh every step of the way. "I love it when you shake." He manipulated his fingertip over the supersensitized head of Sirus's cock again.

"Ohh shit…" Sirus moaned and pushed out more early seed, his dick swelling unbearably under the pressure of Grey's concentrated touch. "Goddamnit." Sirus shoved his underwear the rest of the way down so he could watch Grey fondle his aching cock. "You already know exactly what I like."

Sirus stared as Grey added his other hand to the mix; the man curled his fingers in a tight fist around Sirus's penis and dragged up and down his length in fast strokes. Grey also continued to torment the head and opening of Sirus's dick with an expert touch.

"Oh God," Sirus sucked in a big gulp of air, somehow getting even stiffer as he watched, "that's so fucking good." Every inch of his body throbbed with wanting. "I like it hard."

Grey cursed and pulled Sirus up against him with his hold on the man's erection. "Jesus, you go right to my head." He leaned in and delivered another savage kiss, bruising Sirus's lips. "I need another taste of your cock, but I want to fuck you so badly I don't think I can suck you without coming." Grey spun Sirus around and rubbed his crotch against Sirus's ass. Slick fingers pushed into Sirus's crease and pressed at his quivering pucker. "Bend over and brace your hands on the chair."

Sirus shivered as a sudden awareness stabbed him in the chest. "No." Every time they had sex, Grey turned Sirus away from him. *Not this time.* Before Sirus could second-guess himself, he grabbed Grey and pushed *him* into the chair in a seated position. "If I'm the one taking it, then this time," Sirus slid his legs in on either side of Grey and straddled his lap, "I want to ride."

Grey's pupils flared, and he opened his mouth. Sirus quickly leaned in and covered Grey's lips with his, afraid to hear the man refuse. He clutched Grey's face and pried his jaw open with the force of his own, alternating between licking, biting, and plundering Grey's mouth with a feast of kissing, desperate to make Grey so hot the man wouldn't care what position they ended up in as long as he could get his cock in Sirus's ass. Sirus kissed Grey with every ounce of pent-up frustration and longing he'd suffered all day long, pushing the inferno of need out of his body and into Grey's.

After one moment where it felt like they did battle, Grey finally released the tension in his body and sank back into the plush chair. He slipped his arms around Sirus's waist and held him close. Grey skimmed his tongue along the nubby length of Sirus's and then took over the inside of his mouth with an intimate probing that Sirus swore he could feel stabbing deep in his chute.

Needing more, Sirus flexed his buttocks over Grey's groin in a fucking motion, swiping his bare ass along Grey's hard, jeans-covered cock, in much the way he had that evening in the rain. Thinking about the first night they'd come together fueled Sirus's basest, rawest desires -- ones that in his mind had *Grey* bent over the chair, with *his* ass open and wanting, begging Sirus to fill him to the brim, just as much as the reverse.

Sirus knew he couldn't shove Grey's legs apart and penetrate his channel, but he was too far gone in the moment, and so damn hot for this man, he accepted whatever kind of connection he could get. He delved his hands between their stomachs and worked open Grey's pants, getting them down just enough to free his cock. "Get the lube and fuck me." Sirus's voice was gritty with his command but he had never felt like he needed to mate with someone more than right in this moment. "There's a bottle tucked down in the side of the cushion." He dug his hand down one side of the chair as Grey did the other. "Hurry." Sirus's fingers felt arthritic and clumsy; he knew Grey could see and feel the naked need thrumming all the way through his body but he could not control or conceal his emotions. "Or I might come before you get there."

Grey's hazel eyes fired with sparks of burnished gold. He strung together a streak of blue words, his motions as agitated as Sirus's. "Jesus Christ, at least let me get inside." He straightened his arms and dug both hands into the edges of the chair. "Where's the damn lube ... wait," he pulled his hand out, a small bottle clasped in it, "I found it."

"Hurry, hurry." Sirus's passage rippled and his bud pulsed. "Just slick up your cock." He rose to his knees and braced a hand on Grey's shoulder, the muscles encased within sculpted and firm.

Grey looked up, his eyes bright as he worked the thick, clear substance over his rigid length. "You sure?" He held his cock around the base, every rearing inch now shiny with lube.

Sirus grabbed his ass cheeks, pried himself open, and then lowered himself onto Grey's thick tip. The head of Grey's cock barely grazed Sirus's ring and Sirus felt the slight contact touch over every molecule in his body. He leaned his weight into Grey, kept their stare connected, and bore down on Grey's penis. "I'm sure," he promised, and gritted his teeth together, rocking, pressing, and burning the snug muscle protecting his channel. He didn't stop working his hole over Grey's erection until, with a gasp of pleasure, Sirus's entrance opened, and Grey eased the fat head of his cock inside.

"Ohhhh God ... God ... Grey." His fingers digging deep into Grey's shoulders, Sirus made a choking sound as the pleasure of the coupling engulfed him whole. Sirus's mouth gaped as Grey held him in place and slowly, oh-so-slowly, forced the rest of his rock-hard length up into Sirus's ass. Sirus's channel flamed with the taking, his ring screamed at the pulling ... and he had never been harder in his life.

Grey groaned, the noise rumbling up from somewhere in his middle. "Damn it," he looked into Sirus's eyes, "you're so fucking hot and tight." He squeezed his arms around Sirus's waist and pulled their front's flush, creating friction between their bodies that had both men moaning with pleasure.

Every muscle in Sirus's being contracted and seized yet at the same time shrieked at the restriction. "Hold yourself inside me." He reached back and pushed one of Grey's hands down to where his cock invaded Sirus's body, entwining their fingers for a second before taking his away. "I want you to stay inside me when I start to move."

As Grey nodded, his jaw clenched, and Sirus's chest constricted with temporary power. This man might not be able to admit to much more than a sexual attraction between them but he could not deny how fierce and consuming that chemistry was when they came together.

Holding Grey's gaze prisoner with his own, Sirus found a hold with one hand on Grey's chest and the other at the crook of his elbow. Stable now, Sirus rocked his lower body in one long stroke over Grey's cock, sliding up the man's length until he was almost all the way out, only to then reverse the motion and impale himself one hard inch at a time, filling his channel with scorching hardness again. It felt so damn good Sirus did it a second time, amazed that he could feel every ripple of his chute latch on to Grey's prick and try to hold it inside, only to close up and have to stretch to accommodate when he shifted forward and pushed Grey's erection back inside him again. Sirus found a steady, darkly wonderful rhythm, one that had his rectum sending shivery tentacles of awareness up his back and down his legs, and had his ability to think or breathe decrease with every slow drive of his passage down over Grey's cock. Sirus watched Grey as they came together, saw the burn sparking in his hazel irises that turned them almost pure amber, and Sirus knew he was lost.

No. I won't let myself fall for the wrong man again. Closing his eyes to ward off the swell of emotion trying to take him over, Sirus picked up the pace and rammed himself up and down on Grey's erection, wincing but loving the roughness consuming his sensitized ass, forcing himself to grasp for sensations that were purely physical and nothing more. Whipping his hips back and forth and side to side, Sirus grunted at the almost painful widening of his tender channel, but he couldn't stop. He sank his fingers into Grey's hot flesh and held on tight while he fucked himself on Grey's cock, needing the force and speed of mad sex to take his mind and heart away from the mistaken belief that he and Grey were making love.

"Ahh, Jesus Christ..." Grey speared his dick up hard, making Sirus open his eyes and cry out with sweet agony. "You're killing me."

Sirus's gaze clashed and got caught up in Grey's, and as much as Sirus knew he should, he couldn't look away. "Fuck me," he whispered, his voice a rough noise he barely recognized as his own. "Fuck me hard." Sirus pumped his hips in an out of control fashion, hoping to suffocate the awareness of new love battling to break free. "Please."

Grey growled, and he clutched Sirus's ass, holding them together as he surged off the chair and slammed Sirus down onto the coffee table, sending books and a coffee mug crashing to the floor. Grey came down on top of Sirus and thrust his cock deep into Sirus's ass, shoving his way inside until he could not take a single centimeter more. He pushed his hands into Sirus's hair and twisted, holding on with a stinging grip as he pounded his hips against Sirus's backside, slapping his balls into Sirus's crack and sawing his prick in and out of Sirus's flaming rectum.

"You want it rougher than this?" Grey uttered the words harshly as he speared his dick into Sirus's hole again, starting a motion that rolled Sirus's lower body off the coffee table with every sure thrust. Grey's eyes held more than a hint of animal savagery, and he looked feral enough to bite. "Tell me." He pulled on Sirus's hair and bit his lower lip. "Now."

"Yes." Sirus pumped and strained against Grey, struggling to find a way to get inside the man's very body. He locked his ankles high around Grey's back and grabbed the edge of the coffee table so he didn't slide off the sweat-slick surface. "Fuck me harder."

Grey reamed Sirus into a confused state of pleasure and pain. His fingers slipped out of Sirus's hair and grabbed at his face, pushing his jaw open. "You want me to fuck you so hard you'll still feel me inside you every minute of the day tomorrow?" His focus dropped to Sirus's mouth, and he licked at the opening. He prodded with his tongue, and roughly squeezed Sirus's jaw. "Do you?"

Sirus couldn't close his eyes or look away any longer, and stopped even trying. "Yes." He lunged up and captured Grey's mouth, needing every bit of connection he could steal for when

Grey went home. Sirus rubbed his tongue over Grey's, shouting silently inside when Grey moaned and kissed him back with equal rawness. Sirus bit Grey's lower lip, pulling at the swollen skin as Grey gave Sirus another hard plunge into his ass. "Oh God..." Sirus's mouth gaped as he struggled to breathe through the incredible friction Grey wreaked on his sweet spot. "Fuck me hard ... yes ... yes."

Grey's face changed; the skin over his cheeks pulled taut and his lips twisted into a snarl. "You want me to mark you so deeply my cum never finds its way out of your tight ass?" Grey went at Sirus with a sharp stab of his shaft, shaking the sturdy coffee table with the powerful vigor of his fucking. "Is that what you want?"

Sirus let go of the table and wrapped his hands around Grey's neck, pulling his face down until their foreheads touched. "Please, come." Sirus scraped his lips across Grey's, unable to hide what he needed anymore. Overwhelming emotions had such control of him that his request barely held sound. "I need to feel you come."

Looking into Sirus's eyes, Grey's lips parted. "I... I..." His eyes squeezed shut just then, his entire body shuddered in one continuous wave, and a second later warm liquid spurted deep in Sirus's ass. Sirus's muscles seized in response, and his ass contracted around Grey's shaft as the man came, drawing Grey's eyes open again and right onto Sirus.

Sirus stared up at Grey, trapped, completely unable to mask whatever showed on his face. "Grey," he whispered thickly. He felt only a split second of tingling swirl through his belly and race down his cock before he shot a load of spunk between his stomach and Grey's, his voice hoarse with a moan as he let go and smeared their torsos with thick lines of seed. Grey jerked above him, and renewed warmth took over Sirus's milking chute, coating him inside with a fresh wave of cum. Sirus's cock twitched again between the sandwich of their stomachs, but other than a little spit of semen, he had nothing more to give.

Grey's arms gave out and he fell on top of Sirus, his weight a heady thing that crushed Sirus into the coffee table. The muscles in Sirus's thighs protested the tight hold around Grey's back, so he let his legs fall alongside the length of Grey's.

For long moments, only the shared sounds of their heavy breathing filled the room. Sirus let himself slip into the fantasy that he would feel this amazing male weight pressing into him for the rest of his days. He knew it could never be; he knew he could never sustain a long distance relationship with someone again, let alone try to build something real with a man who could not give even the smallest piece of himself to a partner. All the same, it still felt so fucking *nice* to talk to someone over a good meal, and to share a bed and body heat when the temperatures dipped as cold as they were right now that Sirus couldn't help the snippets of dreams wanting to take over his thoughts and heart.

"Did you paint that?" Grey mumbled the question into Sirus's shoulder, where he had his head resting and his face turned toward the fireplace. "The picture above the mantel, I mean." His voice sounded drowsy and a little bit slurred.

"Yeah." Sirus didn't have to look. He knew the oil painting of the old couple in rocking chairs on the front porch of their home very well. "Don't know who they are. I drove through a little town in Arkansas one day and saw them sitting peacefully -- the old man was half asleep. I stopped, pulled back to take their picture, and then drove away. When I saw them I just knew I wanted to try to paint them, and that's the result."

"It's captivating," Grey said. "Makes you want to buy a rocking chair and sit with them for a while."

Sirus smiled against Grey's hair. "For all I know they fight like cats and dogs and curse at each other all day, but for some reason they looked like they loved each other and had the ability to endure." He brushed his fingers up and down Grey's back, memorizing the cords and rips of warm muscles he found there. "The image of them made me envious of something that long lasting. I wanted to capture it and have something to remind me of what can be." Sirus's hand stopped on the curve of Grey's buttocks, and he exhaled slowly, fighting through his instinct to hide every bit as much as Grey did. "To have something to aspire to one day myself," he admitted, his tone soft.

The pattern of breathing that touched against Sirus's shoulder slowed, and the body on top of him filled with tension.

"Are you all right?" Grey asked abruptly, his voice just as hushed. "I was really rough with you."

Sirus started breathing and began rubbing his palms over Grey's back again. "I'm okay." His ass was still stuffed full of

Grey's cock, and Sirus loved the sensation. "I asked for it."

"I know. But I also know that fucking you as hard as I did can create a lot of pain for the person on the receiving end." Grey still didn't turn his head and face Sirus; instead, he drew little circles on Sirus's hip with the tips of two fingers.

Wanting, aching for something intimate and personal so badly, Sirus steeled himself for another rejection. "Do you want to tell me how you know that?"

Grey shifted and blinked rapidly, Sirus could feel the brushes of the man's eyelashes against his shoulder. "Yeah," Grey finally said, after what felt like an eternity of silence. "I do."

Sirus closed his eyes, and breathed.

Finally.

"Tell me."

CHAPTER THIRTEEN

You don't want to tell Sirus about Joe, you idiot! Why did you say that?

Grey lay on top of Sirus, his cock still tucked all the way in the man's ass, and cursed whatever masochistic tendency had prompted him to say he would spill his guts about a part of his private life. It had to be a moment of weakness, of feeling a temporary sense of closeness to this man as a result of the incredibly intimate sex act they'd just shared. Grey didn't normally lose control and become so vocal and aggressive as he had with Sirus just now, and he'd experienced a momentary obligation to share a part of himself that would equal the vulnerability Sirus had given him during sex.

But that didn't mean he had to tell Sirus about Joe!

Stupid. Stupid. Stupid. This is what Grey got for showing up on Sirus's doorstep in the middle of the night, pushing something he should have just let end when Sirus had walked away yesterday morning.

"I understand if you've changed your mind." Sirus broke the tense silence. The rumble of his words vibrated through Grey and made him tremble. "If you could move," Sirus shifted and pushed against Grey's waist, "we can go wash up, and get some sleep."

"Oh, sorry." A stabbing sensation pierced Grey in the chest. He scrambled off Sirus, gritting his teeth as his dick slid out of the man's ass. Unable to look Sirus in the eyes after displaying such supreme cowardice, Grey stuffed his cock back into his underwear, adjusted everything back up to his waist, and then pulled up just the zipper on his jeans. *Shit.* "Do you want me to leave?"

The table creaked, and bones cracked, and a second later, the fall of feet on hardwood flooring reached Grey's ears. "Stay, go, do whatever you want," Sirus answered, his tone short and hard. "All I know is I'm getting cleaned up and going to bed. I don't have any control over what you do."

Grey's spine stiffened and his gaze shot up from the floor. "What in the hell is that supposed to mean?" There was no response, though; Sirus had already gone. Grey tore across the living room, his memory of where the bathroom was still very clear. "Arrogant son of a bi…"

Slam! Grey screeched to a halt midstep, right outside the

bathroom door, his voice stolen as he watched Sirus punch his fist into the bathroom wall. Grey gasped at the power behind the curled hand flying at the white plaster. With one tiny sound from Grey, Sirus spun toward the door.

Sirus's eyes burned with mercury moonlight. As Grey stood before the man, unable to deny his glorious nudity, Grey had also never believed himself so close to someone capable of doing real violence.

"Goddamnit," Sirus growled, "why do you always see me when I don't want you to?" His lips, so kissable just a short time ago, flattened to a thin, hard line. "I thought for sure you'd turn the other way and run."

With one narrow-eyed glare from Sirus, Grey's blood raced through his body and had his heart pounding harder than when he'd fucked the man just a few minutes ago. "If that's what you wanted then that's what you should have told me!" He pushed the door all the way open and stormed inside, getting right up in Sirus's face. Jesus, he could feel Sirus trying to control his breathing and his anger, but Grey didn't give a damn about Sirus's mood right now. "You invited me inside! You told me I could stay! Sleeping together was part of our agreement!"

Sirus reared back and dug his fingers into his hair, his face a mask of disbelief. "Oh yes, our agreement. Our *fucking* agreement." He snorted and threw his hands up in the air. "Literally, now that I think about it." Turning away, Sirus tunneled his hands through his hair again, where they then ended up clasped at the back of his neck. The lines of muscle that formed to create the backside of Sirus's body was magnificent. He had one of the tightest asses Grey had ever seen, but right in this moment, Grey held his breath and cared only about what Sirus might say or do next.

It felt as if Sirus stared at the wall over his bathtub for eons. With each moment of silence, Grey deflated a little bit, certain Sirus would not grace him with another word. Just when Grey took a step back to quietly leave, Sirus shifted and found his gaze. The swirling depth of open, *brave*, emotion shining within Sirus's stare gutted Grey from top to bottom, and nailed him right to the bathroom floor.

"You know," Sirus began softly, "I honestly thought I could agree to that deal with you. I genuinely thought I could have two weeks' worth of amazing, guilt-free sex, and not give a rat's ass about who you are as a person. Other people do it, and you're so damned good-looking that you have to know I wanted you like hell from the moment I saw you. All of that made me think I could participate in this kind of agreement. But I've discovered I can't."

"Wh --"

Sirus held up a hand and shut Grey right down. "I need to know more than the name, occupation, and length of the cock of the man I'm letting fuck me. I don't need dark secrets or childhood trauma, or even a promise that this will last more than the time you are on vacation." A tight smile appeared briefly on Sirus's lips. "I do need to know, however, how a man as smart as you are -- and I can see in your eyes that you are damned shrewd and intelligent -- I need to know how you can trust me, *a virtual stranger*, at my word when I tell you that I'm clean and it's safe for us to have unprotected sex. Yet with that same sharp brain and thought process of yours, you are completely certain that it's not safe to tell me even one little thing about your life beyond your sister or your work." Sirus took a small step forward, and his gaze softened. "I don't get how a person as smart as you can twist that in your head so it makes sense. I really don't."

Taking an automatic step back, Grey bumped into the side of the door. The hairs on his arms and the back of his neck stood on end, and he fucking hated that he didn't have his shirt on to cover it up. "You trusted me about my health too." Grey's voice remained steady, and he didn't blink or flinch, even as his heart rate sped out of control. "So what does that say about you?"

Sirus bit off a low curse, and he slapped his hand against the edge of the sink. "That is not my point, and you are damned smart enough to know it isn't, so don't fake ignorance with me. If you don't want to answer me, that's fine, but don't insult my intelligence by pretending you don't understand what I'm trying to say. Excuse me," he pushed against Grey's chest, "I've had enough mind games for one night."

Grey whipped his hand out and braced it against the doorframe, blocking Sirus's exit. Grey's nostrils flared and his mouth turned dry, but he could see in every tightly strung muscle in Sirus's body that the man would not listen to one more word of bullshit.

"My sister and my work are my life," Grey admitted, his voice scratchy. Adrenaline washed over his body and made his limbs numb. He felt more naked than Sirus actually was, but words he had never spoken to another soul sat in a tight ball in his throat, pushing to get free. "Except John, and you already know he's my business partner and best friend. My grandmother was the only other person of real importance in my life. She passed away a little while ago, so now it's just Kelsie and John. There isn't anything else for you to know."

"I don't believe that." Sirus remained so close to Grey that Grey could see every small line and imperfection in the man's roughly handsome face. And his eyes, Christ, his eyes held such strength and kindness Grey never wanted to look away. "I think you've just gotten so used to being closed up, and have gotten so out of the habit of talking to people about anything other than work, that you don't know how or where to start."

Grey's chest rose and fell in big, visible waves, and he found it difficult to swallow. "You could be right about that." Fuck, Grey almost choked on making that one small confession.

Looking Grey up and down, Sirus finally took a step back and leaned against the edge of the sink, allowing Grey to exhale, albeit unsteadily. "So," Sirus began as he curled his hands around the sink ledge, "if you don't bend over for anyone, then tell me how you know aggressive sex can be painful for the one on the receiving end." Once again, Sirus lifted his hand and cut Grey off before he could speak a protest. "I have no interest in sharing your stories or secrets, just as I would guess you would never share mine. I just want you to be able to tell me *something*, and that piece of your life actually pertains to what we did tonight, and what we are doing with this fling, so that's why I want to know."

Oh, Jesus Christ, no. "His name was Joe," Grey blurted, before the voice in his head reminded him to shut up. "He was a boyfriend in college, and he was the first guy I dated for long enough and felt strongly enough about to want to go all the way and actually have intercourse with him. I thought I wanted it; Christ, I was prepared to love it, but it turned out to be the most painful, invasive, violating thing I have ever experienced in my life." His rectum automatically contracted where he stood; Grey could still feel the fire from that day burning in his channel. "It hurt so damn badly that, honest to God, I thought I'd have to go to the ER afterward to make sure nothing was damaged. The idea of going to a hospital was even more humiliating than the act itself." Grey grimaced, remembering the days he'd missed classes while closed up in the apartment he'd shared with John, praying like hell that his backside would feel normal again so that no one -- not even a complete stranger in a hospital -- would have to know what had happened with Joe.

Right in this moment, while sharing, Grey couldn't take his stare off the floor. "The thing is," he went on, "Joe wasn't even that big. Maybe even a little smaller than average. If I couldn't take it with him, I knew I wouldn't be able to take it with any man." Grey couldn't help his focus lifting briefly to Sirus's long, thick cock. "I decided at that point I was meant to be a top." He shrugged, and finally looked up, facing Sirus again. "I've been one ever since."

Sirus continued to lean against the sink. He had his arms crossed against his chest, looking as loose as if they were talking about what to have for dinner. "What did Joe say when he wanted to fuck you again and you said no?"

"He never got the chance. I stopped seeing him shortly after that."

An eyebrow arched halfway up Sirus's forehead. "Seriously?"

"I couldn't keep seeing him," Grey explained, his voice full of rationale. "He was definitely a top, and it was pretty much understood I would always be the one on the receiving end of sex. When I realized I couldn't, it became obvious we would have to break up."

"Or, you could have told him, and you might have been able to work something out."

"No, I couldn't tell him." How could Sirus ever think Grey would confess to such a thing? "He never even knew while he was fucking me that it felt like he was tearing me up inside. I didn't ever tell him I ended it because of the sex."

"And he never came after you?" Sirus asked incredulously. "He never called you or banged on your door asking for an explanation or a second chance, or demanded to know about your abrupt change of heart?"

"No." Grey shook his head. "Joe just accepted me at my

word and moved on."

Sirus looked at Grey, let his gaze slide all over Grey's body, and his slow perusal whispered a heated tremor through Grey. "Then you were better off without him," Sirus finally said, his voice striking. "Any guy I cared about enough to have sex with him, I would have ripped down his door and dogged his ass until I got an explanation that made sense to me as to why he was leaving. Especially knowing it was his first time."

"Joe didn't know it was my first time with a man." Grey's skin crawled at the very idea of giving another person the kind of ego boost and power a confession such as that would have engendered. "He just knew it was my first time with him. Like hell I was going to tell *anybody* that he was the one I chose to fuck me for the first time. No, I didn't do that."

Sighing, Sirus said, "He should have known to be gentle anyway, but geez, man, you should have told him."

"No." Talk about putting himself naked in front of someone. Grey shuddered. "Absolutely not." The scrutiny of Sirus in this moment ate at Grey almost as strongly as he imagined it would have if Joe had known about his virginity. Grey rubbed at his neck and tore his gaze from Sirus. "Can we not just stand here looking at each other like this? Do something." He strode forward, grabbed a washcloth off the sink, and thrust it at Sirus's chest. "Here, wash up. That's what you came in here to do."

Sirus shifted to turn on the faucet but he looked up and found Grey behind him in the reflection of the mirror. Sirus looked as if a thousand words sat jabbing inside him, bursting to break out. Eventually, he just said, "If you're going to stay the night, take off your clothes and clean up too. Leave everything on the floor. I'll throw it in the wash in the morning."

Such relief swamped Grey that his legs almost went out from under him. "Okay." He worked his shoes, socks, jeans, and underwear off in quick order, and by the time he did, Sirus already had a sudsy, damp washcloth waiting for him. The men washed in silence, and while they did, Grey couldn't help his attention dropping to Sirus's ass as the man cleaned his crack and hole. He couldn't miss how Sirus's member twitched as the wet fabric teased over his pucker. Grey's own ass quivered in response, and a flash of himself bent over the sink with Sirus ramming his asshole full of hard cock took over Grey's mind and sight -- and had his dick stiffening too.

No. Grey's reaction had occurred due to the topic of conversation; that was all. He didn't want a man to fuck him. All the same, Grey shifted and finished wiping himself down in fast order, and didn't dare look at Sirus's ass again. "I'm good." He tossed his washcloth in the sink and then stooped down to pick up his clothes, taking the time to drape them over the towel rack. "I'll just leave these here. No need to trip on them if you have to get up to piss."

A distinct chuckle reached Grey's ears. "Right," Sirus said, amusement lacing his voice. "By all means, get them off the floor. Come on," he reached back and slipped his hand in Grey's, giving it a tug, "let's go to bed."

Jesus, Grey liked the sound of that. He paused while Sirus flicked off the bathroom light, and then gripped his hand in a tight hold, letting the bigger man lead him down the dark hallway. Once they reached Sirus's bedroom, a hint of light from the moon reflecting off the snow outside guided them to the bed. The covers were already rumpled, all the proof Grey needed that he had gotten Sirus out of bed, if not actually awakened him. The sight of something so achingly personal like mussed sheets -- that would surely smell warm and woodsy, exactly like Sirus -- had Grey stumbling into Sirus's back.

"Sorry," he mumbled against Sirus's shoulder blade.

Sirus gave Grey's hand a squeeze. "No problem. You crawl in first though." He let go of Grey's hand and stung his ass with a little slap. "And scoot over to the other side. I need to sleep next to the nightstand with my alarm clock."

Before Grey finished shifting farther than the middle of the bed, Sirus crawled in behind and threw the covers over them both. He spooned his front against Grey's back, slipped his arm around Grey's waist, and threaded his fingers through the backs of Grey's. Sighing, Sirus snuggled them even tighter together. His shaft grazed along Grey's crease, kicking Grey's heart right back into high gear.

"God, you feel good." Sirus's voice sounded from right behind Grey's ear. "Is this okay?" He dug his hand between them and adjusted his cock so that it rubbed against the small of Grey's back rather than the cleft of his ass. "Just for sleeping. Nothing more."

Grey exhaled, and he reminded himself that Sirus was not the kind of man to take something he knew his partner didn't want to give. "It's perfect." He relaxed and let his entire weight sink against Sirus. Damn it, the man was an inferno. "Never felt warmer."

"Good." Sirus pecked a kiss to the back of Grey's ear. "Sleep tight."

Long minutes of silence stretched between the men, but Grey knew Sirus hadn't yet fallen asleep. His breathing pattern hadn't changed from the moment he'd climbed into bed, and he continued to rub his thumb in the most shiver-inducing little circles over the back of Grey's hand.

After counting two hundred sheep in his head -- jumping over the fence backward -- Grey chewed halfway through his lip before he couldn't stand Sirus's silence anymore. "What is keeping you from sleep?" Jesus, what in the hell was wrong with him tonight? He couldn't just shut up and let things be. "What is sitting right there on the tip of your tongue clawing to get out? I know it's something."

Sirus chuckled, and murmured under his breath, "Maybe you are getting to know me."

Grey tried to turn around. "What?"

Pushing on Grey's head, Sirus forced him to lie back down. "Nothing. I was thinking some more about how smart you are, and how I figure you must be a logical, linear kind of thinker." As Sirus responded, he continued to rub the back of Grey's hand. "Because of that, logically, you must know that being on the other side of sex can feel amazing, wonderful, and something many people crave. Both men and women, gay and straight. You've been with me, and you see how much pleasure I get out of what you do to me, and how much I love having you inside me. I imagine you must have watched similar reactions and cries of pleasure from the other men you've fucked in your life. Logically, you have to know it can be the same for you -- that you can reach great heights of sexual pleasure by letting someone capable and knowledgeable inside your body."

Beads of sweat popped up on Grey's forehead and, in the dark, he tried to adjust his sightline to the door ... toward escape.

"I'm not trying to proposition you right now, or corner you into anything," Sirus continued, never, never stopping that intoxicating, soothing brush of his thumb over Grey's skin. "I'm not even saying you should ever lay yourself open and trust *me*. I'm just saying that if you take the emotion out of your thinking -- the way you do with so many things -- you have to see that what I'm saying is true. All I want is for you to think about it and consider it. Just let the idea sit with you for a while and see if you don't feel differently than you did when you made that decision all those years ago. Can you do that?" Sirus gave Grey a little squeeze. "Will you? Wait, you know what? Don't give me an answer. I didn't say it to get a response; I just wanted you to know my thoughts. I won't bug you anymore." He nuzzled his face into Grey's neck and pressed a kiss to his nape. "Goodnight."

"Yeah, 'night," Grey murmured. Sirus settled in behind him, but Grey could not take his eyes off a three dimensional landscape carved out of wood hanging on the wall in front of him. He studied the piece intently, certain it was Sirus's work.

His mind a jumble of confusion telling him to get the hell out of this cabin right now, Grey still did not leave. His body wouldn't let him. He couldn't separate his flesh from the heat and solid wall that was Sirus. Something struggling to get free inside him wouldn't let Grey walk away.

Grey stared into the intricacies of the carving on Sirus's wall … and stayed.

———

SIRUS WATCHED GREY BUTTON UP his freshly laundered shirt, and his mouth watered with wanting. They'd given each other a couple of earth-shaking blowjobs upon waking up, and then had jerked each other off afterward in the shower, but watching this extremely private man brush his teeth, hair, and get dressed, comfortably, while in *Sirus's* cabin, struck Sirus as the most intimate moment he'd shared with Greyson Cole since they'd met. With anyone, really.

Ever.

"What's wrong?" Grey asked, yanking Sirus out of his dreamy state. "Why are you staring?" He put his hand up to his chin and wiped. "Do I have toothpaste on my face?"

"No, you look fine." Sirus's face heated, but he held Grey's stare. "You look really handsome this morning. You look sexy in blue."

"Oh." Twin blossoms of red crept over Grey's cheeks. "Thanks." He patted his hands down the front of his shirt, and brushed his fingers over his jeans, straightening everything out, *just so*. "I should get going and let you get to your art." Pointing toward the hallway, Grey backed out of the bathroom and walked to the living room. "Besides," he grabbed his coat off the arm of the couch, "I neglected e-mails pretty much all day yesterday, so I really need to play catch up today."

Sirus shook his head and smiled. "You do know you're supposed to be on vacation, right? That generally means you can get away with a little bit of slacking." He opened the door anyway and followed Grey out onto the porch. The still, quiet cold of morning quickly took root in Sirus's bones. Without a jacket or shoes on, he moved closer to Grey for a little heat. He leaned down to steal a kiss, and instead let his lips linger over the warmth of Grey's breath fanning his face and mouth. "Even big shots like you are allowed to take a couple of weeks off every year."

Grey wrapped his arms around Sirus and dragged him in close. He then tilted his head back as he linked his hands at the small of Sirus's back. Mirth twinkled in Grey's eyes, and it hit Sirus right in the heart.

"You think I'm a big shot, huh?" Grey asked, his voice full of teasing lightness.

Raising a brow, Sirus slid his hands around Grey's waist and smoothed them down to caress his ass. "Oh, I know you are."

He slipped his fingers into the back pockets of Grey's jeans.

"Mmm, that feels nice." Grey rubbed his cock on Sirus's thigh. "You like sleeping with a big shot?"

Sirus smiled against Grey's lips. "Oh yeah," he whispered, his voice breathy, "you know I do." His eyes slid closed, need overcame him, and he captured Grey's mouth with a clinging kiss.

Grey's hands curled into fists against Sirus's back, digging into muscle. Sirus whimpered, loving the sensation. He rubbed against Grey like a cat on a scratching post, and slanted his mouth across Grey's, welcoming a deepening of the kiss.

Moaning, Grey accepted the invitation and sank his tongue into Sirus's mouth, making Sirus weak in the knees with his minty heat. All sense that it was freezing cold outside flew from Sirus's body and mind, and he dug his hands between them, working to unzip Grey's coat. *Damn it, I need hard, hot flesh.* Grey threw his hands into the fray too, and between them they got Grey's jacket halfway down his arms, when then, the distinct crunching of snow penetrated Sirus's brain.

"Hold on for a sec." It took a long moment for Sirus to clear his head enough to comprehend the noise; by the blurriness in Grey's eyes the same held true for him.

By the time *"it sounds like tires on snow"* clicked in Sirus's head, as well as putting together that meant he had a visitor, the smartly dressed woman with dark hair styled in a bob already stood at the foot of his steps.

"Mom," Sirus said, still in Grey's arms, "you're here."

Chapter Fourteen

Wow, so this is Sirus's mother. Grey closed his mouth quickly, shocked to find himself standing ten feet away from the woman who made up one half of the DNA of the man he was fucking. Sirus's hands slid from around Grey's waist, and Grey let his fall too. Even with space for another body now between them, Grey could sense the tightness in the man standing beside him. Sirus was clearly as surprised to see his mother as Grey was.

"Mom, how are you?" Sirus recovered quickly, and treaded down the steps, giving the woman a hug. "It's good to see you."

The stylish, impeccably dressed woman gave Sirus what seemed to Grey a genuinely warm, squeezing hug back. "It's nice to see you too, darling." She pulled away from the hug and looked up at him, light shining in her dark eyes. "But you shouldn't sound so surprised to see me. I understand Nic told you I was coming for a visit."

"Yes, he did." Sirus took his mother's hand and guided her up the stairs, sliding her a sideways glance as he did it. "But I expected I might hear from you a day or so before you arrived so I could fix up the bedroom and get some stuff for your stay."

"No need." She reached up and touched his cheek. "I'm just here for a few hours to visit with my handsome son, and then I have to continue my drive to Asheville. I'll be working there for two weeks. I start tomorrow morning."

"Well then, I'm happy you made a detour to see me," Sirus said. "No matter how brief the visit."

Grey watched the exchange between mother and son, surprised by their comfort with each other after listening to Sirus describe his mother's attitude about his homosexuality, as well as feeling his initial tension upon her arrival.

"Grey," Sirus shifted to include Grey in their twosome, "I'd like to introduce my mother, Mrs. Nia Wilder." He smiled in his mother's direction. "She's an interpreter and speaks six languages. Mom, please meet a friend of mine, Greyson Cole." Sirus reached out and rubbed Grey's hand, making it very clear they were more than casual acquaintances. "He owns the cabin across the lake, and we've been spending some time together while he's on vacation. He's a venture capitalist and owns a very successful firm."

"Co-owns," Grey said, stretching out his hand in welcome.

"I have a partner who shoulders the responsibility equally. Anyway," he grinned at Nia, "nice to meet you, Mrs. Wilder. You have a great son."

"Yes, thank you." Nia Wilder only offered the tips of her fingers for Grey to shake, and a wave of discomfort smacked him in the face. "I am aware."

Brrr. Very chilly. So much for first impressions.

As soon as Grey let go of Nia's fingers the woman shuffled her stance and edged Grey out of the small group. "Sweetheart," Nia paused and adjusted the collar on Sirus's flannel shirt, "I don't have much time to spare this morning, and I have a handful of family matters I'd like to discuss with you before I leave."

Well, hell. Grey didn't have to be dismissed twice.

"Mother," censure tightened Sirus's tone, "you can't pretend a person who is standing right behind you doesn't exist. Especially when I've just told you he's a friend of mine."

Grey reached out and twined his fingers in Sirus's, gaining the man's attention. Sirus's eyes were full of apology, but Grey just shook his head. "Don't worry about it." He brought Sirus's hand up to his lips and pressed a kiss to it, knowing full well he half did it to force Nia Wilder to see her son for who he was. The other half, Grey just did because he enjoyed like hell touching this man. "We're all responsible for ourselves, and I've been taking care of myself for a very long time." He darted his attention to Nia, interested to note that she wasn't so gauche as to turn her head away from her son holding hands with another man. She did, however, keep her focus squarely to the right of Sirus's shoulder, just out of visual range of where Grey stood.

Feeling perverse and stubborn, Grey tugged Sirus down the steps, moving ever so slightly until he and Sirus stood right in Nia's line of sight. He then looked into Sirus's eyes and forgot all about the woman on the porch giving him the cold shoulder. "Do you think you can make it over to my place later? I might even attempt to cook something for dinner. Does that sound like a plan to you?"

"Oh, okay, sure," Sirus replied. The damned sweetest smile lifted the edge of his lips. "Around seven? I have a piece I'd like to spend some time with later, and then I'll come over after I clean up."

"I'll see you then." Grey leaned in, his mouth inches from Sirus's, but abruptly halted, yet remained so close they shared the same square foot of air. "Is this okay?"

Sirus rubbed his thumb over Grey's lower lip, pulling it in that way that always hit Grey as so fucking sexy. "Absolutely, ye --"

Grey leaned in and pressed a tender kiss to Sirus's mouth, capturing the rest of his words. Sirus's lips softened; he kissed Grey back, and pleasure shot through Grey from top to bottom. Grey dipped the tip of his tongue out just once, brushed it against Sirus's lips, and then pulled away, reluctantly letting go of Sirus's hand as well as his mouth. This time, *Grey* took a second to rub his thumb across *Sirus's* lips. He just barely suppressed the goddamned silliest urge to wink. "I'll see you later."

Sirus looked a little dazed. "Yeah, okay." He waved as Grey walked to his car. "Bye."

"Bye." Grey gave Sirus one last lingering stare, almost moaning at how fucking sexy the man was, no matter how much or little he wore. Grey opened his door, but lifted his stare to the porch, finding a very stoic woman still standing there. "It was nice to meet you, Mrs. Wilder." He lifted his hand, and he smiled as if he didn't give a shit that she had snubbed him without having the tiniest idea about who he was. "I hope you have a lovely visit with your son. Have a safe trip to Asheville. Bye."

Nia Wilder merely lifted one hand and studied her nails.

Grey shook his head, smiled one more time at Sirus, and then drove away.

Sirus stood rooted in the snow, his feet freezing like hell, but he didn't move or so much as breathe until Grey's car was gone from sight. He then closed his eyes and counted to ten, then twenty. After that, he bit his lip, knowing if he opened his mouth he would say something very ugly to his mother that he would never be able to take back. Right now, Sirus believed with every fiber of his being she deserved whatever he threw at her, but he would not put his father and his siblings through a Mother/Son feud. It would kill his father if Sirus never spoke to his mother again.

But hell, how he wanted to run after Grey and leave his mother standing on his porch right this very second.

"Invite me inside, honey," his mother called down to him, breaking him out of his struggle not to tell her where to go. "We'll catch our death of cold out here this morning."

Invite me inside. Sirus chuckled derisively. He sure liked hearing that a lot more coming from Grey than he did from his mother.

Taking a deep, calming breath, Sirus rubbed his hands together and took the steps up the porch two at a time. "You're right, Mom. Let's go inside." He strode past her and held the door open, sweeping his hand in a welcoming gesture. "It's time we had another talk."

Nia stepped over the threshold and walked to the kitchen, her memory of her previous visit clearly intact. "I hope that's fresh coffee I smell," she called back to him as he shut the door. "After getting up early to start driving, I could certainly use another cup."

Sirus moved to the kitchen but stopped in the doorway and leaned his shoulder against the frame. "It is fresh." He found her already pouring herself a cup. "Grey made it a little bit ago. He was up before I was this morning and got it brewing." Sirus just held off the nasty bent that made him want to share that Grey had then come back to bed and delivered one hell of wake-up blowjob to Sirus's morning wood. "He makes a better cup than I do, don't you think?"

Nia cupped the mug in both hands and strolled around

GREY'S AWAKENING | 195

the small space. "You did a beautiful job updating this kitchen, darling." She moved in front of him and paused to squeeze his hand. "It still looks very cozy and rustic, but has all the touches a modern kitchen should have."

"Grey likes it too," Sirus added. "He was mentioning that very thing this morning over cereal and toast. I'm glad you both approve of my taste."

"Mmm… Come, sit with me." Nia slipped her hand in the crook of Sirus's arm and drew him to the table. She took one seat, and Sirus pulled out the other for himself. "I didn't want to forget anything, so I made a list of family stuff I need to share with you." Her mug of coffee now on the table, Nia pulled an organizer out of her purse and leafed through a handful of loose pages. "Oh, I hope I didn't forget to pull it from my briefcase. I can't believe I would have done that. I knew I didn't intend to take my briefcase out of the trunk until I reached the hotel in Asheville. Here it is!" She held the final sheet up in triumph. "I knew I had it."

"I had no doubts." Sirus eyed the list of names and wondered if his ever appeared on her list when she went to visit other family and friends. *Doubtful*, rang clear in his head. Even if it did, it would never say anything like, *Sirus is dating the most wonderful man, and I have great hopes it will turn into something permanent.*

A pointed, *familiar* ache stabbed at Sirus's chest; a pain that had sprouted the first time he'd told his mother he was gay and she'd acted as if he'd never said it; a hurt that every time she

196 | CAMERON DANE

behaved in the same callous way grew a little nagging needle into a thorn that pierced Sirus sharp enough to bleed.

"First --" Nia began.

"*First*," Sirus interrupted, as what happened on the porch reentered his mind, "why don't we start with the fact that you just completely ignored another human being. A man whom I happen to like very much, by the way. Let's talk about the fact that in the two times I mentioned his name since he left you've moved right past it and pretended you never heard it."

"Oh, yes, see," Nia touched her finger to the name at the top of her list. "I'm busting at the seams to share some wonderful news with you." Sirus's mother broke out into a huge smile, his comment about Grey apparently Teflon that slid right over her. "Christina," Nia mentioned one of Sirus's many cousins, "is going to have a baby. After all this time trying. Can you believe it? She just called me about it yesterday. Your Aunt Mina is beside herself that she will finally be a grandmother."

Sirus slumped, his eyes slid closed, and he sighed. This woman. *His mother.* A CIA trained interrogator would never break her single-minded determination. What in the hell was he supposed to do?

"That is good to hear," Sirus said, almost on autopilot. "I will call Christina and Aunt Mina later to say congratulations."

"They will both like that very much, dear." Nia took a sip of her coffee, but abruptly put it down and grabbed his forearm. "All right, this is important. You need to call your sister; keep her on the phone until she tells you about being selected to play with the symphony. She's being very low key about everything, and doesn't want anyone to make a fuss, or even make it a special occasion to visit, but she has a solo during her first concert on Mother's Day. She had to beat out a handful of very skilled cellists to get the invitation."

Rubbing his eyes with the heels of his hands, Sirus mentally added another name to his phone list. "I will give Diana a call as well." At least his sister always asked about his love life and was happy for him when he had someone special in it. *Diana would like Grey*. Sirus smiled to himself as he fantasized about them meeting one day. *Grey would like unpretentious Diana too.*

Sirus jerked at the romantic slant of his thoughts, and he sternly reminded himself that he had no future with Grey. His heart squeezed, but he forced himself to pull back into the conversation with his mother. "I'll be there for the concert. Diana deserves the invitation and the solo, and I will be front and center cheering for her."

"I knew you would. We all will." Nia scrunched up her face, and little furrow lines formed between her brows. "But let her tell you, before you mention anything, all right? It should be her good news to share, but I knew she never would without you knowing how to nudge her toward the conversation."

"Right. Of course." Sirus shook his head and tried not to laugh. He and his siblings *always* knew when their mother spilled important, sometimes private news to another member of the family. They'd all gotten used to getting "just because" calls out of the blue. "You never told me anything. Understood."

198 | CAMERON DANE

His mother flashed him a winning smile. "Thank you, sweetheart. Oh, this isn't on my list," she leaned in and squeezed his hand, "but I must tell you I just met the most strikingly beautiful young woman at a law firm where I was doing some interpreting work. It was for Kline and Sheuster. Do you remember years ago when I worked for them almost nonstop for two years while one of their clients transacted a deal for a European hotel chain? No, of course you don't, you were too young to remember. Anyway..."

His mother went on, but Sirus sat up straight, his proverbial "Meddling Mother" antennae twitching at full alert. *Not on her list, my ass.* She *just so happened* to meet a beautiful young woman recently? Now, finally, Sirus understood the true reason for his mother's little detour up to his cabin. A woman.

Goddamnit.

"...I tell you," his mother raved on, "this girl is as smart and kind as she is attractive, but at the same time she works side-by-side with the big boys and is nobody's pushover. We got to talking about our families, and when I mentioned I had a talented, handsome, artist son --"

"Truck driver, Mom." Sirus gritted his teeth. *Double goddamnit.* "I drive a truck. You have to stop telling people you have a son who is an artist. It gives the impression I earn my living in that trade, when you know I don't."

"You probably could if you became aggressive with it. You just have to want it badly enough to pursue it. Now, where was I? Oh yes, this amazing woman. Her name is Marisa, and I

GREY'S AWAKENING | 199

would just love for you to meet her when you come home for Diana's concert."

Stop. Stop. Stop. Sirus slammed the table with his open palm and then shot to his feet, kicking the chair out and careening it into the wall. "I cannot believe you, Mom." He planted both hands on the table and zeroed his focus in on her face. "If I met her ... what? What do you think would happen? That I would fall madly in love with her, and your gay son would turn straight, and then all would be right in your world?"

Nia did not rear back in the face of Sirus's explosion of emotion, or even blink. "First, don't speak to me in that tone," she said. "I am your mother, and you will show me respect. Second, Marisa is a beautiful, educated, sweet woman. Plus, she has an interest in the arts. You will be completely enchanted by her, I know it."

Curling his hands into fists, Sirus looked away, unable to tolerate his mother's relentless barrage to alter his sexuality. His gaze alighted on his canisters of cereal, all of them now lined up against the backsplash according to size, like little soldiers. They hadn't been that way yesterday. *Grey.* Suddenly, pictures of the man who had spent last night in Sirus's bed flooded him, filling him to the brim.

Sirus turned his attention back to his mother, but it was as if he could feel another person in the kitchen, reinforcing his voice. "Enough," he said, his voice firm. "You need to stop this. Right now."

"Stop what?"

"Don't you dare --" Sirus bit his lip and held himself back from shouting. He straightened his chair and sat back down, his heart heavier than he ever remembered it feeling. It hurt. His mother's behavior *hurt* him. Physically.

He spread his hands on the table and then looked up at her, trapping her gaze. "You know what I'm talking about," he said calmly. "Are you really going to keep doing this? Forever?"

"Doing what?" she asked. A newborn baby would have looked guiltier than his mother did.

Breathe, just breathe. "Okay, if this is how you want to play it, we can." Sirus continued to look at her pointedly. "Are you going to keep trying to fix me up with women, hoping one day one of them will turn me straight? Are you going to continue to refuse to respond to anything I say about a man, and in fact pretend like I never even told you I was gay? I can only assume you're hoping that if you don't acknowledge what I say, then you can also tell yourself my homosexuality doesn't really exist. I'm just your late bloomer straight son who has never had a girlfriend. Right? Is that what you tell your friends when they ask?"

"Watch your smart remarks, Sirus Allen Wilder." Nia slipped into the voice used on Sirus and his brothers and sister when they used to misbehave out in public as children. "No matter how old you get, I will always be your mother. Remember your tone."

Kicking back in his chair, Sirus threw his hands into the air and rolled his eyes. "Oh, that's just perfect, coming from you, after the performance you gave on the porch just a bit ago." White heat filled Sirus's body, completely washing away the cold. "Do you really expect to sit there with a straight face and lecture me about respect after the way you treated Grey today? Let's just ignore for a moment that you were terribly rude to him, not to mention incredibly disrespectful to me in the process. Let's instead focus on how you would have smacked me upside the head if I'd behaved the way you did with Grey. Only, because you refuse to acknowledge I'm even gay, and hope one day I'll move past this 'phase', you think it's okay to say or behave however you want, and that it doesn't matter." Sirus's throat tightened on the consequences of the words he spoke, but he could not keep them contained a second longer. "Guess what, Mom? It's not okay. You cannot keep doing this."

"Sweetheart," reason filled his mother's voice, "you are my son, and I want you to be happy."

Agh! Sirus wanted to pull out his hair. "That is not an answer."

"I just…" His mother glanced at her watch and then to her sheet of notes. "I don't have a lot of time before I have to leave, and I have a dozen more things I want to share with you before I go. You're really going to want to hear about Lorraine and Bobby. They --"

Sirus snatched the list of gossip out from under his mother's hand and flipped it over. "Understand me right now, Mom." As he looked his mother in the eyes, his heart cracked, but he blinked and managed to keep the catch out of his voice. "You can go on talking about whatever you want, and I will listen because I love my family and want to hear about the latest things in their lives. But one day, and it might come sooner than you think," *God, please just open your arms to me right now*, "I am going to meet someone who is as important to me as Dad is to you, and I will create a family with him. When that day happens, you are either going to have to accept that I'm gay, or we will drift apart and become estranged. I will not get family updates from you; I will get them from Dad. I won't come to Thanksgiving, Christmas, or Easter. And when I go into DC, I'll see everyone individually and stay at a hotel, rather than with you and Dad.

"I don't want to cut you out of my life, and it's killing me to just consider it, but you have had better than ten years to get used to having a gay son. Either do it, or don't. That's up to you. But we won't continue as we have been. Today really drove home for me that things have to change. Soon." Sirus looked at his mother, his heart racing a million miles a second with the magnitude of what he'd just done. *No taking it back now.* Didn't matter. It was long past due. He tried to smile, but with the tension coursing through him it didn't quite form. "I just needed you to know that."

Nia didn't say anything for the longest time. She blinked rapidly, and her hands trembled against the table. "Ahh, all right, where was I?" She flipped over her list, and in doing so punched a hole right in Sirus's gut. "Oh, yes, Lorraine and Bobby…"

His hand on his stomach, trying to control the bleeding, Sirus reeled, but listened to his mother share her news.

———

"You're fucking him, aren't you," John said. Grey could hear the smirk in his partner's voice through the phone. "I would bet our firm that you are."

"You can't do anything with our business without my signature, so you know you wouldn't be able to make that bet." Grey paced the length of his cabin, cell phone at his ear, unable to sit still or concentrate on work. He kept seeing Sirus in his mind, and he couldn't let go of a nagging feeling that he should be with the man right now. He glanced at his watch. Five o'clock. Still two fucking hours until Sirus was supposed to come over. *Damn it.* This day had gone on forever. "Anyway, I just called to say hi and see if everything is going all right. Say hi to Kelsie for me; I'll talk to you later."

A bark of laughter echoed in Grey's ear. "Oh, now you're being evasive," John said, still chuckling. "You're more than fucking Sirus. You like him. You're sleeping with a guy you actually like, who is your equal in just about every way, I might add. Will wonders never cease?"

Grey bit down the denial that would have made him a liar. "How in the hell are you figuring all that?" he asked instead. *Jesus.* Grey wiped his brow. *When the hell did it get so hot in here?* "All I said was 'his plumbing is fixed, and Sirus moved back to his cabin.'"

204 | CAMERON DANE

"I've known you forever, man," John answered, his voice sobering. "Do you think I can't read you, even over the phone? Let me answer by asking you this: How did you know I was in love with Kelsie?"

Rolling his eyes, Grey grinned at the memory of John's attempts to hide his need to see and spend time with his best friend's sister. "Easy. Everything gave you away."

"Right." John's voice gentled. "Asked and answered."

Grey's pacing ground to a halt. *Oh Christ. I don't love Sirus. I don't. I can't. I just ... want* him with every fiber of my being. Care about him too. Right now, a twist in Grey's gut that he'd been ignoring all day had him grabbing his jacket and heading out the door.

"Grey?" John's voice startled him back to reality. He'd already forgotten about everyone but Sirus. "Are you still there?"

"Sorry." Grey tore down the steps and tried to put his coat on at the same time. "Listen, I have to go. I'll talk to you later."

"Drive safe," John replied. "And tell Sirus I said hi. See you later."

Already in the car, Grey threw the phone on the passenger seat and gunned the engine to life.

———

KNOWING WHERE TO GO THIS time, Grey followed the silence to Sirus's workroom, his heart already hurting over not hearing the loud blare of eighties rock music. In one of their conversations since the afternoon Grey had found Sirus working to the sounds of Guns-N-Roses, Sirus had admitted that he listened to all kinds of eighties music while creating his sculptures and other artwork. The lack of a song playing rang volumes louder than *Welcome to the Jungle* had done that first day.

The shed doors were thrown wide open, and, as expected, Grey found Sirus working inside. Once again, he had his back turned, but this time he was still fully clothed. Sirus had a huge chunk of stone on the table before him, and he held a stone carving chisel in his hand, but he did not move. Instead, he stared to the side, clearly a thousand miles away.

Grey rapped his knuckles against the doorframe. "Sirus?"

Sirus jumped and spun, his eyes focusing as he found Grey. "Oh, hi." The chisel fell out of his hand, clinking to the table. "What time is it?" Sirus pushed his sleeve up, didn't have a watch on, and then glanced at the clock on the wall. "It's early. Wasn't I supposed to meet you at seven?"

His chest constricting at the disorder he saw before him, Grey slowly moved inside the studio toward Sirus. "I thought you might need a little company." He made a few more tentative steps closer to his goal. "I wasn't sure ... you know ... after your mother's visit."

Sirus jerked, as if slapped, and Grey was on him in a shot.

He wrapped Sirus up tight in his arms, and planted his chin on the man's shoulder. "I am so sorry." Grey didn't need more than that one small reaction from Sirus to know something rough had gone down after he'd left. He hugged Sirus to him even tighter, and pressed his lips high on Sirus's cheek. "I'm sorry it didn't go well."

Shaking, Sirus mumbled into Grey's hair, "I don't want to talk about it." His lips brushed across Grey's hair, over his temple, and down his cheek, ending with a desperate kiss to Grey's mouth. "I don't want to think about it." He tilted Grey's head back and made love to his lips. "I don't want to know about it; not right now." He bit, and his voice caught, tearing right through Grey. "I can't."

"Okay. Shh, it's okay." Grey stroked the tense muscles bunching Sirus's back. "I didn't come here for that anyway." He started dragging Sirus toward the door. "Not unless you want to talk."

"I don't." Sirus eyes were dry, but he could not hide the hurt and vulnerability living within. "Anything but that."

Grey had ached for something from this man, from practically the moment they'd set eyes on each other. In his dreams, and while awake -- all the time. His body still hungered for it today.

"Take me to bed, Sirus." Grey's voice scratched like hell, but he finally said it out loud. "I want you to fuck me."

CHAPTER FIFTEEN

Oh Christ, I did it. Grey buzzed inside, and he felt a little unsteady. *I really asked Sirus to fuck me.*

Sirus stumbled to a halt, and he grabbed Grey by the neck, forcing his face up. The little-boy-lost look disappeared from Sirus's eyes, and wide, clear shock took its place. "What did you say?"

"You heard me." Grey slid his fingers up Sirus's forearm and covered the hand Sirus had curled around his nape. He squeezed and moved closer until their bodies touched. "You called me on it a few days ago, but I didn't want to know it. You were right though. I want to feel someone inside me again." He trembled saying the words. "And I want it to be you."

"Ohhh God…" Sirus blew out an unsteady breath, and his

fingers clenched reflexively around Grey's neck. "I didn't think I'd ever hear you say that to me."

A frisson of panic raced through Grey, and words just started shooting out of his mouth. "Let me suck you off first." Reaching between them, Grey worked the button and zipper on Sirus's jeans, his nerves running the show. "Tasting you in my mouth makes me fantasize about having you in my ass." He rubbed his hand down Sirus's already thickening cock, and his mouth watered for more.

Moaning, Sirus tore off his jacket and ripped open his shirt, revealing a line of olive-toned, hard flesh that stopped at the white band of his underwear. "We could… Ahh, yeah, harder." Sirus covered Grey's hand and ground them both into his erection. "Just like that." He let go of Grey's neck and braced his hand on the doorframe. "Do you…" Sirus paused, hissing as Grey pulled Sirus's length out of the top of his underwear and teased the tip. Shaking his head, Sirus lifted his attention to Grey's face, and gritted his teeth. "Hold on for a minute." He stilled Grey's hand, his eyes softening. "Do you want to go to the cabin first?"

"No way." Grey couldn't tolerate slowing down or stopping now. He vibrated with need and couldn't risk grinding his arousal to a halt. "I wanted to get your cock in my mouth the very first time I saw you working here without your shirt." Grey peeled Sirus's coat and shirt off his shoulders, revealing more beautiful muscles than should be legal. "Of course, that time," he dipped down and tongued one of Sirus's nipples, flicking the tip, "in my mind, I started with licking your back and worked my way down to your ass." With that confession, Grey opened his mouth and bit Sirus's pectoral muscle, sinking his teeth in hard enough to sting.

"Oh yeah…" Sirus hissed, and he stumbled back into the wall, dragging Grey with him. He forced Grey's face harder into his chest. "Do that again." He speared his fingers into Grey's hair and dug into Grey's scalp as he bowed his back off the wall. "Leave your mark on me."

Emboldened, Grey grunted as his cock raged in his jeans. He bore down on Sirus's chest again, the act of biting arousing the hell out of him. Grey had never cared for biting as foreplay before, but with Sirus, he wanted to leave visible signs of aggression all over the man's amazing body.

Going for Sirus's nipple, Grey latched on and sucked, pulling the slightly raised flesh into his mouth and licking it all over. The sharp, salty taste of sweat covered his tongue, spurring Grey to bigger sweeps over Sirus's chest, across to his other nipple, where he attacked with incredible suction. Sirus held Grey's head tightly, and he made throaty little murmurs of encouragement, urging Grey to bite and suck and nuzzle, all while rhythmically stabbing his erection against Grey's stomach and leaving smears of precum on Grey's shirt.

As Grey kissed his way down the man's flat, solid abdomen, he looked up at Sirus through half-closed lids. "Hold some of that excitement in till I get there." He flicked his tongue into Sirus's belly button, teasing the little indentation enough to make Sirus's stomach quiver.

With eyes shot full of silver, Sirus breathed heavily and looked half-drunk. "Take it quick." He grabbed hold of his cock and held the rearing length out in offering. "I don't know how much longer I can hold off coming."

Lowering himself to his knees, Grey felt his entire mouth tingle at the sight of the huge, thickly veined penis jutting toward his face. The long slit held a pearly bead of seed, and Grey swore the entire beautiful shaft pulsed with a visible heartbeat. He swore it beat *Grey-son, Grey-son, Grey-son* in time with Grey's pounding heart. As Grey stared, mesmerized with wanting, the drop of precum grew and started to slide from the opening. Grey dipped his tongue out and caught it, teasing the saltiness of man over his taste buds as the tip of his tongue grazed Sirus's slit.

A tremor rocked through Sirus, and he pushed the head of his cock at the seam of Grey's lips. "Please," Sirus released his lock hold on Grey's hair and then folded his arms over his head against the wall, looking erotically angelic, "make me come in your mouth."

Undeniable longing and fire combusted inside Grey, his need for *this* man's cock -- well beyond the need for just *any* man's cock -- engulfed him in the flames, consuming him whole. He growled and opened up over Sirus's straining erection, stuffing almost the entire length into his mouth in one wide push, his throat already naturally relaxing to take the extra size. Hot, throbbing cock took over every bit of space in Grey's mouth; musky male smells invaded his nostrils and slipped into his bloodstream. Rough needful noises from Sirus had Grey bobbing up and down the man's burning thickness, voracious for every taste he could get.

Grey shoved his hands between Sirus's thighs and massaged his weighty balls, alternating between rolling and tugging on the lightly furred sac. Sirus groaned from above, his eyelids sliding closed as Grey tormented his sensitized member and testicles. Sirus squirmed as Grey sucked him down deep; Sirus moved his backside so frantically he surely scraped his bare ass raw with every swipe of his buttocks against the rough plaster of the wall.

Sirus's inability to remain still or silent fed Grey's desire to let everything loose with this man and scream "bring it on," in the face of the disastrous emotional consequences. Grey let go of Sirus's balls and grabbed hold of his hips with both hands, sinking his fingers into the steely flesh hard enough to create bruises. The thought of leaving even more evidence of his presence on Sirus drew a growl of ownership up through Grey, and the tangible, audible need vibrated over Sirus's cock buried deep in Grey's mouth.

"Oh yeah ... yeah." Sirus bucked his hips at Grey's face, the power behind his thrusts nearly strong enough to dislodge Grey's hold. "So ... ahhhh," he pounded his fists into the wall above his head, "fucking close."

Grey grew harder and harder with every open, visible response from Sirus. His cock and ass pulsed with the need to come, but he ignored the desire to touch himself, caring only about the man before him. He went down on Sirus's length again. As he did, he slid the flat of his tongue along the underside of Sirus's cock and forced the top half against the roof of his mouth. Precum leaked out of Sirus and dripped near Grey's throat, giving torturously wonderful hints of the flood trapped in Sirus's balls. Grey got Sirus to the back of his mouth and then went right on going, pushing the mushroom head down his throat ... and then a little bit more. When he could take no more, Grey swallowed. Once, twice...

Sirus roared on the third swallow, his entire body locking straight. A split second later, he pulled back and took hold of his cock, pumping his saliva-covered prick with his fist as he spurted a load of seed all over Grey's tongue. Grey held onto Sirus's hips and kept his mouth open to take this man's spunk, eagerly accepting every thick line of bitter ejaculate Sirus gave to him, and then lapped it up like a dog getting its first taste of water in a week. Eventually, the last drop fell. After Grey swallowed it down, he wiggled the tip of his tongue into Sirus's slit, making sure there was nothing left to drink. Sirus shivered, but he was sucked dry and not another drizzle of semen leaked out of his dwindling erection.

All right, Cole. Do it now, before you chicken out.

Grey looked at Sirus's dick, still well above average, even without a raging hard-on. Gulping silently, Grey shot to his feet and backed up as he looked at Sirus -- so fucking sexy -- and then darted his focus away. "So, where do you want me?"

Bumping into the center worktable, Grey recovered by hoisting himself up onto it. "Right here?" He pushed across the surface to the center, and reached for his belt.

Sirus stuffed himself back into his underwear and jeans and moved across the room in two fast strides. He wrapped his hand around Grey's ankle and dragged him back to the edge of the table. "I'm not fucking you on my studio table, baby." Sirus flashed one of his quick smiles, and Grey didn't know if his heart sped up for that or the endearment. Before Grey could decide, Sirus lifted him right off the table, holding them face to face. "At least, not the first time." He pressed a ridiculously sweet kiss to Grey's forehead, one that almost had him crying like an infant. "Now put your legs around me." Sirus wrapped one arm around Grey's back and slid the other down to hold his ass as he started to walk. "Hold on tight. I'm taking you to bed."

———

HIS HEART PUMPING FAST ENOUGH to make his entire body quake, Grey stared down to where Sirus kneeled at the foot of the bed. Already naked as the day God put him on this earth, Sirus slipped Grey's jeans and underwear off and let them fall to the floor, leaving Grey completely nude. Sirus slid his gaze up Grey's body, his eyes wide as if he had never seen Grey before. Grey shivered at the exposure, feeling almost as if this *was* the first time Sirus had looked upon his naked body.

Sirus raised a brow. "Cold?" Shifting, he crawled up Grey

214 | CAMERON DANE

and settled on top of him, wiggling into the space between Grey's spread legs. "Do you need a hot, live blanket to keep you warm?"

"Not anymore." Grey pulled Sirus down, kissing him again and again, fast and hard as he wrapped his legs around Sirus's waist. He grabbed the lube Sirus had thrown on the bed and tried to shove it into his lover's hand. "Now fuck me." His voice sounded a little stripped and high to his own ears. "Please."

Stilling Grey's hand, Sirus broke the kiss, pulled back, and looked into Grey's eyes. "Darlin'," intensity and softness somehow merged in the slate depths of Sirus's gaze and wound its way right into Grey's soul, "if you think I'm going to start and end this by shoving my cock into your ass then you don't know me very well yet."

"I want to work like hell to give you pleasure before I take you." Sirus's words from the other morning flashed in Grey's mind, and Grey felt like someone splashed icy water over his burning hot body.

"It's okay. You can fuck me right now." Grey rolled over under Sirus and thrust his ass against the man's cock. Sirus's length stirred against Grey's crease, and Grey's channel contracted tight enough to turn coal into diamonds. At the same time, a place deep inside screamed for Sirus to force him open and fill him to the brim. "I promise I want you inside me."

"Yeah." Sirus chuckled and nipped Grey's earlobe. "You really feel like you're all relaxed and ready for it." He slipped his tongue into Grey's ear and fucked it, but occasionally pulled back and swirled around the shell, stopping every so often to blow the wet skin dry. Grey trembled with the cool torment, and Sirus whispered against his ear, "You'll be shaking like that and begging for more by the time I fuck your ass. I won't push my dick into your hole a second before I know you're crying for it just as much as I am."

Grey sank a little bit deeper into the mattress as the tightness knotting his core loosened some. "I think you just got me a little closer."

"Good." Sirus eased down and nibbled on Grey's shoulder. "Let's see how much fun I can have with you before I get you all the way there."

Grey felt Sirus's lips turn up in a smile against his nape, and Grey had to bite his cheek to keep from grinning as well. Grey's rectum still clenched involuntarily with every graze of Sirus's dick against his buttocks, but his cock responded to every brush of Sirus's mouth or fingers over his back too, as if fighting to prove his body wanted this as much as it feared it. It was up to Grey's mind to override the fear and let his desire for Sirus win the battle.

Sirus stopped planting kisses about a third of the way down Grey's spine. "You're tightening up on me again, baby." He pressed the flat of his palms down Grey's sides and poked at his waist and hips, making Grey laugh and squirm against the tickly sensation. "There you go." Sirus pushed a hand under Grey's body and stroked his rapidly growing cock. "Stop

216 | CAMERON DANE

thinking so much and just let me help you enjoy yourself."
He trapped the head of Grey's prick against the mattress and
created a snug cocoon between the bed and his hand.

"Not an easy request of a man like me. Ohhh fuck, fuck…"
Sirus teased the tip of Grey's cock, and a trilling little noise
escaped Grey as a shiver of delight ran down his spine. Out
of his control, Grey circled his hips and started humping the
little cavern of Sirus's cupped hand, half slipping back into
adolescence when he'd first become curious about the many
things he could do with his cock to make himself come.

"Yeah, that's it. Don't stop." Sirus picked right back up
dipping his tongue down Grey's spine, leaving a wet trail of
shivery flesh in his wake. He kneaded Grey's hip with one
hand, and the other remained trapped beneath Grey's body, a
temporary place for Grey to pump his cock.

Perspiration began to break out in a thin film over Grey's
flesh, but even the heat pouring off his body as it mixed with
the chill in the air had no power to put a damper on his
quickly growing arousal. Sirus murmured incoherent words of
appreciation into Grey's skin. With every noise Sirus made he
took bigger sweeps with his tongue across some point of Grey's
back, licking up every salty droplet of sweat as it formed on
Grey's skin. Grey loved that Sirus seemed to want every bit of
offering his body had to give, no matter how insignificant. The
unabashed enthusiasm pushed Grey's excitement to higher and
higher levels, and soon he shoved up to his knees and thrust his
ass high in the air, dislodging Sirus from his back and his hand

from Grey's cock.

Suddenly, big strong hands smacked Grey's buttocks and then gripped his ass cheeks, splitting his crack open.

"Oh God." Reverence filled Sirus's voice. A spitting sound reached Grey's ears just as a dousing of liquid coated his asshole. "That is a thing of pure beauty."

Sirus whistled, and Grey squeezed his eyes shut, preparing himself for the pain. Instead, the softest whisper of nubby wetness flicked over his ring, jolting right through Grey in a rolling wave of pleasure.

Oh Christ. It was Sirus's tongue rimming his ass.

Grey whimpered, and his cock somehow throbbed more and got even harder. Painfully so.

"Mmm…" Sirus's moan vibrated against Grey's asshole, and the sensation rippled up Grey's passage, making his channel flutter rather than squeeze in abject terror. Sirus quickly laved the flat of his tongue from Grey's perineum all the way up to his cleft and back, tasting Grey everywhere.

The mental image, along with the beautiful torment of Sirus's mouth and tongue all over and around and almost *in* his ass, sent Grey into a tailspin and had him grabbing for his cock. Grey jerked himself off, feeling wildly out of control but powerless to rip his hand away from his dick or crawl away from this man to a place of safety. His penis burned from the rough handling he delivered to it but Grey felt almost like a puppet whose strings were at the mercy of someone other than himself.

At Sirus's mercy.

At the command of Sirus's tongue.

At the will of Sirus's bruising fingers that held Grey wide open so his talented lips and tongue could suck and eat deliciously at Grey's pucker, relaxing his entrance so goddamned much Grey swore Sirus could get a fist inside him without Grey so much as flinching.

Grey beat at his cock relentlessly, the hardness within screaming for release. "Now," Grey said. His lips were parted against the pillow as he struggled to breathe through too many exquisite pleasures attacking his strung-tight body at once. "Oh fuck, Sirus," Grey pushed his ass into the man's face, "give it to me now."

Sirus surged over Grey in a flash, and he dug his hand into Grey's hair, yanking his head back until their gazes clashed. Sirus pulled them both up to their knees, stinging the hell out of Grey's scalp. Sirus tucked his knees in between Grey's spread thighs. Then he smashed his mouth against Grey's and forced his way inside. As Sirus kissed the breath out of Grey, he uttered into Grey's mouth, "Now."

A sizzle of pressure tickled over Grey's hole, and then, a flash of hot burning. With one stabbing pierce to Grey's teased ring, Sirus slipped his finger inside his ass. Grey bit Sirus's lip as his entrance and channel closed in around Sirus's finger, flashing panic and discomfort in his rectum.

Sirus finished pushing his finger all the way inside, but didn't move. "Kiss me, Greyson." He brushed his mouth over

Grey's, and the coppery tinge of blood reached Grey's tongue. "Kiss me like you don't care about anything else but getting me to kiss you back."

With his torso half turned, Grey hooked his arm around Sirus's neck and held their faces blurrily close. "I always want more from you," he confessed. He then closed his eyes and crushed his mouth to Sirus's, afraid to know anything more than what was happening in exactly this moment.

Sirus met the force of Grey's kiss and gave him equal rawness, the battle of taking and giving coursing tangibly through both men.

"God," Sirus murmured, making Grey *feel* it, "how you get to me." He opened his mouth wide and became almost violent, and at the same time eased his finger out of Grey's ass, holding at the ring, and then pushed it all the way back inside.

A shock of deep-seated physical joy spiked up and down Grey's spine and raced to his toes, forcing his eyes open and his hand back down to his cock. Through the haze of their proximity, Grey watched Sirus's stare deepen to charcoal as he pulled his digit out and then penetrated Grey's ass again, to a burgeoning quiver of delight in Grey's passage. Grey's prick had remained hard through every second on this bed with Sirus. With the third slide of Sirus's finger into his ass, Grey dragged his hand up and down his length in time with the other man's pushing in and out of his channel, the small pain now mingling and becoming part of Grey's pleasure.

Just when a hint of arrogance hit Grey, made him think he

could do this forever, a flash of confidence cleared the haze in Sirus's eyes. The man whispered seductively, "Now I'm gonna make you come." He forced another finger into Grey's ass. Grey gasped, but before he could fully process the added thickness, Sirus crooked his fingers, rubbed right over Grey's sweet spot … and like a switch, he sent Grey straight into the heavens.

"Ahh … ahh…" Grey jerked at the fierce concentration of pleasure. The coil in his belly compressed tightly and then released, shooting orgasm throughout every inch of his body. Sirus's two fingers seemed to hold down a button inside Grey that demanded total submission of his very being, and Grey had no ability or desire to fight it. He whipped his hand over his cock, shouting hoarsely as he spewed cum all over Sirus's bed, giving Sirus the physical proof of his release. At the same time, a pinball-like sensation zinged back and forth and up and down over every inch of Grey's insides, leaving tag after tag of physical pleasure in its wake. A convulsion ripped through his body every time, leaving him awestruck, sated, then exhausted, one right after the other.

Eventually, Sirus eased his torment of Grey's ass and gently withdrew his fingers, leaving one more shiver at the empty sensation in Grey's chute. Grey's legs trembled, and he let himself fall face first to the bed. His breathing was still erratic, but he forced himself to roll over and find Sirus in the first shadows of early evening.

A half smile quirked Sirus's kiss-swollen mouth. "Haven't touched your prostate in so long you'd forgotten how insane it feels, hadn't you?" He crawled over Grey and straddled his stomach, his erection looming and unmistakable, big with wanting. "I'm guessing by what just happened," his focus slid briefly to the semen dampening the bedding, "you won't forget again for a very long time."

Grey's attention dropped to Sirus's rearing dick, and he swallowed. Then his ass pulsed with eagerness for more, and Grey breathed a silent sigh of relief. "Give me a minute to recover, and you can show me again right away." Reaching out, Grey started at the root and slid his finger up the length of Sirus's long cock.

Sirus covered Grey's finger, stopping him midstroke. Grey looked up, and as if Sirus had been waiting for him, he said, "You took one finger wonderfully, briefly dealt with two, and God," Sirus's eyes darkened and his voice thickened, "I loved seeing it and feeling you squeezing me inside. But you're not quite ready for my cock."

For a few seconds, Grey's heart stopped beating. "What?"

"First," Sirus braced one hand on Grey's chest and leaned over him, reaching for his nightstand, "we're going to play a little bit more. With this." His hand came out of his nightstand drawer with a black butt plug.

A big one.

CHAPTER SIXTEEN

A *butt plug?*

Grey quaked inside as he stared at the thing Sirus held in his hand. It wasn't so much the size, although Christ, the width of the lower half was enough to break Grey's upper lip out into a sweat. It was the very object itself. Playing with sex toys struck Grey as so extremely personal, and as something a person should do alone. The way a piece of plastic, silicone, metal ... whatever, looked stuffed inside a body, and the way a person moved and reacted to the sensations a toy created -- *because they were used to being by themselves while they used them* -- sent Grey's heart into racing at triple speed and turned his mouth dry.

Sirus crawled off Grey and reached into the drawer again. In the split second Grey's mind raced with his panicked thought, Sirus pulled out a bullet and slipped it into the base of the butt plug.

The addition of vibration. In his ass. With Sirus watching him take it.

Oh Christ.

Grey blew out a long, slow breath, silently counted to ten in English, Spanish, and Japanese, and reminded himself he could get through this -- for Sirus. "Okay." He hooked his arms under his knees and spread himself open, offering Sirus his reddened asshole. "Give it to me."

Sirus's eyes twinkled with the various shades of the moon. Then he looked over the position of Grey's legs, and his stare flashed with the start of a storm. "I will give it to you." Sirus pried Grey's arms out from under his knees and lowered his legs back to the bed. Climbing on top of Grey, plug still in hand, Sirus forced Grey's legs straight down, trapped them within his, and squeezed. "You'll get it when you're ready, and not a second before. Same with my cock." Sirus rubbed his length against the tightly closed V of Grey's thighs, leaving streaks of early ejaculate on Grey's skin. "Remember, not until you're screaming for it, baby." Dipping down, Sirus brushed a kiss over Grey's lips, teasing them with his tongue as he glanced up and found Grey's gaze again. "And you will." He winked. "Scream for it, I mean."

Employing a one-armed push-up stance, Sirus drew a line with the tip of the butt plug over Grey's forehead, cheeks, and nose, stopping it against his mouth. "I've never used this on or with another person before; only by myself." The rounded tip danced slowly back and forth over the seam of Grey's lips. "Suck it." Sirus's focus dropped to Grey's mouth. As it did, his pupils flared, and his erection swelled with burning heat against Grey's thigh. "Take it, and get it all nice and wet for me."

Sirus's obvious excitement stoked the cooling embers inside Grey, sparking the hidden fire still alive under his skin. He opened his mouth and accepted the first inch of the plug, wanting for himself whatever would arouse Sirus the most. The unnatural, but not unpleasant taste of silicone covered Grey's tongue as Sirus pushed more of the toy past his lips; a faint hint of the artificial material filled his nose too. Sirus kept feeding the toy to Grey, and Grey struggled only a little bit to fit the widest part into his mouth, realizing the plug wasn't quite as big as he'd thought when it was first pulled out of the drawer. Grey's lips eventually closed in around the smallest part near the base; the entire plug filled his mouth, making his jaw stretch a little, but not hurt.

"Holy shit." Sirus dropped to his elbows, and he ground himself against Grey's leg, digging his rigid length between Grey's closed thighs. Grunting, Sirus pulled the toy out of Grey's mouth, about half the way, and then licked in a circle around where the toy emerged from Grey's lips, joining in the base, raw act. He shoved the toy back in and whispered, "You look so fucking hot." The mercury in Sirus's eyes scorched like the hottest flames of a fire as he played with the plug, pushing it in and out of Grey's mouth. "You might make me come when I see this thing in your ass."

Jesus, Grey wanted nothing more than to make Sirus come. He accepted the toy fucking his mouth with greater enthusiasm, licking all over it, and tangling with Sirus's tongue when the man dipped down and joined in the anointing of the butt plug. Grey wanted Sirus to lose his shit all over the place; he wanted the man to spew his orgasm repeatedly, covering Grey with semen until no part of his skin was untouched. Grey squirmed under Sirus, and he scratched his blunt fingers down his lover's back, grabbing Sirus's ass and squishing their dicks together, begging without words that their bodies become one.

Abruptly, Sirus tore the plug from Grey's aching mouth and swollen lips, biting Grey as their gazes found one another. Sirus didn't say a word, but his wide pupils and erratic breathing did all the explaining Grey needed.

Oh yes. Grey had this man as close to the edge as he was.

Sirus buried his face in Grey's neck and nuzzled his way down Grey's chest. His cheeks, forehead, lips, nose, and even the top of his head touched all over Grey's heated flesh as he worked his way down to Grey's cock, the butt plug still in his hand.

Reaching his goal, Sirus finally pushed Grey's legs apart, and stuck his face into Grey's sac. A wonderful noise rumbled through him as he inhaled. "God, you smell like great sex on a warm spring day. I want you outside one day." Sirus glanced up as he dropped the plug, picked up the lube, and clicked open the cap. "Hard and deep. Right up against a tree."

Grey wanted to promise that Sirus could have him whenever and wherever he wanted, but right then Sirus rubbed cool lubricant over Grey's sensitized hole, stealing any thought that didn't center around his ass. With his entire body tingling, Grey stared, fascinated, through half-closed eyes, as Sirus fingered his rim, miraculously relaxing the small muscle, and then pushed his finger inside.

Shit. Grey burned with wanting all over, and his entrance blossomed like a goddamn flower, allowing Sirus's entire finger to slip deep, past the second knuckle. Whimpering, Grey spread his legs more and lifted his hips, forcing friction over his anal walls, although Christ, the gentle sensation wasn't nearly enough to suit the clutching need for more taking place in his ass.

He could not believe how much he wanted -- ached -- for Sirus's cock.

"Look how fucking hard you are," Sirus said, his gaze fully on Grey's straining cock. He kept up the small pumping of his finger in Grey's passage, but leaned over Grey's dick and licked the leaking tip, teasing Grey even more. "I knew you would be." He suckled the head of Grey's penis, swirling his tongue around it like it was a Tootsie Pop. At the same time, he finger-fucked Grey's ass with ever increasing speed, something that sent Grey's channel into a flurry of shivery responses, each tremble reaching farther and farther into the extremities of his body.

"More." Grey moaned, and lifted one leg high and wide, panting heavily as he searched for as much visual and tactile access as he could get. He shoved his other hand between his legs and grabbed for his balls, tugging on himself to add to the pain and pleasure. He looked to Sirus, knowing full well that every open, raw desire shone bright in his eyes. "Give me more."

In a flash, Sirus withdrew his finger and replaced it with the tip of the butt plug, easily sliding the tip into Grey's opening. Grey watched Sirus push the top part of the black object into his ass, each increment widening his hole with toe curling, incredible torment and filling his tunnel on the other side. With more than half of the plug buried in his rectum, stuffing him so fucking good, Grey gasped and clutched the bedclothes; Sirus attempted to push the rest of the toy into Grey's squeezing ass channel, but pain suddenly locked Grey's muscles tight.

Sirus looked up, his sooty eyes locking on Grey's. "God, you're taking it so damn beautifully." He parted two fingers and rubbed them over Grey's stretched ring, somehow easing the tension and flash of fear that had temporarily assaulted Grey. "Keep bearing down, baby." Sirus dipped down and licked a line up the length of Grey's still hard cock, making it jump and drip precum onto his belly. "Let me get it all in." Sirus opened up over Grey's dick and took more than half in his mouth, sucking him so damn hard Grey bucked and cried out. *Right then*, Sirus shoved the rest of the butt plug into his ass.

"Ahhh!" Grey's entire being went up in flames. "Good …

oh fuck…" Grey somehow pulled his leg up even higher and wider. "So good." Sirus stayed right with every twist of Grey's body, and Grey simultaneously fought and reached for the mind-blowing pleasure Sirus offered him with this intimate act.

Grey groaned long and low as Sirus dragged his mouth up and down Grey's cock, as well as pulled the toy out of Grey's ass, only to force it back inside in one fast thrust, spinning Grey's confused nerve-endings into a frenzy. Sirus withdrew the toy again, leaving Grey's ass open and greedy for something to fill it. The toy didn't take him again, so Grey looked at Sirus through lust-blurred eyes and found the man staring up at him, silver piercing the blur clear as day.

Sirus swirled his tongue around Grey's raging erection, made him sweat, but then let the length slip from his mouth. "Ask me." He nibbled on the head of Grey's sensitized cock. "Tell me you want the plug inside you again."

Grey didn't know how much more pleasure his body could withstand. "Please." His body hummed as if his nerves were a series of exposed live wires. "Please. Give it to me."

Sirus smiled against Grey's penis, and eased the plug back into Grey's hole with excruciating slowness, turning it so that it caressed his walls as it filled his ass again. Then Sirus pushed the base, the bullet started, and vibrations consumed Grey's passage in crushing waves.

"Mnn … ohh … ohh, God." Grey jerked, his upper body shifting to the side as he battled the extreme delight the plug claimed in his ass -- as well as the strong vibrations coursing through his channel and into his body. Sirus was relentless, though, and continued to plow Grey with the butt plug, sliding the vibrating toy in and out of his quivering asshole, to Grey's moans and writhing for more. As if Grey weren't already near enough to screaming and wanting to scratch his fingers down a wall to tear it up, Sirus went back down on Grey's cock and sucked him off as if he'd never have the chance to do it again.

Half on his side, with his elbow hooked under his leg and pulled to his chest, Grey arched his back and tried to jam his ass down on the plug with every deep thrust in from Sirus's capable hand. "Don't stop," Grey ordered recklessly, "please don't stop." Barely able to hold his head up so he could see, Grey somehow managed to grab Sirus's hair and hold the man's face to his crotch, frantic not to lose the most enthusiastic blowjob he'd ever been given in his life.

Pure pleasure surrounded Grey in a furnace of sweltering proportions, one from which he could not escape. Every twitch of muscle and every small pant of breath he took brought Grey into deeper contact with either the toy in his rectum or the mouth wrapped fully around his straining cock. Sweat poured off his body, dropping down from his hairline and stinging his eyes, but he just blinked it away, never taking his attention from the vision of raw sexuality before him as he watched Sirus deliver such pure physical joy to his body.

Sirus reached up, dislodged Grey's fingers from his scalp, and trapped his palm firmly on the bed. Grey curled his hand into a fist and grabbed hold of the blanket just as Sirus moved from Grey's cock to his balls and stuffed the weighty sac into his mouth, pulling it hard against his throat. Grey's mouth dropped open at the incredible suction, and he snapped his eyes closed, fighting the shooting lines of joy zinging from his cock, balls, and ass, into his belly and up his spine.

"Too much…" Grey gasped, struggling for his very breath. "Ohh fuck, it's too much."

Sirus ignored Grey's pleas; he wrapped his hand around Grey's dick, giving him one hard pull while he sucked Grey's nuts and twisted the plug in his ass … and Grey could not hold off the inevitable anymore.

"Ahhhh … ahhh!" Grey convulsed in sharp, jerking waves, shouting Sirus's name loud enough to damage his vocal cords, not to mention for every neighbor around the lake to hear him. Orgasm tore through Grey. Sirus ripped the butt plug out of Grey's ass only seconds after Grey spewed, leaving Grey's channel and hole clutching for something to hold. Sirus released Grey's sac from the prison of his mouth, and he moved up to Grey's stomach, lapping up Grey's cum with big sweeps, licking up every little bit of seed. While eating Grey's ejaculate, Sirus reached between Grey's cheeks and rubbed his fingers over Grey's pulsing entrance, settling the confused muscle back into place.

Closing him up.

Without fucking him.

Grey blinked, plummeting at the emptiness in his ass …

and heart. "What?" His leg fell to the bed with a thud, but he hardly felt the sting of returning circulation. Grey found Sirus's gaze, and he reared back as Sirus sleekly crawled up his chest. "Why --"

Sirus covered Grey's mouth, keeping him quiet until he lay between Grey's legs. "You needed to know you could love it." He took his hand away and brushed a light kiss over Grey's lips. "For this." Holding Grey's gaze, Sirus took a second to reach between them. He fitted the head of his cock to Grey's asshole, and then pushed just the tip inside. Grey gasped, and Sirus gritted his teeth. Sirus shook his head, let go of his cock, and linked his hand to Grey's on the bed. "Hold on." He twined their fingers together on either side of Grey's head, looked right into Grey's eyes, and sank his penis deep into Grey's ass.

"Ohhh." Grey bucked, and a rough, moaning emerged through the tightness in his throat, making him sound like an injured animal. "Jesus ... Jesus." He had never felt more full or taken by another person, or more connected to one either. Grey's jaw dropped, emotions choking him into speechlessness right where he lay, trapped by another man on him, *inside* him, reaching into what felt like Grey's most secret soul. Sirus's cock sat all the way inside Grey's body, not moving, but Grey swore he could feel the steady beat of Sirus's heart pulsing through the man's dick; Sirus's life force pinned Grey prisoner right to the bed.

Most terrifying of all, Grey didn't want to escape the hold. He grabbed Sirus's hands and held on, knowing that no fingers

232 | Cameron Dane

or butt plug could have prepared him for intimacy like this.

Sirus shifted on top of Grey and somehow lodged his cock a little bit deeper inside Grey's ass. Grey jolted, and Sirus did too. Desire clouded Sirus's eyes, and he lowered his forehead to Grey's. "Tell me you're okay," he whispered roughly.

Grey's channel clutched Sirus's shaft in a quick series of spasms, and Sirus hissed through clenched teeth.

"Fuck, I'm sorry." Sirus withdrew, and then penetrated Grey again, pushing all the way into his rippling passage. "You're so goddamned hot and tight, I have to move." Sirus seared his lips to Grey's, locking on in a clinging kiss, and started to move his hips, fucking Grey … in exactly the way Grey had fantasized in his most fevered dreams.

Letting go of every screaming voice in his head, Grey slashed his mouth over Sirus's and kissed him back with everything in him, moaning as their tongues tangled in a fast dance. He'd never experienced a more pure, *real* moment in his life than this one right here, where adrenaline flooded him so completely that all barriers inside him washed away, leaving him open and raw.

"It's okay." Grey tore his hands out from under Sirus's and tunneled them through the man's hair, holding his face so close their foreheads, noses, and lips all touched. "Fuck me, Sirus." Grey pumped his hips up to meet the slide of Sirus's thick, long cock, moaning with every claiming of his ass. "Don't let me look away."

Sirus clutched Grey's face in a bruising hold, his fingers

digging into Grey's cheekbones and jaw. "Won't." He looked over Grey's face, and uttered gutturally, "You're so beautiful." The color of his eyes turned pale, and he focused with such intensity Grey shuddered.

"You..." A suffocating band squeezed Grey's chest, overwhelming him with untapped emotion. Unsure what to do, he darted his tongue against the tip of Sirus's again and again, their mouths open against one another as they struggled to breathe.

Grey held on tight, his thighs squeezing Sirus's hips as his lower body strained and twisted frantically in a fevered fucking. Sirus picked up the pace, spearing his prick in lightning-fast strokes in and out of Grey's abused, tender channel. This time Grey welcomed the sweet pain of another man taking him, and even shifted his legs and locked them around Sirus's waist, caring only about clinging to Sirus and thrusting his hips up for more of his incredible cock.

Sirus altered his angle and sawed right over Grey's prostate, drawing a sharp cry from Grey and sending his rectum into a screeching series of contractions. For a split second, Sirus clenched his teeth and went stiff as a board. "Oh shit." Grunting, Sirus jerked and shoved his cock even deeper inside, nailing Grey right to the bed. "You have an incredible ass." He stole a series of hard, aggressive kisses, and took over Grey's swollen, sensitive mouth. Speaking into him, Sirus's voice was muffled and breathy. "Tell me I can have you again." He thrust his tongue into Grey's mouth and licked. "I want you again."

Grey held Sirus's face in the gentlest of holds, his heart exploding on the desperation in Sirus's kiss. "Yes." He kissed Sirus back, sharing one breath. "Yes." He didn't know how it happened, but his dick filled with blood and raged a hard-on between their stomachs, aching once again. Breaking the kiss, their gazes found one another in the blur of closeness, locking in place. "Whenever you want." Grey brushed his fingers over the hard lines of Sirus's face. "Yes."

Sirus's entire face changed; his eyes darkened, his skin pulled taut, stripping everything away to a place of open need. "Grey." Sirus bit his lip and pumped his hips, creating dark, wonderful friction again. "Grey," he repeated, and lifted to his hands, separating their torsos. Sirus briefly looked down to the merging of their bodies. Grey did too, and they both trembled.

As if he couldn't break an invisible line between them, Sirus brought his focus back to Grey's eyes, and said his name again. The chant almost became a whimper, with Sirus's face a twist of longing. "Grey." He penetrated Grey's ass one more time and then froze, sweating, his mouth open.

Each invoking of Grey's name tightened the coil inside Grey, stretching his nerves to the edge. He rubbed his thumb over the man's half-open mouth. "Sirus."

Sirus needed nothing more than that. One whisper of his name, and he drove his cock balls-deep into Grey's flaming ass, shouting Grey's name once more, his voice stripped bare. His entire body jerked, and his muscles popped in stark beauty. His shaft swelled inside Grey, pushing with unbearable pleasure against Grey's anal walls, making Grey cry out as Sirus came; he unloaded burning hot cum into the farthest reaches of Grey's ass.

Scorching liquid branded Grey inside. Jet after jet of seed coated him with every burst of Sirus's hips, painting a mental picture of being marked in a way Grey could never wash away or remove.

In a way I don't ever want to remove.

The truth punched Grey in the gut, and then reached in and ripped right through his balls, cock … and heart. He choked on words he didn't know how to say, so he surged up to Sirus instead, capturing his mouth in a violent, taking kiss, right as his body overtook his will and he came. Grey plastered his mouth to Sirus's with an unforgiving roughness, and he dug his fingers deep into the hard muscles covering the man's shoulders, holding on with everything in him as his cock pulsed and pumped seed between them, shooting a stream of ejaculate on his and Sirus's stomachs that felt like nothing he'd ever spilled before.

It felt like love.

No. No. No.

CHAPTER SEVENTEEN

Oh Christ. Jesus Christ. Fucking Jesus Christ. I'm in love with Sirus. Grey blinked, fighting rising panic as Sirus's body went completely lax and fell on top of Grey in the aftermath of sex. *How did I let this happen?* Squeezing his eyes shut, Grey took a breath and talked himself down, convincing himself he was mixing up passion, respect, and liking with the vulnerability of allowing Sirus to fuck him. His head was confusing his feelings and naming it love, when in truth Grey didn't even know what in the hell this kind of love felt like. *Absolutely no idea.* He opened his eyes and stared up at the ceiling, breathing easier now. There was no way he could be so certain he was in love with Sirus. He wasn't sure he was even capable of the emotion; he'd always known that.

Except you want to hold Sirus forever and never leave his bed. The damning voice inside reared its judgmental tone again, mocking Grey for the liar he had become.

Sirus scraped his palms down the sides of Grey's body and buried his face in the crook of Grey's neck. "Your heart is racing so fast," he said, his voice muffled. Abruptly, Sirus pulled up and looked at Grey, a wrinkle marring his brow. "Are you all right?"

"Yes… Sorry…" Grey put his hands on Sirus's chest, covering half of the rearing mustang tattoo. His fingers itched to move and touch more. Already. So quickly. Again. Grey wanted to create another memory with Sirus, and then another, piling one on top of the next. He wanted to have so damn many moments together that Sirus would only think about Grey when they were apart, even when he looked in a mirror and saw the permanent mark of another man inking his chest.

Go ahead, Greyson, the cynical voice mocked again, making Grey gnash his teeth, *try and tell yourself that's not love.*

"Grey?" Sirus gave Grey a firm shake, jerking him away from his nemesis voice. "You sure you're all right?"

"I'm okay. It's just…" Grey opened his mouth to shade the exact color of his crazy thoughts, but that damned *truth* thing they shared washed out the lie he wanted to spill. "I was thinking about everything that happened just now." *Technically*, that was true. He lifted his head and brushed a soft, lingering kiss on Sirus's hard lips, coaxing them to open for a slide of their tongues. Lowering back to the pillow, Grey curled his hand around Sirus's nape, rubbing the warm skin as he added, "You were amazing."

Sirus nuzzled into the touch, but he also studied Grey with a piercing scrutiny for an uncomfortably long moment. Just when Grey didn't think he could tolerate it anymore, terrified he was revealing something unspoken, Sirus said, "Come take a shower with me." He reached down and gently pulled his cock from Grey's ass, slicing a shiver through them both as he severed the connection. Sirus rubbed Grey's entrance until it closed, and then jumped to his knees. "Come on." He tugged Grey's hand and pulled him out of bed. "I'll wash you down and then tuck you under the covers to get some rest."

Grey balked, holding back as his attention drifted to the window, and then the alarm clock on the nightstand. "But it's barely dark outside. It's not even seven o'clock."

Chuckling, Sirus leaned in and pressed a fast kiss to Grey's cheek. "You are too damned cute for words." He took both of Grey's hands and with one tug got him moving. "Don't worry, I'll keep your secret. No one will ever know you closed your eyes and took a nap before it was actually bedtime."

"But…"

Sirus stopped at the bathroom door. The mirth in his eyes muted, and the quick change in his demeanor brought Grey to a standstill. In response, Grey moved in and cupped Sirus's cheek; his chest squeezed with the need to comfort even though he didn't know what was wrong.

His breath hitching audibly, Sirus turned his head and

kissed Grey's wrist. "Let's just stop and enjoy this moment, right now." His eyes were lakes of liquid silver, and Grey wanted to fall right in. "Let's not worry about anything else beyond tonight." Rawness, the need for a yes, scratched at Sirus's voice. "Okay?"

Just for tonight, Greyson, let go. Don't worry or overthink the moment; just let this be about spending time with Sirus.

Grey's heart pounded like a son of a bitch, the potential risk of permanent injury shaking his insides. He nodded anyway, unable to turn this man away. "Okay." Grey took Sirus's hand and led him into the bathroom.

———

SIRUS REMOVED HIS BOOTS AND the last of his clothes, and then he slipped back into the warmth of bed, snuggling in behind a dozing Grey.

"Holy shit!" Grey yelped and bounced about a foot off the mattress, spinning to face Sirus as he did. "Your skin is freezing."

"Damn it." Sirus reached out to touch Grey, but quickly pulled back his hand before he made contact again. "Sorry about that. I didn't even think that I would still be cold when I crawled in beside you."

Grey slapped his cheeks in that cute way of his, studying Sirus as he blinked himself fully awake. "Yeah, well, I'm not going to make it a federal case or anything." Pushing himself up against the headboard, Grey grabbed Sirus's hands between his, put his mouth to them, and blew wonderful warm breath over Sirus's tingling fingers. "Where did you go? I didn't even feel you get up."

Sirus shivered as his extremities slowly heated under Grey's care. Rolling his shoulders and head, he found Grey's gaze. "I woke up around nine thirty and remembered I hadn't shut or locked the door to the shed when we came inside. I'm not so much worried about people, but I didn't want an animal to get in there and tear up the place."

Grey winced, looking truly pained. "Is everything okay? I shouldn't have attacked you like I did in there." He let go of Sirus's hands and dug his fingers into his own hair, and in doing so made an even bigger, sexier mess of the brown stuff. "I'll replace anything that was damaged -- by animal or by weather. At least the stuff that I can. Obviously, your work is irreplaceable. Shit."

"Hey." Sirus crawled over Grey, straddled his lap, and pulled the man's hands down to his sides before he could give himself a bald spot. "I like that you attacked me in there." He rubbed the backs of Grey's hands with the pads of his thumbs, creating little swirling designs over his warm skin. "It was a damn good frontal attack." He quirked a brow. "I'll take one of those kinds of interruptions any day of the week."

A trace of a smile curled the edges of Grey's lips, and twin lines of pink stole over the slash of his cheeks. "What came after wasn't bad either."

"It wasn't, huh?" Sirus sat on Grey's thighs and just savored being with him. "You weren't expecting the butt plug, were you?"

The pink suffusing Grey's cheeks burned full red and crept down to his neck. "Can't say that I was, no."

Sirus's heart twisted at Grey's obvious discomfort. "You've never used a plug, or dildo, or any kind of toy with a partner before?" He didn't really need Grey to answer that. "And clearly no one has used one on you."

Grey scratched his chest, and he broke eye contact, putting his focus on the wall. As Sirus watched an internal struggle play itself out on Grey's sharply angled face, a frisson of uncertainty chilled Sirus.

Sirus's throat grew tight, and he cleared it before he spoke. "I apologize if I crossed a line and did something that made you uncomfortable."

Grey's focus jumped back to Sirus, pinpointing on him. "No, please don't think that. I loved what you did to me." He touched Sirus's cheek, and the hardness slid away from his face. "It's just," Grey bit off a low curse, "I always viewed stuff like that as a very personal thing, and I didn't want to look like an idiot in front of you. I'm pretty damn sure I did."

"Oh, baby." Sirus leaned in, kissed Grey, and melted into a goddamned puddle of longing all over the man. "With every single little response you gave me, you got me harder and hotter than I've ever been. You could never look foolish in my eyes. If you want," Sirus sat back, and he brushed his fingers through Grey's hair, taming it just a little bit, "next time you can use whatever thing or toy you want on me, and watch me lose it too. That way we're even. Okay?"

Grey opened his mouth, but his stomach grumbled loudly first, beating out whatever he'd intended to say.

Sirus tapped his finger against Grey's abdomen, chuckling. "That rumble is familiar. Okay, so I can take a hint. You want me to feed you first." He reluctantly crawled off Grey's lap, and once again pulled Grey to his feet, tugging until they stood flush against one another. "Will sandwiches work?" Sirus reached between them and ran his hand down the length of Grey's long cock, getting an immediate stir out of him. "Or do you need something heartier in order to regain your stamina for round two?"

His hazel eyes heating to green flecked with amber, Grey snaked his hand around Sirus's neck and pulled him down, stealing an openmouthed, hot kiss. He thrust his tongue past Sirus's lips, sweeping deeply as he grabbed onto Sirus's hips and sank his fingers into Sirus's flesh with exquisite strength, weakening Sirus at the knees. Grey kissed Sirus thoroughly enough to turn him into a puddle, and then pulled away. "That ought to hold me." He flashed a wolfish smile. "For now." Grey smacked Sirus's flank and headed out of the bedroom, his bare ass the most enticing invitation Sirus had ever been offered in his life.

Already out of sight, down the hall, Grey's voice drifted back to Sirus. "You coming?"

"Very likely I will," Sirus muttered to himself. There was

no talking his cock down around Greyson Cole. "More than once."

Shaking his head, Sirus chased after Grey, totally besotted.

———

"YOU MUST HAVE YOUR FATHER'S eyes," Grey said, breaking Sirus out of their silence.

They both leaned against Sirus's kitchen counter, munching on turkey sandwiches, chips, and sharing a beer. Naked. Eating. And completely comfortable, with occasional spurts of conversation, or companionable silence.

"Your mom has dark eyes," Grey added, when Sirus looked at him funny, "so that leaves your father. His must be the same intriguing slate color as yours are."

Sharp pain pierced Sirus's chest, taking him back to his conversation with his mother today. The hurt made him feel twice as heavy and incredibly alone. His food turned to the taste of cardboard in his mouth, killing his appetite. Sirus put the half eaten sandwich down and took a fast swig of beer, clearing the blockage in his throat.

"I'm sorry." Grey banged his fist into the counter, and muttered a foul word. "That was so stupid of me." Regret filled his eyes. "After this morning… I shouldn't have mentioned your parents."

"No, it's all right." Sirus turned and leaned his hip against the counter, facing Grey. "It's kind of nice that you noticed. Yes, I have my dad's eyes and build, and my mother's coloring."

Grey's gaze traveled up the length of Sirus's naked body, ending at his face. "It's a nice combination."

Sirus's skin heated from top to bottom, and he couldn't take his stare off Grey. "Thanks."

"It's just the truth." Grey wiped his mouth with a paper towel, put it down, then picked it up again and twisted it with his fingers. "Can I... I don't know... Just tell me if I'm imposing, and I'll shut up. You won't hurt my feelings. It's just..." Grey pursed his lips, but then blurted, "You were obviously upset earlier. Is it okay for me to ask what happened with your mom?"

Caution butted up against hope inside Sirus; Grey had set the rules for their brief affair, but now he seemed to be changing them. "You really want to know?"

Grey chewed the corner of his lip, and nodded. "If you want to tell me, I do."

Oh God, he really seems to want to listen. Sirus trembled, the knowledge heady. Scary too.

"All right." Sirus's hand shook as he picked up the beer and took another sip. If Grey noticed, he very sweetly didn't acknowledge the reaction. "After you left..." Sirus proceeded to give Grey a blow by blow account of his conversation with his mother -- only leaving out the part where he'd mentioned that he might have someone serious in his life very soon. While Sirus *had* been picturing Grey when he'd spoken those words, he knew they were only his most secret hopes, not a comment upon anything real Grey had given him about their future.

About what would happen to them when Grey's vacation came to an end and he went home.

By the time Sirus finished sharing what had taken place with his mother, he and Grey had finished their beer and moved back to bed. Grey leaned against the foot of the bed, and Sirus sat against the headboard.

"So that's it." Sirus picked at the rumpled bedding, unable to keep completely still. After sharing, his throat felt rubbed raw all over again, almost as bad as when having the original conversation with his mother. "It's up to her now. I can't do anything more."

"I'm sorry it went down that way," Grey said. Softness in his voice and openness in his eyes backed up his words. "It's interesting, though, and unusual, that your dad openly accepts you while your mom cannot. Most times you hear it's the other way, if either parent is willing to accept at all."

"I don't know what it is with my mom." A swelling need to share bubbled up in Sirus, one he could not ignore. Fuck, it felt so good to talk to someone who might understand him. "I think her inability to acknowledge me as a gay man is all tangled up in my grandfather and the disappointment he still shows over the fact that my mom fell in love and married my dad."

Grey drew his legs up and rested his elbows on his knees, his focus purely on Sirus. "What in the hell is so wrong with your dad?"

Sirus smiled, his heart lightening just picturing his father.

"My father is this giant of a man from the Deep South, and is a strange combination of a redneck liberal who also happens to love the opera and country music. He grew up dirt poor -- what people call white trash." A swirl of darkness moved over Sirus's gaze. "He fucking hated that phrase, and so do I. Anyway, my father got himself through college, and he's a professor with a mechanical engineering degree now. He teaches at a college in DC. He loves to talk politics, and loves a good argument about ideas even more. Oh," Sirus made a face, "and, obviously, he's not Greek."

"Ah." Grey nodded knowingly. "Is the non-Greek thing the biggest strike against your dad with your grandfather?"

Scrunching his face, Sirus shrugged. "It's just one of many. My grandfather is one of the most conservative people I know, so I'd say he pretty much disliked everything about my father on sight. But my mother does passionately love my father; all of us kids could always see that as clear as day. She married my dad -- his name is Whit -- and moved away from New York in the face of what she knew was my grandfather's great disappointment." Sirus paused, the pull to understand his mom still locked firmly in his heart. "I think it hurt my mother deeply that my grandfather couldn't be happy for her. My dad says she was really afraid of losing her father when she ignored his wishes and chose to get married."

Sirus stopped again, memories of visits to his mother's family still vivid in his mind. His voice dropped as he spoke, the thick tension in some of those moments as alive today as when he had been there in person. "My grandfather is one of those people that to this day, forty years later, still makes those under the breath comments that let everyone in the room know how he really feels, without out and out saying something hostile to your face. My mother knows my grandfather hasn't fully forgiven her for defying him, and I think in a lot of ways she's still trying to get back that love he openly gives to his other daughters."

"I would think that would make her even more sympathetic to openly accepting you, not less." Tucking his legs against his chest, Grey laid his chin to rest on his folded arms. "Don't you?"

"You would think, but I can't get her to talk to me about why she won't acknowledge that I'm gay, which is so frustrating, because I can only guess at where's she's coming from." So many excuses and reasons for his mother's behavior had come and gone from Sirus's mind over the years. One came back to him time and again, but he had never talked about it with his father or any of his siblings out of fear of creating a tear between his mother and another member of the family. "I think in my mother's mind, if she acknowledges and accepts that I'm gay, then she'll feel like she *has* to tell my grandfather that his grandson is gay. Right now, my grandfather doesn't know about me, and for a lot of reasons it's just a good idea that we never tell him. There are others who don't know either, and I'm okay with that. I don't see my grandfather that often, and we're not very close. He always kind of scared me when I was little, and that never fully went away."

Sirus looked to Grey and found a man quietly focused, listening intently to every word Sirus shared. The intensity caused a flip-flopping in Sirus's stomach and tied up his tongue. Grey was so attractive, smart, successful, and decisive in his choices that Sirus had to wonder if his own worries and fears seemed small and silly to this man. He began to sweat a little as he considered whether in his wildest dreams, even if he somehow got Grey, that he'd be an exciting enough person to hold his attention for long.

Don't get ahead of yourself, Wilder. Not this time. You got to fuck him once, and he has asked about your family. Neither thing amounts to a marriage proposal. Not even close.

"Do you want to stop?" Grey asked, making Sirus realize he must have been silent for longer than he had thought. "Did you decide you don't want to talk, after all?"

"No. Sorry." Sirus scrubbed his face and wiped away the worry. "It wasn't that." He rolled the conversation back in his mind and found the place where he'd left off. "I think acknowledging my homosexuality is twisted up in my mom's head with knowing that if she does, and is proud of me in every way, and brags about me or a partner, then she'll have to tell her father that I'm gay. That will sever any tie they still share for good." It killed Sirus just to think about cutting off communication with his mother, so his heart bled for her position, even though it affected him too. "In my grandfather's eyes, not only will my mother have gone against his wishes and married beneath her, but then she went and had a son who turned out to be a fag... Nope, that would do it for my grandfather. Not only would I not be welcome in his home, but I'm pretty sure he'd fully disown my mother too." Sirus grimaced. The idea of tearing apart two families, even as he knew he couldn't change who he was in order to keep them together, weighed heavy on his soul. "I think my mother is hiding in this in-between place, pretending what I am doesn't really exist. If she did, she would have to deal with it on a lot of fronts, not just with me. She's clearly not ready to do that. I suppose I can even understand it, on some level." Suddenly, Sirus shook his head, cleared the heaviness of family history, and put his attention back on Grey. "Of course, that's all just a theory. If she'll never even talk to me about it, that's all it will ever be. I'll never know for sure."

Grey nodded, his cheek rubbing against his forearm as he did it. He stared at Sirus, quiet for a long moment, his eyes looking as if they tracked back through the conversation like words on a page. Eventually, the internal mapping seemed to stop, and Grey settled his focus on Sirus again, his gaze full of sympathy. "I would guess the fact that your mother so obviously loves you must make it tougher on you. I think it might be easier to deal with just being tossed out on your ass; at least you know where you stand with someone like that." Grey's face hardened, but in a flash the hint of emotion disappeared. "Your mother is clearly not homophobic -- at least not in the sense that she's afraid to touch you or be near you, a *gay* man.

Her hug and happiness to see you looked very real to me, and I'm not half bad at reading people. There was never even the slightest cringe toward *you*. She just wouldn't *see* me."

"Yeah, but I'm old enough now and clear enough about what I want in my life that accepting me also means accepting a man as my partner. I need that now." Visions of some of Sirus's siblings and their spouses filled his head. The love and acceptance he constantly witnessed in their marriages twisted a ball of envy and wanting in his gut. "I don't have the patience or energy anymore for bullshit and games. Least of all from a member of my own family."

"Families are complicated and messy." Grey closed his eyes, blocking Sirus's one constant avenue to reading this man. In front of Sirus, a shudder jerked through Grey, leaving *Sirus* cold. When Grey opened his eyes again, the bleakness living there ripped right through Sirus's heart. "I broke mine up when I was nine years old," Grey said, his voice agonizingly soft. "Tore Kelsie right out of the arms of my mom and dad, and we never saw them again."

Oh God. He's giving me something personal. Sirus held his breath, and he tried not to make the slightest movement, noise, or anything that would alert Grey to the fact that he was once again sharing something intimate, and as a result possibly shut him down.

"My parents were not exactly what you would call capable or functioning members of society," Grey said. "Even less so as caretakers of two children." He looked at a place beyond Sirus, but Sirus could see his eyes clear as day. The unforgiving glint in the hazel depths did war with a film of moisture battling not to fall. "Not everything can be turned into a fun wilderness adventure, you know? Kids need a specific amount of calories in their everyday diet and certain nutrients for their bodies to grow properly. They need hot running water to keep clean, and heat when the weather turns cold. If you willfully don't even try to give your kids those things, then they should be taken away from you." Grey's voice grew rougher with each statement, and, with each sentence, he successfully blinked the threat of tears away. Finally, he looked at Sirus, back in control, and said, "Even if one of their own kids is the one that makes it happen."

"You mentioned a grandmother," Sirus said, treading gently. "Kelsie has in passing too. She's the one who came and took you from your parents?"

"Yeah." Grey lifted his head; his hands trembled just the slightest bit as he ran them through his hair. "But I found her number, and I'm the one who called her. She was my mother's mother, but they were estranged. I deliberately made that call and alerted her to the squalor Kelsie and I were living in. I told her she needed to come see it for herself and then make a decision about whether she wanted to do something about it before I took Kelsie and ran away."

"God, Grey." Sirus couldn't keep the shock out of his voice. "That must have been so hard. You were just a kid. They were your parents."

Grey frowned and went stiff. "I had to do it. They didn't

give me any choice." Sharp defensiveness rang in his tone. "I was already very linear, even back then. I surmised that if these two people didn't care enough to pull their heads out of their 'la-de-da, isn't the natural way of living beautiful' asses and give proper care to their two children, then they weren't really my parents anyway. By the time my grandmother came, assessed the situation, and took us under her care, I didn't think of that man and woman as Dad and Mom. They didn't fight for us, at least not more than a token few words with my grandmother. I knew they wouldn't. They were just people to me by then, and we happened to share some DNA." His mouth thinned, his lips turning pale. "Kelsie didn't, though." Shadows darkened Grey's hazel eyes to almost pure green. "Christ, she was so mad when my grandmother took us away."

"She knew you did it?" Unable to help himself, Sirus crawled across the bed and faced Grey, wrapping his arm around the man's bent legs. "She turned that anger on you?"

Grey nodded, the movement jerky. "I didn't lie to her about it, but I also didn't tell her about it beforehand, just in case my grandmother didn't come. The situation was bad at our house. I needed to get her out of there, but for Kelsie it ended up being a blindside. She hadn't disconnected from our parents the way I had, and I underestimated how terrifying leaving would be for her."

"For you too, I would imagine."

"No." Grey shook his head, absolute vehemence in the sharp shake. "The only thing that scared me was every day that went by where Kelsie refused to talk to me. I was so scared I'd made a choice that would end with me losing the only thing I ever wanted to make sure I had: my sister. I never cried when I made that call to my grandmother, and I never shed a tear when I walked away from my parents, but dealing with Kelsie's anger … that's where I was weak. That first night away, and every night afterward for two weeks where Kelsie didn't talk to me, I cried myself to sleep, so terrified I'd done the wrong thing." Grey turned away, giving Sirus the back of his head and the stark, naked lines of his back. "Goddamnit, though," a hand went up and swiped at his hidden face, "I knew it was the only thing I could do."

"Hey, hey." His heart breaking, Sirus turned Grey back around and forced damp eyes to meet his. "She came around. From what I hear in your voice when you talk about her, I think she's right up there with John as your best friend. I know she feels the same about you. You both look so different, and you present opposing personalities to the world, but deep down I think you're very similar in who you are at your cores."

Grey nodded within the tight hold of Sirus's fingers. "John says the same thing."

"John's a really smart man."

A choppy burst of laughter escaped Grey, and some of the spark of amber light returned to his hazel eyes. "Ergo, you are too, huh?" He peeled Sirus's hands off his head and pressed a kiss to the palm of each one. "I guess you are, at that." He looked away and put his attention on the wall, holding it there.

"You're certainly a very talented artist; there's no doubting that."

Sirus gritted his teeth against correcting Grey's comment. This moment wasn't about him and his hobby.

"You did that piece on the wall." Grey jerked his head toward the three dimensional mountain scene. "Didn't you?"

Okay, so he wants to change the subject. All right. I can live with that. He's given me more than I ever thought he would, and it has clearly taken an emotional toll.

"I did," Sirus answered, almost reluctantly. "I like to experiment, and that was my second attempt to create a textured piece that had a flat back and could be mounted on a wall, as you can do with a painting. The first attempt was truly awful, but while this one has a ton of mistakes, I ended up liking how the shades of the wood grain seemed to hit in just the right places and give the image lots of depth. If you look at it closely, you can see it's not good enough to grace anyone else's walls, but I didn't want to get rid of it, so I ended up hanging it there. Lots of the stuff that ends up in my house are the first stages of trying something new, with lots of mistakes and flaws."

After letting go of Sirus, Grey got up and walked up to the carving. He started at one end and scrutinized his way to the other, occasionally lifting a hand and running his fingers over the ridges. "I can't see any mistakes, and I don't think you'd have any trouble selling it."

"Trust me, they're there." Reluctantly, Sirus stood and walked to the wall too, stopping at Grey's side. "See?" He pointed to the lower left side of the piece. "Right here I miscalculated the scale of the trees to the mountain, and in the overall dimensions they're so big they could be toothpicks for giants."

Leaning in and then back, examining the area Sirus had pointed out, Grey finally said, "They're not that big." He glanced at Sirus and rolled his eyes. "You're being overly critical. There's so much detail over the whole piece that I wouldn't have even noticed them if you hadn't pointed it out."

"Doesn't mean the mistake isn't there. Or a half-dozen others, for that matter. And no," Sirus held up his hand when Grey opened his mouth, uninterested in keeping the focus on his artwork, "I'm not going to point them out to you. If you stare long enough, you'll see them for yourself. You can do that if you want. Or," he trailed his finger down Grey's chest, ending at his thatch of pubic hair, "you can come back to bed."

A half-smile touched Grey's lips, and it reached all the way up into his eyes in a way that got Sirus's heart thudding. Grey lifted his fingers to Sirus's chest and started to slide them down his middle too, but he abruptly stopped on the edge of his tattoo. "Do you regret getting this?"

Sirus rubbed his palm over the mustang tattoo, long ago having memorized its exact position and intricate design. "For a long time it hurt to see it," he admitted. "But ultimately I think looking at it every day made me face the break-up with Paul faster than I might have otherwise." Sirus made eye contact with Grey and raised a brow. "I literally could not run from a very real symbol of my relationship with him."

"You could have had it removed," Grey said. "I understand it hurts like hell, but it can be done."

Sirus shook his head, and he took a step back, letting Grey's hand fall away from him. "I couldn't have done that." He put his hand over the tattoo, almost in protection of the very idea of laser removal. "I thought about it, for about a second, then I remembered how hard Kelsie worked on getting the design just perfect to her high standards, and I couldn't just have it removed like it was nothing."

"Right." Nodding, Grey let his attention drift from the tattoo to Sirus's piece on the wall, then moved back to Sirus. "One artist respects another's work."

"No." With effort, Sirus bit his tongue and kept the irritation to correct Grey's mistaken "artist" label out of his tone. "One friend respects the time and effort another friend took in the creation of the design on his behalf. I think of Kelsie's hard work now when I look at it. Rarely do I think of Paul." As Sirus said those words, the truth of them settled in on him in a way they never had before.

I'm over Paul. Completely. Wow. Sirus was momentarily stunned that the realization wasn't even that big a deal to him. It just ... was.

Sirus looked at Grey; he took in the stunning beauty of the naked man before him, whose heart and mind he was getting to know very well. A deep sense of rightness -- well beyond what he'd ever experienced for any other man -- settled on him and sank straight into his heart. It didn't matter that Grey might not ever love him back, or that this fling might not last beyond next week; Sirus knew and accepted he was a better man right now for having known Greyson Cole.

He didn't intend to waste a minute of the time they had together talking about a tattoo or a carving on his wall.

"Come with me." As Sirus walked backward around the bed, he beckoned Grey with the crook of his finger.

Grey followed, his eyes already filling with dark heat. "What is on your mind, Wilder?" It suddenly felt as if Grey stalked Sirus, rather than allowing himself to be led.

Sirus's heart rate kicked up, his cock twitched to half-mast, and his pucker started to pulse in a fast beat. "I believe I owe you a piece of my ass in fair trade." He reached back and slid open his nightstand drawer. "Pick your poison," he stepped aside, revealing a plethora of sex toys, "and tell me how you want me." He caught Grey's gaze from two feet away, and held it. "I'm yours."

Grey growled and lunged. Rather than going for a toy, he grabbed Sirus and branded him with a hard, hot kiss, and tumbled them onto the bed.

Laughing in between kisses, Sirus didn't fight the fall.

CHAPTER EIGHTEEN

K *nock. Knock. Knock.*
Grey glanced at the clock on the fireplace mantel, and smiled. *Right on time.*

"Be right there!" he called out, taking just a few seconds to put down his laptop before jumping to his feet. He hadn't been able to concentrate on work anyway. Not with thoughts of Sirus invading his brain every five minutes ... and leaving him hard. He'd already gone to his bedroom and jerked off twice, and he had only been away from the man for five hours.

Won't be long before you see him again. Excitement hummed through Grey as he raced to the door and swung it open. *Sirus is going to be so fucking thrilled.*

"Rebecca," Grey drew the woman on the other side into a

hug, "you made it."

"Of course I did," the woman answered. Grey stepped back and allowed her to enter the cabin. "You send me pictures of some beautiful creations and then text me that I have to meet this man and see the rest of his work. You knew I would work a visit into my schedule." She stomped snow off her boots and unwound a black cashmere wrap from her slender frame. As Grey took the cover-up from her and shut the door, Rebecca shot him a pointed look. "You could have told me with the first message that he wasn't in Raleigh, though, and that I'd have to clear an entire day to drive halfway up a mountain to see him."

"He's worth it." Grey couldn't keep the pride out of his voice. Rebecca was an old friend from college who now owned a prestigious line of galleries that operated in seven states. She traveled all over the country searching for new artists, but she maintained a home base with her husband and children in Raleigh. "You'll see that for yourself."

"Considering you've never approached me about who or what to sell in my galleries in the past, you certainly piqued my interest with your photos and messages." Grey and John had financed Rebecca's first gallery, as well as her eventual expansion. She owned her business outright today.

Grey led the way to the kitchen and poured Rebecca a cup of coffee. After handing a mug to her, he got one for himself, and said, "No pressure to take Sirus's work." He pulled out a chair at the table for her before sitting down himself. "You don't owe me or John anything anymore. You know that."

Rebecca reached across the table and squeezed his hand. "Don't worry. I didn't think you were trying to bully me." She pulled her long blonde hair back and tied it in a knot at the nape of her neck. "Now, why don't you find me a cookie, or a muffin, or anything chocolate, and tell me all about this talented Sirus Wilder."

Talented. Yes. Grey's insides heated, and he couldn't keep the goddamned smile off his face. Sirus was talented. In so many ways. Sweet as hell too.

Grey couldn't wait to introduce him to Rebecca.

———

"DID MOM PUT YOU UP to calling me?" Sirus asked, his voice going tight as he struggled not to shout at Nic. "Is that what this offer is all about?" Out of the blue -- after never having shown a bit of interest in Sirus's art -- Nic had suddenly thought Sirus would be the perfect person to create an oversized sculpture that his office building's management wanted to put in their outdoor garden. "Is this some ploy to get me to DC?" Sirus couldn't forget how badly his mother wanted him to meet that woman lawyer.

"No." Irritation laced Nic's voice, and in the background it sounded to Sirus like he moved through a crowd. "I haven't talked to Mom since before the last time I talked to you."

"Seems strange that you're all of a sudden approaching me about my art." Sirus held the phone to his ear while he paced. He circled his large worktable, his focus on the series of sketches he had scattered all over the surface. "You've never shown any interest before."

"That's because I don't know dick about art and never know what to say," Nic snapped. "Not because I don't care that you love it. You are my brother, you know. Just because I don't get to see you that often doesn't mean I don't love you and care about the things you love. Look," Sirus heard what sounded like a car door slamming, "I have to get going or I'm going to be late for a meeting. The offer for the artwork isn't even a done deal. Building ownership is going to look at the proposals of every artist interested in the commission, and they'll choose what they want from there. I heard about it, and it made me think of you. That's why I called. Do whatever you want with the information. Now, before I have to go, will I see you in May for Diana's opening concert?"

"I plan on being there." Sirus's chest squeezed when he thought about how strained his relationship with his mother might be by then … as well as what might remain of him and Grey. He cleared his throat, but it didn't quite ease the rawness living inside him. "Looking forward to it."

"Me too. Should be good material to tease Di with, at least through next Christmas." Nic's chuckle, one that brought Diana endless torment, filled Sirus's ear. "Right?"

"Depends on who you're asking." Sirus shook his head, and he wondered if Diana sometimes regretted being adopted by the Wilder family. "Be good."

"Ain't no fun in that." Nic's chuckle briefly turned into

a full-bodied laugh. Just as fast, the humor left his voice. "Seriously, though, think about the commission, and let me know if you want me to send you any further info. I think you should consider pursuing it. Gotta go. Bye."

Nic hung up before Sirus could say goodbye. Sirus severed the call on his end, put down the cordless receiver, and tried to put his attention back on his sketches. He couldn't seem to focus on his main piece -- the one that kept wanting to turn into an abstract version of Grey -- so Sirus had put his tools down and picked up a pencil to doodle some ideas for Noah's sculpture. Sirus wanted something large, but somehow subtle, that would reflect the quietness inside the big man. Sirus knew in his gut Noah would end up buying the east house on the lake, and he wanted something ready for his new neighbor's home whenever that day occurred.

His fingers drifted over the dozen papers strewn about the table, but his thoughts jumped from the piece for Noah, to the strange phone call from his brother, and then to Grey and the two nights the man had stayed at Sirus's house since they'd talked about their families.

Grey appeared content and relaxed in Sirus's home, at least most of the time. There were flashes where Sirus swore Grey looked like he wanted to stay forever. At the same time, Grey insisted on going home every morning and working at his cabin during the day, only coming back in the evening for dinner and to spend the night. Sirus wanted to attribute Grey's choice to return to his cabin to the fact that they both knew being together would cause endless distractions, such as crawling on whatever surface they happened to be nearest to and fucking until neither one of them could walk. Sirus wanted to believe that was what was behind Grey's leaving every day, but he couldn't quite make it happen. He couldn't quite shake the worry that Grey hadn't given him even a hint of anything personal since their talk two nights ago.

But he makes love to you like there's no tomorrow, with a desperation that defies words. Lets you do the same to him too.

True. Sirus ached for the moments when he was buried inside Grey to the hilt, the man's body clutching him like he never wanted them to part. The way Grey looked at Sirus in those moments, and in the times when Sirus opened himself and gave Grey the same… God, if only Grey would give him even half the promises of tomorrows he conveyed during sex -- only do it when they weren't in bed.

"Knock, knock." Grey's voice broke into Sirus's thoughts and had him whipping around to face the open shed door. Sirus immediately ate the man up with his eyes, hungrily, as if he hadn't had Grey's cock and ass for a meal just this morning.

"I have a friend with me," Grey said, slipping his arm around an attractive blonde woman. "She's actually here to meet you, if you have a few minutes."

Sirus's focus shifted to the woman, who murmured "Hi," and wiggled out from under Grey's embrace. She immediately walked to Sirus's unfinished "Grey" piece, her interest clear, and the first line of cold trickled down Sirus's spine.

"Oh wow, this is going to be amazing," the woman said. "I want it when it's finished."

She said that just as Grey said, "This -- that," he pointed, "is Rebecca Hardy, and she owns a number of prestigious art galleries."

The wind went right out of Sirus; he felt punched in the gut. He wanted to ask Grey what in the hell he'd done, but the woman, Rebecca, had her hands on his incomplete project and demanded his attention first. Sirus moved across the floor to Rebecca's side and fought the most powerful urge to tear her hands off his work.

Rebecca glanced up, her pretty face open and her eyes piercing. "This is going to be something incredible," she said as she caressed the half-carved block of stone. "The lines you have half formed are already beautiful."

"Thank you," Sirus murmured. "This piece is very personal to me." His gaze flashed on Grey, and his skin heated before coming back to Rebecca. "Thank you for your interest, but I don't see myself parting with it when I'm finished."

Nodding, Rebecca rubbed Sirus's forearm, and then began to peruse the rest of his pieces. "Of course it's personal, Mr. Wilder," she said. "It's all personal, or they wouldn't be any good. Grey wouldn't have contacted me to come take a look at your stuff if he wasn't damn sure I would be interested in selling it. He retains the nuts and bolts knowledge of every business he ever helped create." She flashed Grey a fast smile. "Mine included."

Grey held up his hands, waving off Rebecca's words. "I don't have any financial stake in how you run your galleries anymore." His attention slid to Sirus, the amber chips sparking brightly in his hazel eyes. "I saw something in Sirus's work, and I thought you two might be able to form a partnership."

Of course you did. Son of a bitch. Sirus's entire body itched to ram Grey into the wall and take a swing at his face. *You might not directly financially benefit from my art, but you'll get something you want out of it, and you know it.* Sirus looked from Grey to Rebecca, light dawning, and every nerve ending inside him lit like the flint tip of a match. His heart plummeted right into his stomach. *Question answered; I'm not quite good enough for Grey after all.*

"All of your stuff is very good," Rebecca said, forcing Sirus to put his attention back on her. "Although I will be honest and say I wouldn't be able to sell a lot of it through my storefront. This more literal stuff isn't really what my clients are interested in purchasing. Although, damn," she stooped down and ran her hands over a life-size rendition of a bobcat, "this is insanely good technique and interpretation. I almost think he's going to arch his back if I scratch him behind the ears." She rubbed the cat's head and stood back up. "There is definitely a high-end market out there for work like this as well, even if it's not with me. I will leave you a few phone numbers for gallery owners who carry them."

"Thank you. That's very kind." Sirus bit his lip, and he behaved with the good manners his parents had instilled in him, even though all he wanted to do was turn around and yell "Bastard!" in Greyson Cole's face.

Rebecca walked to Sirus's main worktable, and her eyes immediately lit up as she spotted his array of sketches. "Oh, now these ideas all have a ton of potential."

Possessiveness slammed Sirus hard. He wedged himself between Rebecca and the table, partially blocking her view. "These are ideas for a specific piece, for a friend of mine." Sirus turned, gathered the papers up into a neat pile, and slid around to the other side of the table with the sketches trapped beneath his hands. "Whatever I end up creating from them will be a gift for him."

Rebecca's eyes widened, but just as quickly, she schooled her features and slipped into a professional smile. Her attention quickly shifted behind Sirus to Grey, then came back to Sirus, and Sirus could tell she now understood that Grey had never mentioned her visit.

"Listen," Rebecca said, her voice kind, "I have to turn right around and drive back home, so I really can't stay, but I thank you for allowing me to view your pieces. You have real talent, Mr. Wilder."

"Sirus. Please."

Rebecca dipped her head. "Sirus, then." She pulled a business card case out of a small purse and produced a card. "My number is already on here, but I'm going to add two more for dealers I believe will be interested in some of your work." Leaning across the table, she snagged one of his pencils and scribbled a few lines on the back of her card. "Take as long as you need, but I would ask you to seriously consider giving me a call so we can talk." Understanding infused her voice and softened her eyes, giving her beauty a surprisingly motherly appeal. "If you choose to, and if you like, I can tell you more about what I do and how I work. If you find you're comfortable with me, I'd really love to sell some of your pieces." Rebecca pressed the card into Sirus's hand and curled her fingers around his, applying a light pressure. "Please think about it. Can you give me that?"

"I will think about it," Sirus answered. He had to. Hell, it wasn't this woman's fault she'd been thrown into the middle of a manipulation. "Thank you for understanding. It was nice to meet you."

"Nice to meet you too," she said. They exchanged a firm handshake. "I'll show myself out."

Sirus turned, watching as Rebecca walked up to Grey. The woman rose up on her tiptoes, giving him a hug. She pressed her cheek to Grey's and gave him a kiss, then whispered something that made Grey's brow furrow and his focus shoot to Sirus. She pulled away, gave them both one last smile, and waved as she walked away.

Counting each second that went by, Sirus kept his focus solely on Grey. In return, Grey drilled him with an equally probing stare.

Bastard. Bastard. Bastard.

Sirus waited until he heard an engine rev up, then slammed

his fist into the worktable and exploded on Grey. "You son of a bitch." His voice raged low, sounding like it came from the depths of hell. "You just had to do it. You couldn't just accept us and leave something that was going pretty damn good alone. You had to go and put your hands on it, try and manipulate it, change it, and turn it into something *acceptable* and *worthy* of your time and interest."

"What in the hell are you talking about?" Grey shouted, his hands thrown in the air. "Do you have any idea how successful Rebecca's galleries are? Do you even understand what a fucking big deal it was for her to take an entire day to come see your work? For her to express an interest in someone she thinks is talented enough to promote?"

"Of course I know she's successful." Sirus shot each word into the air with the precision of flying daggers. "She has to be, doesn't she? You wouldn't have anything to do with her otherwise." Grey reared back, but Sirus made up the distance and got right in his face. "Another one of Greyson Cole's successes. And that's what you're all about, isn't it? Take something unique, but small and inconsequential, and figure out how in the hell to pretty it up to sell it to your investors. Me included."

"I don't know what you're talking about, or why you're so angry with me," Grey spat back. "I was trying to help you. You have an artistic gift; Rebecca is one of the best at putting that gift out to the public. She can turn your art into a career."

"Oh, and you would love that, wouldn't you." It wasn't a

question, and Sirus's lips twisted in a sneer. "We start to open up to each other, you start to feel something for me that you want to take beyond a vacation fling -- and I know you feel it." He grabbed Grey and savaged his mouth with a brutal kiss, only to shove him away and point in his face. "Don't you dare fucking tell me that you don't. But you can't possibly feel something for me, this guy," Sirus waved his arms up and down his stained jeans and flannel shirt, "a mere truck driver. No, not you. Not Greyson Cole, a successful venture capitalist who owns his own gazillion dollar business and heaven knows what else. You can't possibly have real feelings for a truck driver. And God knows you don't dare introduce me to your friends and colleagues. Not as I am right now. If I'm an artist, though, well, that's respectable, that's admirable, that's maybe even a little bit coveted. But a guy who drives a big rig…" Sirus laughed, and it sounded awful. "That's not something you can dress up and put on your mantel to show off. That's not something you even keep hidden in your nightstand drawer."

"You fucking prick." Grey grabbed Sirus's shirt and shoved him into the edge of the worktable, unleashing incredible strength. "You need to be very careful about the words you're putting in my mouth," he whispered, his voice lethal. "You are painting my motives with some awfully broad strokes that you know nothing about. You might want to shut the fuck up before you say something you can't take back."

"What do you plan on threatening me with?" Sirus snarled the question. "Leaving?" His chest heaved, and he put up a token struggle, spoiling for a fight. "You're doing that in five days anyway."

Grey shoved hard at Sirus, cracking Sirus's head back as he took him all the way up onto the table. "We can make it a whole hell of a lot sooner than that, if you keep talking."

"Hey!" A deep, rough voice rang through the tension-filled air. "Get the hell off him right now!"

Grey was suddenly lifted off Sirus and thrown in the direction of the door.

Standing between Sirus and Grey, like some avenging angel, stood Noah Maitland.

Chapter Nineteen

Noah Maitland.

Oh, this was just fucking perfect.

Grey took a step forward. "Si --"

"Stay the hell back," Noah said, his voice cutting and low. His eyes flashed with something more than mere friendship. "If you don't, I'll tie you down and call the sheriff; I swear I will." The man loomed large, standing in front of where Sirus kneeled on the table. Sirus shifted and put his hand on Noah's shoulder.

Grey seethed, at both Sirus and Noah, and fought down the heady desire to do serious physical damage. He wanted to tear Noah's arm off and beat the shit out of him with it. He hadn't felt the urge to savage an entire building since he was nine years old, but right now he had to take a huge step backward and curl his hands into painfully tight fists so that he didn't rip this studio to shreds.

Fucking bastard Sirus, accusing me of thinking he's not good enough for me. If he only knew how wrong he was...

Great sweeps of swirling, volatile emotion consumed Grey, making his entire body quake. It felt as if every piece of his heart -- *that this fucking man had awakened* -- was exposed and on display for everyone to see. For Sirus to see. To judge. To reject.

Grey *could not* have that. Nobody got that kind of power over him. Not anymore.

Sirus pushed himself to the edge of the table and swung his legs over the side, stumbling to a standing position. "Grey, listen --"

"No." Grey held up his hands, praying the tremor vibrating through him did not show. "I think you've said plenty enough already. You have a guest." His tone was pleasantly sarcastic in the face of wanting to snarl. "Stay and talk to him." Grey looked Noah up and down, his heart growing even sicker at the rough attractiveness he found in every line of Noah's hard body. He swallowed, and shifted his attention back to Sirus. "Maybe you'll find something more to your liking here." Blinking, he turned away. "Goodbye."

"Grey." Sirus's voice held Grey in place. "Stop."

"Wait, Sirus," Noah said. From the corner of his eye, Grey saw Noah wrap his hand around Sirus's forearm. "I need to talk to you." Noah's jaw clenched visibly. "It's important."

Sirus hesitated, his attention going to Noah, and that was all Grey needed. Without looking back, he walked away.

Fast.

———

"Stupid idiot son of a bitch." Grey slammed the door to his cabin with a resounding crack, shaking everything on the front walls. He threw his coat on the floor and tore to the bedroom. "Spilling your guts and making yourself vulnerable; showing weakness and giving him the power to use it against you. You fucking deserved exactly what you got."

Grey yanked the closet door open and snatched his suitcase, throwing it on the bed. He unzipped the thing, cursing the stubborn zipper that he knew was actually the clumsiness of his own fumbling fingers. Wanting to rail and shout blame at Sirus for this raging hurt eating its way through him, Grey turned it all inward, knowing it was his own fault.

He had broken all of his own rules, and he had done it willingly, so he had no one to blame for this awful twist of anger and heartache but himself. *Idiot. Idiot. Idiot.* On the very first night of his vacation, when he'd heard Sirus moaning, Grey never should have taken that step to the man's door. And he *never* should have kissed him that first time, let alone play with fire and start a sexual affair. He never should have come to this cabin in the first place. That was the only way to guarantee he and Sirus never would have met. Not meeting that man was the

274 | CAMERON DANE

only way to ensure Grey wouldn't be suffering these ridiculous sweeps of emotion right now, ones that had him fighting the urge to run back to Sirus's house and fuck him right in front of Noah, staking a claim in the most primal of ways.

Grey stalked to the dresser, pulled a drawer right off its tracks, and took it back to the bed to upend its contents into his bag. There could be no peace in this cabin now, not with Sirus right across the lake being all wonderful, sexy, stubborn, passionate … and open, in a way Grey could never be.

He couldn't do this. He did not have the right skill-set for a relationship. Grey had forgotten his limitations for a few days, but he remembered them now.

Just look at how everything with Sirus had gone to fuck so quickly after just *trying* to share a piece of his soul. It couldn't be a coincidence that it all went to hell only days after Grey had cut open his guts and told Sirus about Joe, and then showed him pieces of his childhood. Christ, Grey had become the very man that had caused him to become celibate in the first place.

Someone weak, clingy and needy; someone desperate for love.

Grey caught a glimpse of himself as he passed by the mirror, and his heart stopped at the man reflected back at him. Gone was the put-together businessman with the piercing, cool gaze. In his place stood something almost feral, with flushed skin, hair in wild tufts, and hunted, fear-drenched eyes.

All because of one man.

"Christ."

Unable to look at himself anymore, Grey slung a handful of ugly words at his reflection and then strode to the kitchen, needing a drink. He couldn't stand himself in this pathetic state; no wonder Sirus had let him walk away with hardly a word.

Pain tightened a band around Grey's chest, making him stumble. Jesus Christ, he barely knew Sirus; there was no way this suffocating pain of loss could be real.

You know the most important thing; you know his soul.

"Yeah, but he doesn't know yours." Grey swung open the refrigerator door and leaned his hand on it, talking back to himself. "He proved that today."

The rafters suddenly shook with a slam of the front door. "Greyson!" Sirus's voice rang right on top of the slamming door. "Where the fuck are you? We need to talk."

Grey grasped the fridge door in his hand, squeezing until the tips of his fingers turned pure white. His heart raced madly, but he stared at the contents inside, refusing to turn around, even when the air crackled and heated, and Grey knew Sirus now stood in the kitchen too.

"What is the matter with you?" Sirus's voice reeked of combativeness. "We were talking. You don't walk away in the middle of a discussion."

Go away. Grey squeezed his eyes shut, and spoke through gritted teeth. "There isn't anything else I want to say to you."

A growl erupted from Sirus, and a screeching noise assaulted Grey's ears, making him think Sirus had kicked a chair out of his way. "Then maybe you need to shut up for a minute and listen to me."

Every word Sirus spoke stabbed at the open wound in Grey's chest. At the gaping hole Sirus had created, the one Grey could never let him see. "Go tell it to Noah."

Sirus cursed something low and foul. "What in the hell is that supposed to mean?" Suddenly, pure heat rode Grey's back, and he knew Sirus stood right behind him. "Look at me, damn it." Sirus grabbed Grey's arm and spun him around, trapping him in the V of the open refrigerator door with spread arms. Mercury burned in Sirus's eyes, turning them deep silver. "Are you trying to make something out of Noah being my friend?"

"I saw that wedding ring on his finger, but don't for one second think I don't know Noah is gay." Grey looked Sirus in the eyes, meeting the depth of passion and intelligence there. "And don't you dare try to tell me that you don't know it either."

Red crept up Sirus's neck from beneath his shirt and jacket, turning his face ruddy. "I do now. He told me today."

"He wants you." Grey shook, fighting sickness as he flashed back to the muted longing in Noah's eyes that evening at the diner, and then jumped forward to the aggressive protective streak that had reared its head today. "For more than a quick fuck too."

Sirus looked Grey up and down, slow and lingering, making Grey feel it along his skin, like one long caress. "And you're just going to let him have me? Is that what you want?" Smoldering heat worked its way into Sirus's eyes, and the sight of it ran frissons of uncertainty through Grey. He had no idea if Sirus's gaze had turned hot for him … or Noah. Sirus lifted his hand and brushed his rough fingers across Grey's cheek, catching his thumb on Grey's lips. "You want to walk away," Sirus said softly, "like you did today? You want me to stay with Noah and help him discover what it's like to be with another man?"

A crushing wave of denial rocked through Grey, terrifying him to his core. He saw himself crawling into a hole and dying, and *could not* concede such power over his wellbeing to another human being. He schooled his features to his best, no-fear business face, and looked at Sirus through dead eyes. "Do what you want." His voice was cool, but he turned around, needing to break the contact before it killed him. "It's your life."

Sirus moved in behind Grey, and dipped his head down, putting his mouth right next to Grey's ear. "So you want me to go home, pick up the phone, and call Noah." Sirus's voice sank into Grey's very being, each word contaminating his blood. Sirus stepped in even closer, not stopping until his chest seared itself to Grey's back. Slipping his arms around Grey's waist, Sirus tugged Grey's shirt out of his jeans. "You want me to invite Noah over, make him dinner." Sirus paused, licking Grey's ear as he unbuttoned Grey's shirt and slipped his hands up his stomach. "Take him to my bedroom and fuck him." Sirus drew Grey shirt off his shoulders and arms, letting the fabric hang between his chest and Grey's upper back where their bodies were fused together. Sirus rubbed Grey's nipples, abrading the sensitive flesh, and twisting the dark circles to hard points with his sandpaper fingertips. "Is that what you want?"

Grey pushed back against Sirus, grinding his ass into the man's cock. Blinding, rage-filled jealousy reared inside Grey and did battle with the need to save himself from such an all-consuming passion, rendering him mute. Christ, he wanted Sirus to be his with every fiber of his being but the fear of falling choked Grey's throat, blocking the words.

"Maybe I should undress Noah." Sirus pushed the flat of his hands down Grey's torso, digging one hand under the waistband of his jeans. "Like I've done a dozen times with you." He worked Grey's buckle open with his free hand. When the belt gave, Sirus's fingers slipped farther inside Grey's underwear, to the root of his cock. "I could touch him," the button on Grey's jeans opened and his zipper slid down, "make him hard." Sirus took Grey's erection in hand and stroked his rigid length with a tight, dry hand, drawing a sharp cry and shiver from Grey. "Make him moan for more."

Sirus held Grey at the mercy of his slowly pumping fist, as well as the dark evolution of Grey's imagination. "Do you think I'll love fucking Noah as much as I love fucking you?" Sirus asked, his voice gravelly at Grey's ear. "Will I want to taste every inch of his body the way I crave learning yours?" Letting go of Grey's dick, Sirus pushed Grey's underwear and jeans down to his knees. "Will I think his is as beautiful as yours?" Somehow, through the mingling haze of pain and desire, Grey processed that Sirus removed Grey's shoes, socks, and the rest of his clothes, leaving him naked in every way.

All the while, Sirus didn't let up his verbal and mental torture. His wicked mouth went right back to Grey's ear. "Do you think he'll be eager to suck my cock, the way you are?" Sirus pushed two fingers into Grey's mouth and started an abbreviated, fucking motion. "Will he take it all the way down and make me scream, the way you do?" He added a third finger and filled Grey's mouth to the throat.

Like a starving man, Grey lapped and sucked at Sirus's fingers. Moaning, slipping to a place of pure reaction, Grey anointed the salty flesh of Sirus's digits as he remembered the feel of blowing his thick cock.

Sirus slipped his fingers out of Grey's mouth, leaving him bereft. Hot breath constantly tormented Grey's nape, never letting him forget Sirus loomed close, pulling every raw response out of Grey like a puppet on a string. Sirus pushed his arm in between their bodies, and the agonizing sweetness of his fingers on Grey's asshole had Grey whimpering. Pressure played at Grey's pucker, ever more insistent with every swipe of Sirus's rough fingertips, making Grey squirm. Sirus licked at the shell of Grey's ear and flicked his tongue into the opening.

Sirus's voice, Svengali-like and low, whispered, "Will Noah's ass be hot and tight, and cling to my cock the way yours does?" *Right then*, Sirus shoved two fingers home, breaching Grey's asshole in one sure thrust.

Grey jerked and his cock spiked at the invasion,

unprepared, even though he had known it was coming. He bit his lip to keep from crying out; only this time he did it because it was so damn *good* he almost couldn't stand to feel it. Sirus penetrated Grey's channel again and again with full, deep strokes, scissoring his fingers and exquisitely widening Grey's entrance, making Grey's legs shake as he struggled to accept every layer of sensation without coming. When Sirus forced a third finger inside and started a corkscrewing motion, Grey shuddered, his mouth falling open. He grabbed onto the open refrigerator door, clutching the width in his fingers, keening through the pleasure of what Sirus did to him.

Sirus wrapped his arm around Grey's chest, holding him upright as he plowed his fingers in and out of Grey's rectum. "You think Noah will respond so completely to me being inside his ass, like you're doing right now?" Sirus's taunting invaded Grey's mind, consumed him, and spurred his emotions as invasively as the man's fingers did in his chute. "You think I can make him hard and make him come without doing anything other than plugging his hole, the way I can with you?" Sirus shifted his fingers in Grey's body and crooked the tips over Grey's kill spot, shooting direct lines of zinging joy to every corner of Grey's being, pushing him into overdrive.

His body and mind weakened with longing and wanting, Grey felt as if he hung suspended from Sirus's arm and fingers; his balls were painfully full, and his cock ached with the need to release. He shoved his ass back on Sirus's embedded digits, trying to find that one extra touch that would throw him into orgasm. Grey reached, searched, almost sobbing for it, but couldn't make himself come.

"Should I walk away from you right now and invite Noah into my bed?" Sirus asked, slipping the words into Grey's soul. "Leave you unfulfilled, and go fuck him, hold him, love him, the way I do you?" Sirus's fingers started to slide from Grey's ass, and Grey had never felt so frightened and alone in his life. The final inch of Sirus's fingers left Grey's body, *left him*, and Grey's entire world went hazy red. "Tell me to leave you --"

No!

Rage and loss tore through Grey, leaving him ragged and raw. He spun around and grabbed Sirus by the neck, yanking him in until mere inches separated their faces. His bare chest brushed against Sirus's jacket with every heavy breath they shared. "You are mine," Grey uttered, his voice so guttural he didn't recognize it as his own. "I don't care that you're angry at me, or what you fucking think I tried to do to you today; you are mine." His throat was clogged, and he barely scratched out the words. "I wasn't trying to change you or hurt you." He crushed his mouth on Sirus's, clinging in desperation. His fingers brushed through the hair at Sirus's nape, and he somehow pulled the man even closer, whispering against his mouth in between kisses. "I swear I wasn't."

"I know." His eyes unnaturally bright, Sirus held Grey's head in his bruising hold, angling his mouth for a deeper kiss. Tongues swirled and fused together, bringing light back into the brief darkness of Grey's world. "Now." Sirus scraped his lips against Grey's, sipping there. "I know now."

Grey dug his fingers into Sirus's coat, possessive fire scorching a trail through his core. "You'd better have told Noah to get the hell out." He pulled on the bigger man, stumbling them both against the counter. "He better fucking never try to shield you from me again."

"Noah understands how I feel about you now," Sirus said in between kisses. He tilted Grey's head back and nuzzled his neck, sucking the sensitive flesh there. "He knows the score."

Hardness coated a shell around Grey's fear, making his voice harsh. "You belong to me." Insecurity smothered the softness his soul ached to give Sirus. "He can't have you."

"I want to be yours." Sirus brushed his lips all over Grey's face, leaving not an inch of it untouched. "Just yours. I don't want anyone else."

A crack in the foundation of Grey's resolve to stay strong weakened his knees, but he fought to stay upright. "I gave you my ass." Roughness filled his voice, and his throat was tight, hurting like hell, but he couldn't shut up. "That better fucking mean something to you."

"It does." Sirus broke the savage depth of their kiss, and pulled back, putting a small distance between them. His chest rose and fell in visible waves, clearly breathless, but his eyes were clear and focused, and trained right on Grey. He lifted his hand and swept his knuckles softly over Grey's cheek. With a catch in his voice, Sirus said, "It means everything to me." He held Grey's gaze, keeping him prisoner with just his eyes. "You mean everything to me."

"Oh Christ." Unsteady, unable to catch himself and pull back, Grey fell. "I love you." He mangled the words with the depth of his emotions, and he shook all over. "I love you." Complete vulnerability rocked through him. He turned away and gave Sirus his back, terrified to let Sirus see such need in his eyes. The words just kept spilling out, though, ones he had never spoken to anyone in this way before. "I love you."

"I know." Sirus slid his hand around Grey's waist, and Grey swore the other man knew he needed the extra strength to help hold him up. Sirus brushed his hand across Grey's lower back, and the warmth created a shiver. The snap of a button and the soft sigh of a zipper caught the evening air in the cabin, and then the rigid length of Sirus's cock slid between the cheeks of Grey's ass, teasing his pucker and crack. "I love you too, Greyson," Sirus finally said softly, and tore right through what was left of Grey's cool. He kissed the side of Grey's neck. "Always."

"Oh fuck." Grey's legs buckled, the enormity of hearing Sirus say those words to him -- and knowing they were true -- stole the strength from his body.

"Shh, shh, it's all right." Sirus took hold of Grey and slid them both down the cabinets to the floor. They landed with Grey on Sirus's lap, his legs spread wide on either side of Sirus's open thighs. Holding Grey around the waist with one arm, Sirus reached out and knocked the tray of butter off the shelf in the fridge, letting it fall the short distance to the floor. He smeared his fingers in the oily stuff, and then lifted Grey just a few inches to lube his hole. Sirus then fitted the head of his cock to Grey's tender ring, drawing a whimpering gasp of need from Grey. "Slide down, baby," Sirus said, pressing on Grey's lower belly, "and take me inside."

Grey did as ordered, moaning as the pure, physical *rightness* of Sirus penetrating his body and making them one consumed him. Letting his eyes fall closed, Grey dropped his head against Sirus's shoulder, and he blocked out every single thing in the world except the thick length of Sirus's shaft pushing deep into his ass. Grey's passage was still sore from the newness of fucking this way, but he welcomed the slight pain that mixed and became confused with the pleasure, knowing now that with Sirus this meant he was *alive*. With Sirus, Grey wanted to experience everything. And he wanted it forever.

Lips brushed against Grey's temple, and then the flick of a warm tongue. "Look at me, Greyson," Sirus said, his voice husky and a little bit harsh. "Don't hide. Not anymore. Not from me."

Turning his head, Grey opened his eyes and found Sirus's gaze, so fucking full of love, waiting for him, and he fought the need to cry.

"No. Not hiding," Grey promised. He touched Sirus's stubbly cheek, and it looked like Sirus fought tears. "Just…" He looked into Sirus's eyes, falling into their depths, while at the same time breathed through the stuffed-full sensation the man's hard cock wreaked in his ass. "Feeling." The scrape of the zipper on Sirus's jacket rubbed Grey's bare back, and the fabric of his barely opened jeans scratched Grey's buttocks too. Sirus's fingers dug into Grey's legs, holding him spread open, pulling at Grey's inner thigh muscles in the most exquisite way. Cool air caressed the front half of Grey's body, but every inch of his flesh that touched Sirus burned hot enough to scorch his skin. Early cum leaked in a steady stream down Grey's rearing erection, and his balls were pulled up tight against his body, painfully so. "Feeling everything; for the first time." Grey gritted his teeth, fighting the onslaught of release, struggling to process everything and make this moment last forever. He stared into Sirus's slate-colored eyes, and tumbled the rest of the way home. "Because of you."

Sirus's pupils flared, blackness nearly overtaking the silver. "Son of a..." He left the curse in the air and latched onto Grey's mouth in a bruising kiss instead; at the same time, he surged up with his hips and stabbed his cock deep into Grey's ass. Grey jerked and cried out, but never took his mouth off Sirus's, craving the mingling of need and desire more than his next breath. Sirus curled his hands under Grey's upper thighs and manipulated Grey's movement, lifting and lowering Grey's ass to slide up and down his piercing length, and sent Grey's anal walls into a rippling frenzy.

"Oh yeah, oh yeah..." Grey clamped his teeth, biting Sirus's lower lip as he bore down and squeezed his chute all around Sirus's embedded cock. Blinding pleasure raced through Grey and tingled every nerve ending in his body to life. Sirus groaned and let go of Grey's legs, but quickly snaked one arm around Grey's waist and tied them together in the middle. He jerked his other hand up and down Grey's rock-hard dick in a suffocating, tight grip, rendering Grey temporarily incapable of anything more than grunting and moaning.

Grey's rectum flamed with the heat of Sirus's invasion, but he needed the scorching-hot fire of friction or he thought he might die. His upper body fell forward, and he shifted his legs, bending at the knee as he planted his hands on Sirus's jean-covered knees, searching for a hold. He dropped his head, his mouth gaped, and his hair dripped sweat as he started to pound his ass down on Sirus's cock in shallow, fast strokes. Grey's knees lost traction on the hardwood floor, spreading wider and wider with every hard fuck. His left foot eventually hit the edge of the refrigerator and gave him a hold, but Grey didn't care how he looked; he only cared about Sirus and coming.

His nuts crying for release, Grey became a frenzy of erratic gyrating, and he pummeled his aching passage down on Sirus's massive penis. "Fuck me; oh yeah, fuck me good." He howled low with the fierce stabbing of Sirus's member into his hole. "Again, again." Grey couldn't keep the need or pleading out of his voice, and no longer cared. "Oh Christ, make me come for you."

Sirus yanked Grey back up to his chest and fused their mouths together in a hard kiss. He buried a hand between Grey's legs, but forewent his cock and balls. He went right past them straight to the pulled-tight, thin membrane of skin between Grey's stretched pucker and sac, and gave it a good, hard rub with his butter-slicked fingers.

Grey exploded on contact, shouting into Sirus as his entire body convulsed on top of the other man, shuddering as orgasm took him over completely. His channel squeezed mightily and repeatedly around Sirus's cock, triggering not only a second wave of orgasm in himself, but he pushed Sirus there too. Sirus held onto Grey with a bruising hold as his cock swelled in Grey's ass. He then pumped within, filling Grey's rectum with steaming lines of cum. At the same time, Grey grabbed his cock and directed it upward, spraying a ridiculous, endless amount of seed, splashing the warm liquid onto his stomach, chest, and Sirus's forearm. All the while, Grey kissed Sirus with every ounce of love in him, trying to invade the man, *infect* him, brand him, in every single way.

He had to.

Grey was terrified.

Nothing was resolved between them, but he didn't want this to ever end.

CHAPTER TWENTY

Sirus let his head fall back against the cabinet; he exhaled, exhausted, as the last wave of orgasm rippled through him.

Good God. He had never had sex with anyone in the way he'd just had with Grey.

Never had sex with someone he loved so deeply, who also loved him back.

Holy shit. How in the hell did I fall so fast?

Grey suddenly tensed on top of Sirus and started to pull away.

Sirus flexed his arm in an even tighter band around Grey's middle, holding him in place. "No way." He finally eased his fingers off Grey's perineum, but deliberately kept his dick tucked all the way inside the man's tight ass. "You're not going anywhere yet. We're not done talking." Sirus smiled, but didn't have the energy to lift his head. "God willing, we never will be."

Grey's muscles bunched up tight on top of Sirus for a long, drawn out moment, pushing against the python-snug hold of Sirus's arm. It felt as if the man waged an internal war, but he eventually relaxed and leaned against Sirus once again.

Swallowing the shout of victory, Sirus rolled his head and pecked a kiss against Grey's sweat-soaked hair. Under all his clothing, Sirus perspired like hell too. He didn't dare make a move to remove them though; that would mean letting Grey go.

Not gonna happen.

At least, not any time soon.

"That was mean as hell of you," Grey eventually said, his voice still unnaturally scratchy. "Taunting me with threats of going to Noah."

"Never a chance of it happening," Sirus murmured. "Deep down, you know that." He rubbed his fingers over Grey's stomach, his heart constricting at the pain he'd caused Grey, no matter how temporary. "You needed to see it, though, in your mind, to know how much it would bother you if I ended up with another man."

Grey snorted, and Sirus swore he rolled his eyes. "I didn't need the extra visual, thank you very much." He shifted his legs, grunting as he unfolded them one at a time and let them fall straight next to Sirus's jeans clad ones. Sirus held on to Grey's middle the whole time, never letting him move far enough away to risk his semi-hard penis slipping from the smothering hold of Grey's passage.

Picking at Sirus's bunched up jeans, Grey added, "It bothered me plenty enough to see Noah in your studio, protecting you like that ... from me. Goddamnit." Fire erupted in Grey's voice again, exciting the hell out of Sirus. This was his Grey. The real one beneath the cool façade. "He dared to protect you from me. I wanted to kill him."

"He thought you were trying to hurt me," Sirus explained. "When you shoved me up on my worktable, my head banged into the surface pretty damn hard."

"I'm sorry." Grey turned his head and looked at Sirus, his hazel eyes deepening to nearly green as he searched Sirus's face. "I didn't mean to do that. I was about one second away from crawling on top of you, and probably tearing off your clothes to fuck you. I was so angry at your accusation, I could barely speak, but I was strung too tight with too many emotions to turn around and walk away." His jaw clenching, and his eyes narrowing, Grey started to look a bit like a trapped animal. "At least until Noah showed up and played a damned effective knight in shining armor. You were right behind him, as if you were hiding from me. Then when you put your hand on him... Well, it looked to me like that's where you wanted to be."

"I don't. You never have to worry about that." Sirus caressed Grey's face, trying to soothe away the hardness still living there. "I promise. Noah didn't know the full scope of what went down between us; he reacted to the final piece he witnessed.

There wasn't anything more to it than that."

"That man has feelings for you," Grey said. Certainty sharpened his gaze. "Trust me when I say there was a little more to his quick jump to help you than simply lending a fellow citizen a hand."

"*That man* is struggling to find a place where he can admit to his family and friends that he's gay." Sirus closed his eyes, breathing through the short conversation he'd shared with Noah, and the sheer volume of emotions Noah had radiated during those few minutes. When Sirus pulled himself together, he faced Grey again. "Noah has children, and he has been married for a long time. He's in his forties, and he's just now facing who he is. Try to imagine that, and then tell me you don't have any sympathy for how mixed up his feelings and life must be right now."

"I didn't say I don't have any sympathy for him." Grey bit off each word, and tension filled his body once more. "Again, don't put words in my mouth. That's what pissed me off so much earlier."

Sirus immediately put his forehead to Grey's, and then kissed away the hard line of his lips. "Okay, okay; I'm sorry," he whispered. "You're right. I did do that. Both times."

Grey pulled back, but he did link his hand over Sirus's against his stomach. "What I said was that Noah has feelings for you. At the very least, he has a crush, if not more." Grey still looked a little surly, and Sirus had to bite down a laugh. His man was a little jealous, and it was sweet to see.

292 | CAMERON DANE

"Whatever Noah has will pass, and it's not reciprocated." As much as Sirus loved and was committed to Grey, he didn't feel it was right to discuss the feelings Noah had admitted to having for him. The man knew they couldn't go anywhere; he'd spoken very clearly about intending to work past them, and about not letting them interfere in their growing friendship. Sirus believed him. "Mainly Noah wanted to apologize to me for speaking to you at the diner." Sirus arched a brow. Grey had certainly not told him anything about said conversation, although it did make the certainty of Grey's reads on Noah so much clearer. "He realized he overstepped his bounds, and he was afraid he might have hurt something you and I were trying to build."

"And then he saw me attacking you and probably wished he'd interfered some more." The grumble stayed in Grey's voice for a moment, but then his eyes softened. "I am so sorry I cracked your head against the table like that." He wrapped his arm around Sirus's throat and tried to reach around to the back of his head. "Are you okay?"

Grey's fingers probed at the back of Sirus's skull, but Sirus grabbed his hand and pushed it down to his side, trapping it there. "I'm fine," Sirus said. He figured he would have a little bump, and maybe a headache later, but nothing more than that. "My head is as hard as it looks."

"And what about the other?" Grey glanced away, and when he came back, his eyes were shadowed. "Are you fine with me introducing you to Rebecca? Or do you still believe I had ugly motives for what I did?"

"I don't... No..." Sirus let go of Grey's hand and ground his knuckles into the floor. Banked hurt lived in Grey's hazel eyes, and it cut Sirus up inside to know he had put it there. "Let me see if I can have this all make sense." *God, please let Grey understand me.* "I see now that you genuinely thought you were doing something good for me. You did it in your way -- the way you understand and know how to -- which is to team someone up with a person who can hopefully make them commercially successful and wealthy. That's what you do; it's how your brain operates. I'm not judging it or saying it's a bad thing, believe me. I've seen you incredibly focused when you're working on something, and it's totally sexy.

"I just got so damn angry because I thought you were ignoring everything I ever tried to tell you about my art and where I place it in my life. Creating is something I love and do on the side, and it seemed like you were trying to push me into a place I have no interest in going, so that I was a more ... I don't know ... respectable person in your world. I was angry and I got insecure, and all I could think was that you wanted me to sell to Rebecca because you didn't think I was special enough just as I am. Once I got past my initial flash of anger, I saw that you truly didn't understand my position, and that you thought you were doing something really nice because you care about me and thought it would make me happy."

Grey's lips thinned, and his eyes became very focused on a point across the kitchen. It looked like he chewed on his cheek, and his fingers drummed a one, two, three beat on the back of Sirus's hand. He wiggled on Sirus's lap, reminding Sirus with a sharp jolt of pleasure that he still had his cock embedded in the man's ass.

Seemingly completely unaware of the effect his shifting had on Sirus's dick, Grey suddenly swung his head back around to face Sirus. "Don't get defensive," he started. "I'm just asking a question, not trying to nudge you away from your position. But can I ask you why you're so opposed to making a leap into a more commercial market with your art? Do you think it's selling out, or that you'll lose creative control; something like that?" Grey clamped his hand on Sirus's mouth. "I'm not trying to change your mind; I just want to understand where you're coming from. Your view is leaps and bounds away from the world I function in on a daily basis, and I guess for that reason I cannot wrap my brain around it. All right," he took his hand away, "you can answer now."

"Gee, thanks," Sirus said dryly, but pecked a quick kiss on Grey's lips. He rubbed his thumb back and forth against Grey's jaw while searching his mind for words that Grey's way of thinking could understand. "Painting, sculpting, drawing, carving... It's all such a wonderful outlet and release for me. It always has been. I get to go into my shed and just let myself go, not ever having to think or worry about anything other than what I'm doing right in that moment when I'm in there. I don't ever want to stop loving what I do in there or have something practical infect it. I don't want my art to become a job that I *have* to do to earn a living. I don't want to resent something that has given me peace and joy all the way back to when I was a kid.

"I also don't want to ever feel like I can't attempt something completely new and fail at it miserably simply because I can't afford to give it a try." Passion infused Sirus's voice, making it sharp and strong. "I don't want my income and livelihood to depend on art." He focused in on Grey, his vision for his future clear. "Aside from all that, I do own my own rig, and I do like driving my truck. It's actually one of my greatest sources of finding new things to try in my art. Some of the unusual stuff you see at my place isn't born in my imagination. Take the three dimensional piece I have in my bedroom, for example. I saw a bunch of pieces in that style when I was in Kentucky. I thought they were interesting, so I spent a good amount of time studying them and talking to the artist about them, then I came home and gave it a shot myself. Nothing much really came of it; I didn't have the hand for it, but for better than six months I enjoyed the hell out of trying." He shrugged, out of steam. "That's what my art is to me, not a business. That's it."

Grey nodded, but the eyes of a hawk still studied Sirus. "Hear me out." Grey didn't blink, but his voice was conversational, not instructive. "This is what I do, and you're right in a lot of ways, I can't turn it off. For you, there is the option of giving Rebecca two or three pieces a year, if that's all you're comfortable creating for high-end sales. If you're firm about your position with Rebecca, and you tell her you're not interested in putting yourself in the middle of a big show or meeting clients, then just say so. She is a businesswoman with a good eye, and she is not going to risk pushing you away by demanding more. You can continue to drive your truck while at the same time give Rebecca -- or someone else -- the occasional piece to sell. Even Ginny, since I would imagine you have a friendship with her." Certainty and confidence lived in Grey's eyes, and Sirus knew this was the Grey that thrived in his work. "There is middle ground, Sirus. It doesn't have to be all or nothing. You can be financially successful with your art, and continue to drive your rig, on your own terms."

Sirus chuckled, his heart feeling truly light for the first time since starting this fling with Grey. "Yeah, but you're an all or nothing kind of guy, Grey, so when you brought Rebecca to my shed I thought you were trying to turn me into a career artist. Someone you can brag about to your friends." It was amazing to Sirus that he could hear a laugh in his voice even though he spoke about such a sensitive subject. His heart kicked into overdrive with a skitter of nervous racing, just in thinking about searching for a middle ground with his art.

Just as quickly, as Sirus mentally slipped back to the flaring tempers of a short while ago, he shivered beneath his layers of clothing. "I'm sorry I snapped in front of you earlier, and I apologize for shouting over your attempts to explain yourself. You eventually got this cold look in your eyes, and you scared the shit out of me when you so coolly walked away. I thought you were coming here to pack your bags and leave."

"I was." Grey dropped his head back against the counter again. He looked weary, and Sirus's chest ached for his struggle to open himself to another human being. "I started to do it, but I stopped to get a drink." His eyelids fell to half-mast and his Adam's apple worked overtime. "Christ, I've never felt so much for one person before, and I've never hurt in the way I did when you accused me of not thinking you were good enough for me." He turned his head and looked right into Sirus's eyes, no longer hiding the brightness shining in his. "Nothing could be further from the truth. But when you thought I did…" Grey exhaled shakily. "I just wanted to get the hell away from everything you were making me feel. I figured the quickest way to do that would be to get far away from you."

Cupping Grey's cheek, Sirus noticed his hand tremble. "I would have followed you." His body shook with wanting, but his voice remained rock steady. "I would have chased you down and demanded that you talk to me. I am not Joe." He kissed the protest out of Grey before it left his lips, and then curled his hand around the man's neck. "I would not have let you slip away without a fight." They touched foreheads, their gazes holding one another. "Maybe not even then."

Grey wound his arm around Sirus's neck and closed the small distance between them with a desperate tasting, clinging kiss. Their upper bodies contorted to somehow face one another, while their cores remained connected through the unyielding grasp of Sirus's arm around Grey's waist. Grey dug his fingers into Sirus's jaw and forced his mouth open, deepening the kiss with the rough thrust of his tongue. Mutual moans of pleasure escaped Sirus and Grey as Sirus's penis grew hard in Grey's ass, pushing at Grey's channel and ring once again. Their kiss turned hot, wet, messy, and aggressive with shared need for more.

Suddenly, Grey pushed his hand between their mouths, breaking the kiss as fast as he'd started it. "Wait, wait." He panted heavily, fanning quick breaths of warm air over Sirus's face. "Help me." His eyes were a mixture of open lust and raw fear, and both seeped into the roughness of his tone. "Tell me how we're going to make this work. I need to know."

So, so like my Grey. He needs a definite, clear answer. Offering a gentle smile, Sirus said, "You already gave us the answer, baby." He brushed his fingers through Grey's hair, taming the drying thickness. "Middle ground. We just have to find middle ground. With our jobs, with where we live -- whatever we need to do to make it work -- we will compromise and make it happen."

Grey's chest heaved with a sharp intake of breath, and hope lit his eyes. "I can do that." His voice held such earnestness that Sirus fell in love with the man all over again. "I can spend time up here with you. I want to. I like this place; I like being here with you."

"I like Raleigh too. I can build a life there with you when you can't be here." Sirus stepped through the fear of change, *about everything.* He could do no less than what he asked of Grey. "Maybe reintroduce myself to Rebecca, to start."

Grey's eyes widened, and Sirus could feel the pick-up in his heartbeat. "Only if you want to." His voice held complete conviction. "I swear you don't need to change anything for me."

"I know. I think I want to talk with her, and we'll see what happens down the road. But right now," he circled his arms around Grey's chest and flipped them both forward, facedown, onto the floor, "all I can think about is making love to you again." Sirus covered Grey's back completely with the weight of his body. Then with a hiss of pleasure, he pushed his cock all the way home.

Grey melted into the floor beneath Sirus, relaxing completely for the coupling. "Christ, I love the way you feel inside me." Grey moaned, the sound rolling all the way through him as he nudged his backside up, teasing Sirus's invading length. "Take me. Please."

Sirus chuckled and buried his face in the side of Grey's head. He had never been happier in his life.

Kissing Grey's temple, Sirus whispered seductively, "I love it when you say please." Holding tightly to Grey's hands, Sirus started to move.

EPILOGUE

G rey smacked Sirus's hand before it reached his neck. "Stop fiddling with your tie, babe." He took Sirus's hand in his before the man could go for his attire again. "You're gonna mess up the nice knot I tied for you."

Sirus glared at Grey, and flashed his teeth with a growl. "I don't like getting all dressed up. You're used to living in monkey suits like this; it's not comfortable to me. I'll touch if I want to." He used his other hand and slipped his fingers into the neckline of his dress shirt. "God, I'm sweating worse than when I have you spread open and am pounding away at your ass."

"Jesus, honey." Grey's neck heated, and so did his cock. He talked the latter down while taking a fast look around the performing arts center hall to see if anyone had overheard

300

Sirus's comment. "At least get me in the bathroom before you say shit like that." Taking another discreet glance around the hall's foyer, Grey didn't see his sister or John, or anyone who looked remotely like Sirus. "I don't think you want me meeting your family while sporting an erection."

"Damn it, maybe this wasn't such a good idea." Sirus had his stare trained on the series of front doors, tracking them back and forth. At the same time, he put a finger to his mouth and started gnawing on a hangnail. "Maybe we shouldn't have put so much pressure on Diana's big night. We're stealing some of her thunder by setting up this dinner."

"Which she told you she would welcome with open arms." Grey could feel the tension running through Sirus, and he hurt for the meeting that might, *or might not*, take place between the man and his mother tonight.

"Look at me." Grey took Sirus's face in his hands, and made his partner focus only on him. "You don't have to make any decisions tonight, no matter how Nia treats me. It is not going to change how I feel about you, and from what I know of the rest of your family, it's not going to influence whether they decide to accept me." Grey had already met Diana, and had also spoken to Nic, as well as Sirus's father on the phone a few times. "Okay?"

"Okay."

"You don't need to worry at all," a beautiful blonde woman snuck up behind Sirus, and she headed up a small entourage that included Kelsie and John, "because some of us have already met. In between finding out some dirt," Diana winked at Grey, "we already like each other just fine, with or without you."

"Diana, you look beautiful." Sirus hugged his sister while Grey hugged Kelsie and then shook John's hand. "You slipped in without me seeing you."

"You need to calm down, big brother," Diana said to Sirus, a smile on her face. "I'm the one who's supposed to be a nervous wreck tonight, not you."

A man nearly as handsome as Sirus, but with dark brown eyes instead of gray, tugged on Diana's hair; he then clasped Sirus's hand in his and pulled him in for a brief hug. "If it were up to Diana she'd have slinked in through the side and not faced anyone until after she played. I grabbed her --"

"Scared the crap out of me is more like it," Diana interrupted. She shot the man a glare that reminded Grey of the one Sirus often employed. Grey recognized the man's voice from their phone conversations as belonging to Sirus's brother Nic. Diana added, "One of the other cellists thought I was being accosted."

"But then I revealed that I know she pukes before every concert," Nic shared, "and he realized I must know her very well. He happily handed her over and said I was welcome to hold her hair."

"Oh God." Sirus burrowed his forehead into Grey's shoulder and shook his head. "You're going to get two hours of this over dinner and are not going to want to be with me anymore by the end of tonight."

Grey bit down a laugh. He wrapped his arm around Sirus and tucked his partner against his chest. "Don't worry about your colorful family." He bussed a kiss to the side of Sirus's head, but smiled at Diana and Nic as he spoke. "I can handle them." He turned Sirus around and angled the man's sightline in the direction of magenta hair, tattoos, and a multitude of piercings. "You have met my sister, right?"

"Hey!" Kelsie whacked Grey in the arm with her purse. "Pregnant woman here." She pointed at her rounded belly. "Be nice."

"I was dragging Diana inside when I saw a woman with pink hair, and then an imposing, fierce looking dude with his arm around her," Nic explained. "Figured that had to be the Kelsie and John I've heard so much about from Sirus."

"So Nic went ahead and accosted Kelsie too," Diana muttered. "Thank God I introduced us really quickly, because I think John was about slam Nic to the ground."

A smile *almost* lifted John's lips. "Nobody puts a hand on my wife." His pale blue eyes flashed with quick mirth. "Except me."

Kelsie rolled her eyes and rubbed her very pregnant stomach. "Yeah, I think they all figured that out, McBride."

Nic looked at Kelsie, and another fast grin lit up his dark eyes. "He put more than a hand on you, Kelsie. Unless he has one hell of an immaculate touch."

Sirus groaned, John blushed, and everyone else laughed. "In case you hadn't figured it out yet," Sirus finally said, "this

304 | CAMERON DANE

is Nic."

"I gathered." Grey stuck out his hand. "Your voice was familiar, and I've heard enough family stories by now to put two and two together the minute you spoke." Grey's voice was dry, but he breathed a sigh of relief when Nic chuckled and shook his hand. "Good to finally meet you."

"Likewise," Nic replied. With a blink of his eyes, the teasing man disappeared, and only a stone-cold serious older brother remained. "I've never heard more happiness in Sirus's voice than in the last few months since you've been together. I've heard through Diana's visit that it's clear you adore him. That makes you a welcome addition to the family in my book."

Grey's emotions rose to the surface and he found it difficult to swallow. "Thank you." He dipped his head. "That means a lot."

"And that's why we keep Nic around." Sirus cuffed his brother's neck and gave him another fast hug. "He can be a poet when he cares."

Sirus leaned back against Grey's chest. He barely settled when he stood back up straight, his eyes locked across the room. Grey followed his stare and immediately recognized Nia Wilder, tonight dressed in a beautiful, formal navy-colored gown. She held the arm of a big, bruising man with salt and pepper hair, and behind them was a decent sized group Grey could only assume were the rest of Sirus's siblings and their spouses.

Nic turned too, and his demeanor altered again. He slipped

his arm around Diana, and turned to Kelsie and John. "Why don't you guys come with us, and I'll introduce you to my other brothers and their wives?" Nic's gaze shifted to Sirus and Grey, and Grey could tell the man fought to grab Sirus and throw him behind his back.

Damn, Nic doesn't know how this is going to play out either.

Nic added, "We'll give you guys some time to do this alone, okay?"

Diana squeezed Sirus's arm. "Call us if you need us," she said, but let Nic lead her away. John and Kelsie followed.

Slipping his hand into Sirus's again, Grey nodded. "Don't worry. We'll be fine."

Grey let the small group walk across the open hall and make some introductions before turning Sirus to face him. Sirus's hands shook, and too much brightness brimmed in his eyes, breaking Grey's heart.

"Look only at me," Grey said. Once again, he took Sirus's face in his hands, holding the other man until the light sparked in his beautiful, deep gray eyes. Christ, Grey's heart ached for how much Sirus was still tied to his mother's choices, no matter how hard he tried to sever that love. Mother and son had not spoken since that day months ago in Sirus's cabin. "You okay to do this?"

Sirus exhaled slowly, and rolled his neck, joints cracking. "I'm okay now." His shoulders lifted, and the small tremors left his body. He looked at Grey, and his normal confidence infused his voice. "I promise."

306 | CAMERON DANE

"Good." Grey pressed a gentle kiss to Sirus's lips, uncaring who saw them or what they thought about two men as life mates. He pulled back and pecked another kiss on each cheek, loving the hard mixed with the soft in this man. "I love you, Sirus. No matter who does or doesn't walk over here, or how they treat me or you in the process, I'm still gonna love you and we're still going to be together. You fought through too much of my shit to get me to open up to you; I'm not going to let anyone break us up now. Got me?"

"Loud and clear." Sirus lifted his hand and soothed Grey with his touch, as he always did. "I love you too."

A rough clearing of a throat broke the men apart. They both turned, and Grey stood face-to-face with Sirus's imposing father and cool mother.

"Son," Sirus's father pulled Sirus into a bear hold, "give your old man a hug."

"Hi, Dad." Sirus hugged Whit tightly, his flexing muscles straining against his suit jacket as he did it. "I've missed you." A slight catch hitched his words.

"You too, kid." Whit planted a kiss on the top of his son's head. "It has been too long."

Sirus's gaze slid to his mother, but Whit shifted and demanded Grey's attention first. "You must be Grey." The guy stuck out his giant hand. He smiled suddenly, and it lit up his entire face in the same way the move did for Sirus. "It's nice to finally put a face with the name and the voice. Good to meet you."

A breath Grey hadn't even realized he'd been holding escaped, almost making him dizzy. He took Whit's hand and was met with a strong, sure handshake. "It is my honor, sir," Grey said, humbled to meet the father of the man he loved. This man had no idea how much Grey already admired the parent he was. "Truly, my honor." Grey became momentarily tongue-tied, and did a quick scan of his memory for the content of their few talks. *Yes.* Grey smiled. "I look forward to a game of chess while I'm in town. If you're interested, of course."

Whit clapped Grey on the shoulder and boomed with a burst of laughter. "Now you're talking." His granite eyes -- Sirus's an almost perfect mirror of them -- held only welcome. "You give me a call and we'll set something up."

Good Christ, Grey might just want a father after all. *If it could be this man.* "Will do."

Stepping back, Whit slid his arm around Nia's waist. Nia looked up at her husband, and Grey could only see love in her eyes. It reminded him of the similar, gentle way she had looked at Sirus that morning on the porch.

Nia shifted her attention to Sirus, and her chin wavered a little bit. Grey slipped his hand into Sirus's and gave him a reassuring squeeze. He breathed a little easier when he got a strong squeeze back.

We'll be all right, the hold conveyed. *No matter what happens.*

Nia opened her mouth, but snapped it shut again, and she put her attention on Grey. "Mr. Cole," she held out her hand, "it's very nice to meet you. I hope we can talk over dinner."

Her gaze slid back to her son for a moment. Her eyes filled with moisture, and a nervous smile lifted her lips. Something passed between them, and she came back to Grey, her hand still outstretched. "I'd like to get to know my son's partner, if you'll let me."

Grey brought Sirus's hand up to his lips and pressed a kiss to the back. As soon as he let their hands fall clasped between them, Sirus did the same, and kissed Grey's hand.

Smiling, Grey finally took Nia's hand in his and shook it. "Mrs. Wilder," he said, his heart full for Sirus, "it's very nice to meet you too."

THE END

ABOUT THE AUTHOR

I am an air force brat and spent most of my growing up years living overseas in Italy and England, as well as Florida, Georgia, Ohio, and Virginia while we were stateside. I now live in Florida once again with my big, wonderfully pushy family and my three-legged cat, Harry. I have been reading romance novels since I was twelve years old, and twenty-five years later I still adore them. Currently, I have an unexplainable obsession with hockey goaltenders, zombies, and an unabashed affection for *The Daily Show* with Jon Stewart.

FIND ME ON THE WEB AT
WWW.CAMERONDANE.COM

Made in the USA
San Bernardino, CA
12 January 2014